dreamt my death in a field of poppies. They were lit with that brilliant white summer light that makes of them a vibrant red tissue: butterfly-wing gossamer fluttering its insufferable fragility, pinned to stems like crane-fly legs. But of course I've forgotten the dream. Only the poppies remain. You forget everything eventually, if you try.

First Edition 2014

Published in the UK, USA & Europe by
Poison Pixie Publishing

**www.poisonpixie.com**

**ISBN 978-0-9571920-1-0**

A CIP record for this book is available from the British Library.

1 2 3 4 5 6 7 8 9

# The Boy With The
# RED HAIR

### and Nothing But A Negro

# Chancery Stone

# Nothing But A
# NEGRO

## The True Story of Robinson Crusoe

Latent in every man is a venom of amazing bitterness, a black resentment; something that curses and loathes life, a feeling of being trapped, of having trusted and been fooled, of being the helpless prey of impotent rage, blind surrender, the victim of a savage, ruthless power that gives and takes away, enlists a man, and crowning injury, inflicts upon him the humiliation of feeling sorry for himself.

### Paul Valery

Aristocracy is always cruel.

### Wendell Phillips

I pray that if I stay here long enough the heat must burn itself out. And so I sit staring into the water, with all the power of my aristocratic eyes, and scorch innocent molluscs in their shells.

I know what is right for me. In the purity of my lineage I am not used to fur without lining. Often, when I first sat in these stinking, ill-cured clothes and felt the roughness of the inner animal against my skin, I avowed that it was not meant to be. But now who am I to kick against such idle fate? I have grown used to picking ape-lice from my hair and the sticky feel of my own oil.

And now I see the bare shadow of myself, stirring like a cunning thing, under the noonday sun. It lurks among the gentle water where a small crayfish, the colour of sand, crawls over my toe. He thinks it is a monument to nobility, a stone statue left by foreign invaders.

Somewhere behind me, lying in the shade with the wisdom of one natural-born, I feel him sensuously stretching, while I, transfixed by the scalding sun, am desperately cauterising my yearning like some ingrown toe-nail. "Grieve me no more," I beg, and geld my own lusts.

And how many years were those lone years? And how many years for The Black? And those black years have been the worst years. Hunger amidst plenty, thirst amidst drowning. And so I send him on errands. I capitalise on his gratitude. I live off his subservient defeat. And what am I?

For all this that I do – nothing but a slave of my own hungers.

And so, here I sit. My shadow has moved another inch and the crayfish has gone. I feel the rock beneath my fingers burn the edges of my skin. Even baked brown, my back stings with sun and sweat. Down, where my feet frolic in the warm blue water, where my toes curl in the sand, there is still a prescient sense of waiting. They would like nothing better than to climb from this pool and walk back along the scorching stones to where the great palms crack like whips and the twisting roots trip my numb toes. And thence into the tree-frog shade, where the great red pokers strut out from the malachite black of the jungle, insistently thrusting their rubbery stamens, sticky with honeydew, against my scorching skin. It is a journey into defeat, and one my body longs to take. Oh, how it would betray me.

No, I shall sit here in the burning light of the beach, with my body blistering in penance. I, a creature of intellect, impeccable lineage, dropping my degradation into the water like so much sewage.

And every hour or so I shall feel him look at me from the fringe of shadow, his eyes cat-gold in the black, staring across the sands, fixing me there, wondering what ritual such a white man plays. For what God he prays. And I shall pretend, in my impeccable way, that I meditate upon greatness, upon the mystic ways of white men, beyond the knowledge of any coal-black savage. And he shall accept my ritual cleansing and return to his shadows without interrupting me, least he frighten away my Gods.

And little does he understand that here, perched on my rock, feet in the water like some ugly lone-hunting seabird, I keep the white man's devil barely at bay, strapped down beneath the clothes he cannot comprehend, lest it eat him up, nectar and all.

I have collected his discarded habits, and still he trusts me. I have delivered him from those who would consume him only to hunger for him myself. I am without honesty… and yet he trusts me.

And so I sit here in the sun each day, praying to my Gods, delivering myself of demons, and he patiently awaits me, stretched out in his dug-out earth like a sun-baked lizard keeping his blood cool.

And at night, when the sun washes the warm and sickly sea with blood, I return to him, where he cooks me food: snake-meat and scorched fruit, salty and sweet, and I could weep at the beauty of him. He looks at me with feral eyes and runs his tongue over his teeth, pleased but uncomprehending, only glad that finally I have come to eat. And I, hot and blistering, let him rub cooling unguent upon me. And it hurts and it makes him more gentle. And my head burns red and my lips split and bleed. And he beds me down and watches by me, sitting with my fevered nightmares, pleased to serve a man so obviously holy, who communes so endlessly with his maker. And I have burnt all the lust from my bones. I am a cinder man and can only lie and see his ebony skin dancing in the firelight, his half-eyes inward looking.

I have no idea what he is thinking, except that he worships me, and so tempts me with his willing sacrifice. 'Ask of me and thou shalt receive.' He has his life to repay and this is a priceless gift to a man who lives only by the grace of the elements. And I, such an honourable man, long to abuse him, but am afraid of my own degradation. For I can foresee, in receiving his complacent body, my own dwindling image reflected in his eyes, and his Great White Priest would become but a lost thing.

But when I go home, when I return to England, he shall be my servant. And there we shall live under the icy restraint of English manners. We shall walk in cold grey rooms and watch the cold grey sky. And the endless rain shall be my chaperone. It shall conspire against his heat and he will be doused, nothing but a negro. And people shall look at him and proclaim his ugliness. And I shall keep my secret, the secret of his beauty. I shall be as one of the women, who will long to touch him, be fascinated by his sleek obsidian skin, his voluptuous mouth, his cat-black eyes. And we shall all keep our secret by crying, "How ugly he is!" and laughing at him.

And thus we shall pin down our demons, even as they would stalk among us, curling their tongues into our ears and whispering urgently, "A little taste. Just a little taste…"

And when he is wrapped in white man's clothes and his skin begins to grey like a flower pressed between leaves, and his tiger's eyes begin to dull and lose their shine – shall he then understand? And shall I ever stop dreaming, in that cold, well-mannered kingdom, of red-phallused lilies dripping their honey into the velvet dark?

And yes, I shall go home. And I know, with each twilight's last look at the sea, that it should be kinder to leave him here, but I am too tortured to offer him any kindness. He will suffer as I have suffered. Eventually, lost in that bleak moorland world, he will perish as surely as a bird in a cage. And finally, when he is dead, and spread out on his funeral bed behind the drawn curtain of respect, I shall lock the door and be alone with him, and there I shall touch him, inside his English clothes, and be hungry no more.

And his beauty, at last, shall be mine.

# The Boy With The
# RED HAIR

### or

### I Dreamt My Death In
### A Field of Poppies

Nothing is quite so wretchedly corrupt as an aristocracy which has lost its power but kept its wealth and which still has endless leisure to devote to nothing but banal enjoyments. All its great thoughts and passionate energy are things of the past, and nothing but a host of petty, gnawing vices now cling to it like worms to a corpse.

### Alexis de Tocqueville

Had the price of looking been blindness,
I would have looked.

### Ralph Ellison

## ONE

Once there once was a boy with red hair; cream skin with that faint tint of pink, so that he looked as if he had been scrubbed with rhubarb stalks.

He had red hair all over – I know you understand my meaning.

I know because I looked.

Often.

It was my delight to imagine licking my tongue along one rhubarb-stained course to another: from belly-button to nipple; nipple back to belly-button. Tasting of tart rhubarb and sour cream, this was how I imagined him. Skin like curds, like the transparent shifting skin of whey. A whey-faced boy. Thus, I called him to his face. 'Here, my whey-faced boy,' let me lick inside your soul, I said, but only to myself, and, of course, he never did. I never asked him, or told him, because if not freely given there would have been no pleasure in it.

Or so I say.

Or so I lie.

In truth, I would have forced him. Forced him hard. Ruptured him into his maker's arms, and for what? To spunk up one is like another. Yet I could not do it, could not even frame the words. He became as bad a dream as a nightmare to me, walking through my rooms, all seeming-oblivious, going about his appointed tasks, while I, clad in the satins of ancient indiscretions, waited for some fictitious moment to exercise my droit de seigneur.

But all that came was cowardice, fear. Fear of rejection, fear that if he said no, if he repulsed my advances, my soul would shrivel and die within me; whatever last gasp of my compassion would expire like a match beheaded.

All ego. All selfishness and ego. I make no pretence at not wanting to hurt, not desiring to pollute.

Desiring to pollute? Ha! I would have rotted his soul in a day and thought nothing of it if I could have once dipped my tongue betwixt his lips.

He was a peasant. They're all peasants, snivelling about my yards. I don't know how old he was when first he arrived. He was a new acquisition of some months before. Not that I had noticed him. Rather he had impinged on my awareness like a change of curtains. Not a bright new arrangement of colour in a well-used room. Rather, an alternative pattern in some seldom slept-in bedchamber.

I have so many faces around me, I who have 'had' so many women. Satiated by my own satiety – Christ, am I not a living legend? The man who lived his life in a circle around his own staff. I was there because I was *tired*, because I was sick of the sight of my Priapal thrust. A satyr whose horns were soft, worn to nubs. I was beyond fatigued. I wanted no women. Yet my servants were afraid for their daughters, their wives.

They were afraid of an old legend. I could no more have tupped their women than their horses. But boys, oh yes, here was a new sophistry, and one I did not even have to cultivate. No intellectual thought, no purposeful rebellion, no offence; no marching through the church with a high whore. All that had been burnt out long ago.

Did I not say I was tired? I was home to sleep. To sleep in my soul. And here was some milk and rhubarb boy – a little tart for my taste. Ha! I saw him and heard myself asking. *Me*, asking after a boy, and the cretins didn't even see it. They who knew and feared the legend didn't see my face flush and my mouth go dry. I felt that dry heat on my body like a plague, a sickness, a disease. That's what my filthy little peasant was, a disease.

I avoided him. I ran away and hid. But once I had seen I could not unsee. I could not unfeel what I had felt. I rode God-lost-count-how-many-miles away, and then rolled on my stomach, pressing my face in the cold moss, almost groaning for the distance I had placed between us. A loss as real as death.

I rode home hell for leather so often I wore my horse out, and I began to see those agitated signs in my groom of a servant who knows he is in a predicament: how to tell a man lower than an animal – for what else was I? – but higher than you that he will kill his horse, riding it like that?

Let it die, I thought in a bitter rage, then I can stay here and be captive.

I interfered with the time and place of his labour. I had him sent from kitchen to stables and thence to the aviary. I created a miasma of fear around the boy. That he had offended me they all knew, *how* he had offended me, he could not say. He, of course, could not know, and they, the illiterates, assumed he was lying. And, volte-face, I confused them further by finally taking the boy to be my valet.

Oh God, curse the day. What madness gripped me? An urge to torture myself? He was immune to me. I swear he did not even fear me. I was a capricious aristocrat to be obeyed in every quarter and otherwise forgotten. He was servile enough. He was obedient – enough. But I could not take his attendance on me dressing. I sent him away and then longed to have him tie my shirt, arrange my cuffs, as if these picky little tasks were my staff of life, my aqua vitae, my sustenance.

The other servants took me now to be eccentric in extremis. I was short of temper. Not dull, as of old, but quick and sullen. The boy was exempted and so they thought he was but the first of my vagaries. They thought they saw a pattern in my madness, and he had been but the unlucky butt of its first directions.

He was accepted, indeed respected, as my valet. Selected by a madman, a drunk, a sybarite. Was it love or lust, or something more bestial than either? How can *I* tell, how would *I* know what it was? I was drunk, mad, incensed. I was being *eaten*.

I created chaos in my apartments that I might watch him rearrange them. I insisted that he come everywhere with me. I taught him to ride a horse, and could not bear to watch the beast between his legs. And for jealousy, by God, for what else?

In the summer, we rode to the river so that I might send him in swimming. The first time I had no such intentions. When I told him to swim, he said he couldn't, and when I offered to teach him, he said he would rather not and would not meet my eyes. And I, consumed as I was, thought he saw my lust and struck him back-handed with such violence that he fell back straight to the ground, as if he had been kicked by a mule. And I, white with rage, roared at him to strip his clothes, but before he had got further than his shirt, I had turned my back on him and ridden home.

And of that, they could make nothing. I knew by their faces when he had returned and told the story. And finally, my oldest servant, my man of all offices, asked if I would still require the boy. "Yes," I said in a voice so low he had difficulty hearing me. "Yes, I still want him." And still he was not afraid.

Would that he had been. I could have stood anything but that bucolic stoicism. He expected irrationality of me. He thought I was mad. He thought I was sick with the diseases of dissipation.

I sent him to be trained by the barber. I wanted him to minister to my grooming. When he shaved me, I could feel his hands on my face and the closeness of his body bending over mine. I wanted to watch him tend my hair in the mirror, press against my shoulders. It became a consuming petty idiocy.

He was duly apprenticed and cut my hair, or at least he tried. Watching his face in the glass, bent over the latest ridiculous fashion of curling-tong and powder, I stiffened as if he was licking me, naked, into a frenzy. I picked up a pot and hurled it at the mirror, threw him from the room with my bellows, and hurled myself onto the bed in a fit of rage.

I thought to myself, "I am sick. I need a physicker. I am ailing." But I knew what I needed to cure me, and all I could do was cast my rescue away from me. I could have taken it, and it was nothing but fear that stopped me. Cowardice. He had beaten me with indifference. And I surrendered to it. I became a sycophant, a dog.

The following morning I asked him to dress me. He had until that point been forbidden to do so. He did not even have the grace to look startled, now the great lunatic had changed his mind once more. I did not dare to watch but stood with my eyes closed, feeling his hands moving over me, and if he saw my hardness, well, he would keep his own counsel.

His hands remained steady, cool, dry. He was as self-contained as an oyster in his shell. He cared nothing. He felt nothing. I was as meek as a lamb, docile, loving the feeble neglect of his hands. Grabbing at crumbs, I.

From then on, my shame and degradation lived as poor relatives dogging my coattails. I took anything from him that I could legitimately obtain. Every service, every right of master over servant. And my pride hung onto that. What matter, I told myself, if every time he touches me, I am harder than ram's horn? No doubt in one so virile, with such a legendary reputation, it is but a manifestly ordinary thing to be.

I don't know if he accepted that. I don't know what he thought. I don't know *if* he thought.

But it wasn't enough. Why is it never enough? He was like rare spirits of brandy, distilled tincture of poppy, a rose sherbet beyond compare: he was never enough.

I wanted to lie with him. And when I wanted it, I wanted it enough to kill for. What my heart had decided, then it simply must have. Women slept with their servants all the time. It wasn't so odd, I told myself.

Why I worried, I do not know. Yet I worried about him. Always him. What did *he* think? What did he think of *me*? But his face never spoke. And how could I ask?

The servants treated it as one more delusion of a madman.

*I shall move another bed in, sire.*

*No, let him sleep in mine – God knows there is room enough.*

*Very well, sire.*

Never a blink. And I do not feel, even to this day, that they found it strange. If I could have spent my life and a day thinking up a plausible disguise for my lustful heart, I could not have conceived a better plan than my omnipresent 'madness'.

He came to my room after his supper and knocked on the door. When would I wish him to come to me? Now, I said.

He came in. He had washed, and in the dull hiss of the candles, he looked waxen, with that damp blood-rust hair. The tendrils looked almost black. I told him to undress me and he did. God, I was harder then than in all my life. I might have been seventeen. I could feel the obscene strength of it. I watched his eyes; he neither looked nor looked away. It might have been my arm or a common finger. I suddenly ached to grab his cunning little head and shove him in face first – *see it, you little felcher*. I had a mouth full of words and my lips clamped them so tight my teeth ached with their confinement.

I wore no nightshirt and climbed into bed and lay watching him undress. He could not see me in the shadows, and I thought to hide myself from his all-seeing, never-seeking eyes. But he undressed as he did everything else – with indifference.

But I was not indifferent. No, I watched him untuck his shirt and unlace its ties. His chest was flawless. Hairless but lithe. His muscles corded as he bent to pull off his boots. I had not suspected such an adult body on such a lean and milksop frame. He stood aslant to me as he unbuttoned himself. I saw the cream line of his buttocks before I saw the thick length of that pizzle. Pale as some ungodly snake against the thick thatch of russet hair – darker than his head – curving up over his flat belly. So much of it on one so smooth. It looked outrageous on such a perfect marblesque form. Like a deliberate obscenity. The heavy white staff, the dense wiry satyr's hair on that gruel-thin angel-faced boy. Oh, he was lean enough, muscled enough, coarse and peasant enough to satisfy any noble blood that he was clean animal stock, but this rutting horse-cock, heavy, flaccid, slung, belonged to some other animal. And when he looked at me once – a rare, elusive thing – he was like a different creature. I felt as if I had invited the devil into my bed.

He climbed in beside me without my invitation. The bed was sufficiently wide for us to sleep without touching, but I blew out the candle and lay rigid on my back, as he, I assumed, was lying on his.

I do not know when I slept, I only remember violent confining dreams, like a pinning weight waking me in the night, and lying in the dark, bathed in sweat, pushing the coverings beyond me, and turning to ice in the draughts of my chamber. I remember turning to him and seeing his profile in sleep, intolerably beautiful, like a dead thing carved in stone. It was as if he had never moved.

Even in sleep, he was indifferent. His body left me in sleep. It was worse, harder than before, to see him so detached from me. Not even an eyelid flickered. He chased nothing of a dream; he was not dreaming of me. I lay on my back where I could not see him and wept. I felt the tears slide down my face like the salt coursing of my heart's blood.

# TWO

In the morning, he was up before me. I had not told him to do so, but he was. But then I had not told him anything. I had given him no reasons for wanting him there. He had asked no questions. And that night, and every night thereafter, he turned up at my door after supper and took off my clothes and saw me pared down to my pathetic little lusts and lay with me and felt nothing.

And me? I was once more the meekest lamb in God's stable.

I am sure my household thought I had been cured of my madness. Perhaps they felt I had been prey to bad dreams and the boy had exorcised me. But there were no knowing glances.

Did he tell them nothing? I heard no rumours. Indeed, there only seemed a feeling of content that I had somehow settled down, become an exemplary bachelor squire. And what of the ram, the nightly stallion he revealed with his long white hands? Was there really nothing to tell? Was he blind? Did his eyes not see? Or was mine a simple senile madness? God knows the old aristos get stiff at nights for no reason, the licentious old goats. Was this what they said? Was it considered but a stripling love-sickness? Fit for the pastor, forgettable, God forbid... mere Meadowsweet? I don't know. I only know it didn't last. It wasn't enough. It was never enough. He gave me nothing and I wanted it all.

He washed me, he dressed me, he lay with me. He rode and sat and ate with me. I would not be parted from him, but I did not *know* him. He spoke with me, even occasionally, although I am at a loss to see how I managed my part, sported with me, and still he kept himself locked up, intact, like some convent-schooled virgin. I did not ask him if he had lain with women, I did not want to know, and he never ventured the information.

That day we had ventured down to the river. It was warm and still, with a shimmering veil of dragonflies darting through the verdant air. The sky was a brilliant porcelain blue, cloudless, and the heat was burnt into the very air. I had taught him to swim, overcome that fear that earlier I had thought to be revulsion. We had been in the water – me, for once, God-save-me, not standing up at his very presence – and were now lying, me on my stomach, he on his back, prostrate in the sun, baking like two turtles on a Simian tide.

I felt, for a rare moment, contented, perhaps drugged by the heat, but, for the nonce, I felt not that strong awareness of him, but only a quiescent lassitude. He was but a beloved friend, a companion, not the eternal source of my torment.

I turned to face him and saw the red flush on his body. "Your skin burns," I said and reached my hand over to brush a stray ant from his arm.

His body seemed to shimmer, as if the sun had lent him its quicksilver – I know not – but he turned his head towards me, his eyes opening slowly with the laziness of stupefaction. I remember seeing that they were green, greener than grass or tree, and I was surprised that I had not noticed before – fool that I was, how could I, when he never looked at me? – and his eyes held that same knowledge, that same glint of concupiscence I had seen before, that first night. I could feel his body stiffen, grow tumescent under my very fingers, fill and flow as if some lustful satyr had awoken under my hand.

I could not move my eyes. I could not look. I wanted more than anything to see what I had felt through that brief touch. God knows, I had looked at it often enough before, watched that great thick creature slumber in its nest, and yet I could not move my eyes. I was transfixed by that solid unsmiling gaze.

And then he was gone.

His eyes had slid from mine like a lizard's and he was sitting up, his staff now hidden from me by the glare of the sun, against which he was but an eye-watering silhouette.

And I had to lie there, stiff as I ever had been. Me, grown hungry and gorged, pressing my hot belly into the grass until it subsided enough to let me dress, until he had wandered off to see to the horses. Had I dreamt it? Was this a fevered sundream, half-awake, half-asleep? Had I but imagined that satyr stirring in his body?

My torture became real from that moment. Everything that had gone before was but some youngling phantasm. That dream animal born in the heat was stamping up and down my spine, raging its ropes to be let loose. And I wanted it, I wanted it to rip me asunder in a way I had wanted nothing else before.


From that point, nothing was the same. Everything took on some new secret knowledge. I felt like some pathetic Eve damned by an inconsequential apple. Where before I had seen indifference, even in my more charitable moments innocence, I now saw cunning. Cunning and deceit. He was as one damned by accusation. I watched him with a new perception, questioned everything. He, in turn, remained elusive, mysterious. A two-faced lying little whoreson. I did not know I had held such rage in my heart until it poisoned my spleen. My previous angers seemed like petty tantrums.

But everything remained, on the surface, calm. I watched him and waited, until I grew tired of that. I *would* have some answers, and I would have them by nightfall.

He came to me that evening after supper, the only meal he still took away from me. I enjoyed the piquancy of torturing myself with his absence. He came in and lit the lamps then the candles. The sun was setting in a vast pyrotechnic display across the horizon. His skin seemed feverish in that red-reflected light, and I felt something twist inside me at the sight of those boyish curls, that pristine pink-blushed skin. Everything so neat, so undisturbed in his flawless soul, and I longed to shake him, to wound him as he twisted knives in *my* gut. Every night's torment seemed like years of persecution. I hated him with an intensity that I feared might scorch the skin off his face.

I stood up and crossed to where he had come to rest. He stood stock-still. Like a byre animal, I thought, a horse waiting to be shod. He stood like a milk-beast in a pen, immobile, docile, waiting for the next move of his 'gentle gaoler'. My hand shot out and twisted in the locks that curled down his neck. I pulled them tight, sufficient to lock his head back. And I swear, as God is my witness, he did not flinch an inch. His eyes never shifted; he never recorded a degree of fear or even surprise.

"You lied to me," I said, though God knows why I said it or what he made of it.

But he said nothing, just stood blinking, but unperturbed.

"If I wrung your whoring neck now you'd still stand there like some colic-struck cow, until the very life was choked out of you." My voice hissed like gas escaping from a bottle.

He said nothing. I saw nothing, not even the brightness of reflex tears, in his eyes. He was dry, unmoved.

I let his hair go and slapped his face, there and back in rapid succession. "Say something, you insolent whelp."

I backed him up against the dressing table, my arm pressed against his chest, clutching his shirt so fiercely it almost rent the fabric. I could smell him, close beneath me: a smell of hay and saddle soap and some spice like nutmeg, custard-sweet, and his eyes were green, fixed not on me, but on some point beyond my shoulder. And on impulse, in rage, frustration, an urgency to hurt, I know not what, I grabbed his dirk tight through his clothes and even under my anger I could feel how heavy it was, thick like a cudgel, too large. And what I had thought to say died on my lips as his eyes moved to mine with the surprise of dying eyes coming into focus, as if he had not previously seen me there. And I saw it again, not a smile, but the suggestion of a smile, the ghost of something alive in his eyes, buried in that unemotive face. A lewdness, a lechery, a lust – what? I could no more place it than I could think. I could no more hold it than I could hold his eyes.

I let go of him as if burnt, and his eyes slid away as if they had never been there, and I did not know if I had dreamt it.

I undressed myself with shaking hands, pushing him away when he came to me disguised as the good servant. I stared at the ceiling while he disrobed and felt nothing but a dull icy ache when he climbed into bed with me. He was asleep within half an hour, like a man with nothing to fear.

I think it was the only purposeful, deliberate decision I made with him. I decided to be cruel. I *vowed* to be cruel. And now I am not even sure if it was simply revenge or some more sophisticated plan to force his hand. To force him to what, I do not know. To reveal himself, to give something, playact some emotion, *anything*, as long as I was no longer alone with my passions, my doubt, my fears.

At supper I would not speak to him, as if he had earned my disfavour, then I would summon him to talk, only to snap him down with the implication that he had been presumptuous, insolent.

For his personal services, nothing he did pleased me. I jumped as if he had nicked me in my shave. The bath water was too hot, too cold. He tied my lacings in knots or not tight enough. He could do nothing right. One night I made him sleep on the floor like a dog. I was boorish, insufferable. No man would have served me willingly.

And him? If I had had a plan, it had failed its mark by a country mile – he was more bland, more insipid, tolerant to the point of banality. Even the night he slept on the floor, it was I who lay awake, aching to have him back with me, missing the distant warmth of him, aware that I could not steal those surreptitious brushes against his skin that made my nights tolerable.

## THREE

The next morning I felt I had irrevocably lost that night, while he slept like a king, a lord, a monarch. Content, conscienceless, unmoved. I detested him.

I don't know if I could ever have been called introspective. Certainly, it was something I had never believed myself. I had never questioned my desires, gave thought to my motives. I worked on the irreversible nature of man. My life had been a monotonous round of dissipation. I have said before that I was tired. Well, I *was* tired, or I had been. Now I seemed to fall into a well of philosophical rumination. I looked at my past, I examined my history and knew that I had never entertained such lust. Nor had I ever looked at a man in any way. They were but poor shadows of myself, monotonous in their similarity. Brutal, dull savages. From whence, then, had this lust assembled itself? Out of what half-baked devil's scheme? I felt sure that even if the little milksop succumbed, I wasn't sure what to do with him. All I knew was the fire he had sparked was unquenchable. Without forebears, without logic, and most of all without appeasement.

I began to think of things to please him.

I, please others?

Had it not been so tragic, I would have been distempered laughing. I could not bear to pass myself in the glass. Even the idea of my want sickened me. I had used gifts before, as an oil to soothe troubled consciences. They were part of the armoury of seduction – but to a serving lad? I did not know what to give. I teased him as to what he would have and could gain nothing. I finally had made up, in desperation, a silk shirt the colour of his skin. I had seen the plush weave and been reminded of him and bought a length on the spot. And here was how I sought out whips to thrash myself. The feel of his body through the warm silk. The shadow of that curl of belly hair that showed, pressed against its transparency. The sight of that faint flushed skin against its complementary silkworm cousin. All I had done was draw my eyes to his body. And instead of a remedy, I was pulling scabs from my own sores. There was no healing me.

I bought him a pendant jewel for his ear. One large emerald, cold and green as an under-leaf, and had it mounted in a ruby gold of Africa. We pierced his lobe with a tallow flame and needle. I loved to watch the flinch of pain as it went through his skin – oh that I could make him flinch thus, that I was a needle to pierce his unfeeling hide. I longed to kiss him better like an infant, only it was I who was in pain. Each night I bathed the wound. It healed and the stone sparked like an unwinking eye amidst the red gold of his hair. The lust. The dreadful lust.

His fellow servants thought him a foundling; my bastard surely. I had adopted him like a son, given him gifts that were worth his wages two years over, could not bear to be parted from him.

The fools. The snivelling, carping, cretinous fools. I should have crushed the blood from his parasitic carcase, destroyed the thieving succubus before he ate me body and soul.

God, I loved him. As God is my witness, I would have bled to a desert for him, did he but ask it. My heart was arid without him. I longed for the succour of him like a man without water. I thirsted, I burned.

And he? He felt nothing.

## FOUR

I decided to go away. I would leave him. I would go to Europe, re-live my youthful adventures, leave him here to rot; fuck every woman I met, even try Italian boys, if I was going to start a new pattern in dissipation. I would cauterise my wound. I would leave him.

I saw to my estate, neglected for the lust of a capricious infant. I tended to my affairs. I arranged finances and planned my itinerary. I took him everywhere with me. I said nothing other than that I was going to Europe. I watched his face, like an astronomer reading the skies. I searched as the fateful day grew closer for some sign. I saw nothing.

Nothing.

On the night before my departure, I told him that he should take his supper with me. He acquiesced with all his complacent grace. We sat by my chamber window, I smoking some vile black Turkish stuff only for the pleasure of its bitterness, its gall. If it had been Wild Bryony, it would have tasted sweeter than the bile in my mouth.

He was doing nothing, gazing from the window, his eyes lost on some distant horizon, miles from me. Already he had left me. I felt my heart would break. I had never had a heart before. It had beat in my body in steady oblivion and nothing had ever touched it. And now it pained me so often I could not believe it would not burst from such misery.

I stood up and snuffed the candles, plunging us, in some impulse I did not stop to understand, into the abbreviating closeness of the dark.

The room shrunk into the square of light from the casement. The moon was almost full and as the clouds cleared from its face, the room began to light its forms with the eerie sliver so peculiar to its glow.

I saw that emerald flash once from its fleshy oyster shell as he turned his head towards me. He stood up and began, with what only *seemed*, in that strange ghost light, to remove my garments with an unnatural languor. His hands unfastened the ties on my shirt and slid under, against my skin, to tug at the waist of my britches. Every move he made seemed opposite, pregnant with meaning – or was that merely my enraptured eye?

I felt a soporific heat that frightened me. I lifted each arm, each part of myself, as he moved them, like an overtired child. I saw his teeth glimmer once. What had he done – smiled? Him? Surely a yawn, filled with ennui, longing for this time to be over, to be free of me, exiled in Europe.

He sat me on the bed's edge to pull off my boots. I dropped back on the mattress, hands above my head. I could see myself with a detached eye. My body, well-fleshed, matted with thick red-gold hair, as lionish as he was lamb. Every inch of me the animal satyr, except where it mattered. And him, I knew, smooth as a child. Muscled, yes, but pure and clean in line, untouched, unsullied – except where it mattered, and there he made me look a child. He would have made any man look a child, shamed a stallion.

He pulled my breeches down – lifting my buttocks off the bed, sliding his hands beneath me as if he was going to clamp my loins to his face. I saw myself even through this deep, drugged haze, rampant, peeled back against my belly, sulky-red and glistering taut, as he saw me every night, every single, solitary lonely night and said nothing, expressed nothing. What did he imagine it stood there for – to admire the view? Ah! but, I thought, that's what it did do – admired the view he presented to my hungry eyes.

I lay unmoving on the bed, scythe standing like a bludgeon, and watched him take off his clothes. His skin looked like a dull mirror in the moonlight, so white it reflected the light; his eyelashes a black slash on his cheeks; his hair dark, black in this cloak of shadows. He was soft and ebony, like some obscene statue. He should have been thrust forward, like the god, Priapus, mounted resplendent and worshipped in some temple, and instead he stood here in my chamber, heavy with the thick weight of himself, dull, waiting for my next command, unable to enter the bed because I lay across it, unable to move. He should have been uncomfortable, unsure of himself, and instead he was steadfast, certain. He simply closed in on himself, waiting for the next order.

"Come here," I said.

He moved to my side. I reached out my hand. "Closer."

He moved forward without hesitation. I wanted to touch it more than I had ever wanted anything in my life. As soon as I knew the thought, I felt my mouth gum together, the saliva gone as a spoonful of alum will do. My skin flushed crimson and the hairs on my body stood as live things. I felt my sconce spring up as the skin on my bags dragged tight from its headlong run into the air.

I reached out my hand. He did not stir. I touched it for the second time. But with nothing between us. It felt firm, flexible and muscled, like the flank of some powerful animal. I realised I could not get my hand around it. I tightened my fist. He did not flinch. I pulled him forward by this hair-splitter, like some dray horse, until he was pressed almost off-balance against the bed.

"Do you never get a stand?" I asked. My voice was clamped, my teeth clenched. I sounded sulky, petulant. Like some woman snivelling, 'Do you *truly* love me?'

He remained flaccid. His teeth flashed in the dark. I could see his face arrange itself into a grin. He looked devilish and perverse in that carving light. His face moved into planes and angles that looked alien on him, like a mask.

"Go away," I said, dropping him. "Go away," and I jumped up, striding across the floor, grabbing my robe and stormed out of the room.

## FIVE

My delay was not intentional, no matter how much I may devoutly have wished for it in my prayers. Prayers full of vice and degradation. Prayers for a Devil. I cannot even now remember what caused it. Something unimportant, trivial, and yet it was as if the hand of some malignant God stepped in and, like a fly beneath his thumb, had crushed all my good intentions by his one capricious act. One cycle of sun and moon was enough. Enough to undo everything that I had once held sacred. Every last determination to keep my face free of the muck I longed like a pig to snout in. I, brought down like an innocent lamb to the slaughter, a corrupted child.

We were held up some forty miles from home. And after two hours it seemed unlikely we would make headway. In my highly-strung state it was not far enough to free me from his pull.

I returned to the house, probably to the perplexity of both my servants and the innkeeper, and had already decided in my heart that I would not leave him. I was like some child running away and going only to the foot of his house steps before deciding he has tasted enough of freedom. I returned as if I had gone the full journey's duration, like some lovesick soldier impaled on the saintly love of some black-eyed Susan. I make myself weary to hear it.

Needless to say, when I returned he was not there. I ran up the steps with all the vigour of the young parson returning to his beloved and found my hall as barren and cold as if it had stood empty for three hundred years. My servants were surprised to see me, but not unduly put out. They were used to my volte-faces. And lacking nothing as much as I lacked shame, I asked for him: "Where is the milk-sop?"

Did I detect some hesitation, some colouring, some fluster? I feel sure I read it, but is this just in hindsight?

"Out, my lord. Shall I fetch him?"

"Out?" I said. My voice held all the perplexity of a man who has been told his foxhound refuses to hunt the fox. "Out? What do you mean – out?"

"He went out earlier this evening, my lord. Somewhere past two hours by."

I fixed my eye on this man as if he had sold the boy's body for dog meat. The look was sufficient that he felt impelled to explain himself.

"We did not expect your immediate return, my lord."

I ignored him. "Out where? Out with whom?" I added, my voice suggesting some lewd death for this seducer of innocents. And now I did not *fancy* I saw things. Now I saw his colour rise, and into it I read all manners of guilt, all manners of deceit. In all he was merely at a loss, but I fear he was turned into fifteen types of lying devil in my mind.

I did not wait for further replies; I grabbed this less-than-peasant by his waistcoat. "Where has he gone? *Where?*"

"The stables, my lord. To the stables."

I did, and I do not know by what cunning I decided to move like a mouse, if a mouse as charged by murderous anger as I was could move with stealth. And yet, I was not heard. They were playing at cards. No offence in that, surely?

Why, none, and they were lucky I did not rip off their heads with my bare hands.

I threw open the door on that pretty little tableau and kicked him back off his stool. I threw the table over and only by some miracle did not succeed in setting the whole stable alight.

I picked him off the floor before he even realised it was not a horse that kicked him. "You arse-kissing little maggot!"

I threw him back against the stall wall with such force the rafters shuddered. He had no breath in his body; it was all knocked out by the first blow, and the second left his lungs clutched with the terror of suffocation. His skin was grey and sickly, even under that warm hay-light.

The other must have picked up the lamp with more sense than I had shown in knocking it over. I didn't care, he barely registered, his time would come. For now, I was content to kill this one. *This* one's blood would satisfy me.

He had slumped down against the wall. I dragged him up again with both hands and thrust him against the wall of the stable. A hay manger was fixed beside his head. I remember an ear of wheat hung down stark against the stone. I started banging his head against the wall. "I'm going to make you bleed, you little prong-sucker." I flung his body back again. "I'm going to kill you."

But my arms were effectively stopped by a stranglehold, growing minutely stronger as a powerful hand twisted my neckerchief tighter and tighter. I could see coloured confetto before my eyes; my arms grew limp and fell away from their prey. I saw his grey face, his unfocussed gaze, as we both slid down into the waiting dark.

## SIX

He had damn well near strangled me, this unknown assailant. I lay on my back and stared at the inner canopy of my bed. Dragons ate dragons ate dragons. I felt my tender neck with one cautious hand. I could barely croak. This soft-footed brigand had rendered me into a toad: a horned toad.

As soon as I was able, I sent for him. Craven, pathetic as I am, after nearly killing him I could not wait to see him again. I never doubted he was alive, because I knew my punishment was not yet over. Is not Hell for an eternity? There is no reprieve.

He had not fared so badly. I had not even broken skin. He walked as a man bruised in limbs he never knew he had – with an immense fragility, like one walking on eggs – but he was unmarked. My temptation could not be removed by a godless blemish. He had devils to protect him.

Did he stand a little unsure? I could not tell. I could not see for the dazzling beauty of his gaze.

"Who is he?" I croaked. Even to my own ears, I sounded like some sickly lecher, some ancient crone. All I needed was to paw the boy and coo, 'Pretty creature.'

I turned my head to my pillow, though I felt as if a bar was pressing my throat, and closed my eyes. I could feel the lowness of my belly as it dragged on the floor, the abrasive rip of my humiliation.

I realised he had answered me, yet I had not heard. What new trick now to taunt me? Needs I ask again?

Of course, we did not laugh sufficiently for *heartfelt* pleasure the first time.

"Who?"

He repeated it patiently, without shame. "My brother, my lord."

I looked at him. His eyes were fixed somewhere on a unicorn to the left of my knee. "Your brother," I said. I think it was a question; certainly, he took it as such.

"Yes, my lord, my twin brother."

I did *not* repeat, 'Your *twin* brother,' and at least saved myself that mediocrity.

He stood there docilely. Happy, perhaps, with the simple pleasure that at least I was not beating his brains out on the bedpost.

I dismissed him.

I lay there with my suspicions jeering at me like allies turned enemies. Before, I was possessed with myriad devils of jealousy and fear, and now they were all turned in upon me. A thousand demons laughing at my pathetic little lusts, sneering at my blind cupidity. I had nearly killed him for nothing.

Would that I had.

## SEVEN

It took me time to pick up courage to see this brother. It took me no time to want my boy back beside me.

As soon as I could leave my sick bed, the sheets were changed, the chamber aired, and I had my Good Servant peeling me down nightly as if I had never missed a day. His touch was still as poisonously sweet, his looks more potent, since I had almost wrested them from before my very own eyes. I drank him in as if I had left him for a lifetime. I could not see enough of him. The servants thought both he and his brother protected by the Gods. Between them, they had nearly slaughtered one of the gentry – even if he had set out to slaughter them first – lucky they weren't hanging from the gibbet.

I gave his brother a job. He may already have had a job, but it would have been his life for him to refuse. The servants thought him not only lucky but privileged. Perhaps he knew better.

I wanted to see him, this twin. They are not all identical, twins. I had not seen him that night. I did not ask if he was his copy. I would see this boy for myself.

I put him in the stables. Let me see him in the right setting.

It took me two weeks before I gathered courage to approach my nemesis.

It was a grey, misty-wet day. Autumn was lying among the trees like some great damp dog waiting to shake its stinking pelt and spread its dirty muck all over us. It was a depressing day, and my lust was hurting like a bone out of joint. The relief at my return was passing off, and again he was becoming nothing but a torture to me. So I did what I always did when this lechery became unbearable, I heaped coals on my head.

I would go for a ride.

*On this slippery treacherous day?*

The exercise would do me good.

High-stepping between dripping trees – living on my nerves, waiting for the damn horse to take a tumble?

I needed cheering up.

My conscience refused to even criticise that one. So I walked to the stable.

Perhaps he would not be there.

Of course he was there. He had his back to me, sweeping out the effluent. When a gust of wind curled around my feet, seeking entrance, he turned and shaded his eyes with his hand to see who stood there.

"Come forward," I said.

He stepped out into the light.

You could not tell them apart.

And perhaps I did not want to tell them apart. Perhaps two would be better than one. Two to watch, to love, to lust. Two to undress me, touch me. Two in my bed, naked, pleasuring me. I wanted this boy. I wanted him more than his brother. For in truth, he was different. He had been cast from the first mould, like a piece of fine plasterwork. His were the more definite features: the sharper nose, the broader cheekbones, the clearer eye, the cleaner chin. Somehow, he lacked the soft, milky indefinition of his brother. Everything the same and yet different; even this one's indifference was different. It smacked of arrogance, impertinence that walked its line on cat's paws. A creature to watch for: his lies, his deceits. Here I could *see* cunning in the green eyes, not just feel its presence. This was the man complete.

I stood in the stable doorway. He stood leaning on a besom and regarded me equally calmly, calculatingly, critically.

"You are the eldest twin."

It was a statement. It brooked no argument, but he shifted hands and replied, "Jack is my younger brother… sire." The 'sire' was insolent, too long in coming. It edged me like needles.

"And what do they call you, elder brother?"

"John, sir," he said, smiling a lazy smirk of a smile.

"John? That's the same name, surely? As Jack?"

"Reckon it might be, sir."

"Someone had an odd turn of humour."

To this, he ventured no further remarks, only his line of strong white teeth, saying, *Make what you like of it. I know what your gape says. To me, you are isinglass.*

I felt my eyes shift away from that knowing, languorous gaze. "Saddle my horse," I commanded.

He never even said 'Yes, sir'.


It was the brother who did it: who broke my bonds.

That night I got drunk. I staggered up to bed with only the evil intent of any drunk – to assert his honour, avenge imaginary slights. I was inflamed, helled up by his cunning sloe eyes, this John the Elder, with his insolent ways.

I sat on the edge of the bed, mumbling my incoherent grievances. I had barely managed to struggle with a recalcitrant boot when I heard his knock.

"Come in, milk-sop!" I half crooned, half shouted. "Come in, little Jack, and see what your lord and master has for you." I laughed at this last, inordinately, as if I had made some surpassingly witty remark.

He came in and put down his candle and proceeded to light the others, as was his custom, with a taper. I made a lunge for him as he made to pass me. I don't know if he sidestepped me or if my aim was too poor, but I missed him by a length.

"Oho, Jack's a naughty boy, trying to escape his father of all fellows."

He answered, but I was too absorbed by this new wickedness to hear him.

"Come on, come on, that's enough light, boy. Come undress me. These infernal straps defeat me," and I began tugging at them with purpose.

He knelt down at my feet and began pulling off my boots.

"Very good, Jack. Very good," I commended him as I flopped back on the bed. "Oho, the world's gone upsy-daisy," I added, in my imbecile way, while he attempted to struggle me out of my clothes.

Perhaps I dozed, for I awoke to feel cold on my skin. I was naked, having managed to lift my head up the few degrees necessary to see myself. "Oho, stolen my clothes, have you, guttersnipe?"

Then I was struck by a new marvel. "Look, no peg tonight. Doesn't love you anymore." I let my head fall back. But barely had it rested its drunken weight on the down before I was raising it again to demand, "Why don't you give it the kiss of life, Jack? Go on, see if you can rescue the old boiling fowl from going in the cock-a-leekie."

He went down again, falling to his knees, and pressed his head between my legs. He took me in his mouth as if he had been born to do it.

They speak of the sobering effect of a bad shock, but no shock had ever rendered me powerless before. I felt it then. It was as if I had been doused by a pitcher of cold water. All these months of wistful longing and I had only to ask. He was doing it now, to me, drunk and obnoxious.

It took my body longer to sober up, but it did. I rose myself onto my elbows and saw my flesh stiffen under those lips and teeth. I felt the slumbering coals in my belly burst into flame, like tinder under a summer sun. I groaned, "My God." I could see that curly head go up and down on me as if this were mere practice of his kitchen-work. I felt indescribable pleasure.

He held me tight, making a totem of me, and ran the tip of his tongue under the plum. I could see it, plump and swollen, pushing against his lips. As he sucked me in again, he released the shaft and I felt myself go slinging into his mouth. I pushed myself up to thrust it out from me, months of longing. I groaned as if I were dying. I *felt* as if I were dying. I gripped his hair and pushed his suckling head down further. He drank me down, every last drop, without compunction, and I remembered no more.

## EIGHT

In the morning, I awoke, sticky-eyed and feeling disembodied. I could dimly hear the chink of curtain rings on the rail. I could smell chocolate and heard the porcelain clink from the cup placed by my ear.

I opened one eye and turned my head to the source of the sound. He was there, going about his business, as oblivious as any housemaid. It came back to me and I could feel the dull flush of red through my skin. Hard on its heels came the conviction, the convenient conviction, that I had dreamt it. A lewd, drunken dream.

I followed him about the room from under my lashes. Nothing marked him, nothing gave him away, but I had to know: "Jack…"

He turned to me. If there was any surprise at the unaccustomed use of his name, he did not show it. Had I even known his name before? I did not go on; his gaze transfixed me. "Yes, my lord?" he prompted.

"Is my bath drawn?"

"Yes, my lord."

I went to it and dressed myself and shunned his help.

But night had to fall. The inevitability of the dusk, the evening, depressed my spirits. It was a dank, grey day of early winter and the light was brief and hardly meriting the name. I spent what little there was of it hidden in the library, trying books in a mindless determination to relieve myself of memory, responsibility. But it was no good: the Greeks all looked like him, the poets all sung eulogies to him, and the historians all fought battles over him. I went back and forth from chair to window in an ascension of misery, resembling nothing more than a caged animal. I sent word he would not be required for supper and ate it alone in the library.

At ten o'clock, I found myself staring into the falling ash, deep in a reverie of his twin's head at my belly, eating deeply, a consummation of my lust.

I stood up and shook myself with disgust, shivering with tiredness; the tiredness of long confinement, captivity. I went upstairs to bed.

The candles had been lit and the fire had burned low, but Jack was nowhere to be seen. Would he not come? I undressed, half in relief, half in anxiety. I could not bring myself to extinguish the candles. I fetched a bottle of camphorated rum & opiates from my cabinet, kept there for toothache, and gulped a swig from the neck. Here I was behaving like a virgin on her wedding night. I took another swig, then another. *Enough.* I put the bottle down firmly.

I was asleep when he finally manifested. It seems preposterous, given the state of my mind, but I opened my eyes with a start to see him stripped to the waist, blowing out candles.

"Where've you been?" I grogged out. It seemed too much of an effort to rise up onto my elbows. He left only the bedside candle lit and began to take off the rest of his clothes.

"To the stables, my lord," he answered, his back to me.

"The stables? To see John?"

"Yes, my lord."

I could not see his face. I felt alarmed, convicted in my own eyes, damned by their imagined conversation. I reached for the bottle and took another swig. He watched me, waiting to blow out the last light. I kept my eyes off him, away from his body. "Here, have a swig," I offered.

He surprised me by taking the bottle and gulping two or three long draughts. He was all surprises, my little Jack. He put it down and blew out the candle.

In the darkness, I could feel him shift in bed beside me, then his body leaned over mine. His lips were soft and full. I mewled in surprise, but it was lost under the cushion of his mouth. His tongue frolicked at mine, like an inquisitive kitten. He tasted rich and plummy with the fumes of rum. I sucked his tongue as if it would give me sustenance. His hands ran questing over my chest and belly. He was all child, lost in his wondrous new toy. He kissed into my neck, his teeth nipping against the skin. I felt consumed, eaten.

"Not a dream then," I murmured, feeling his hand's grasp grow fiercer on his new plaything. "Not a dream at all."

His mouth sucked hungrily on mine in reply.

## NINE

One stocking off, one stocking on, tweedle-deedle dumpling, my son John.

John of the wild waves.

It was a strange gesture. I caught it one day when I was haunting the stables, in search of love.

Jack and I had ridden down there, tired and sweaty after a crisp gallop through the cold winter's air of a January morning. Jack had dismounted and led his horse into the stable. I, behind, had been delayed, fiddling with my saddle, steadying the horse. I came in behind him, absorbed in my own thoughts and probably, I realise, the quieter for my self-absorption.

They were standing in the corner of the stable, by the end stall. The horse's rump showed, and the top of her twitching ears. John stood holding, from what I could see, his brother's chin, much as an artist moves his sitter's head to correct the pose. His expression was enigmatic yet faintly unpleasant.

At first, I thought Jack had something in his eye, or some such thing requiring the close inspection of another. But then it struck me as wrong. It looked illicit. Jack's body was arched upwards, as if his face was reaching forwards.

John saw me over Jack's shoulder and lazily, very lazily, removed his hand.

Given the appearance of their positions, his withdrawal looked insolent, like the lover barely conceding to the cuckold. It threw me all of a spin. I was not sure what, if anything, I had seen.

Jack went to see his brother often. Try as I might, I could not feasibly keep him by me always, and he seemed to be at the stables when he was not with me. Nothing odd in that, but I was jealous. It was but a beginning worm, and I was not even sure who it was directed at. Was I consumed by envy of Jack seeing John, or of John monopolising Jack? Or was it simply jealousy that I did not have them both: my fantasy, my dream?

And every night Jack came to me and plied his skills in bitterest silence, and the pleasure he gave me was at once euphoric and shaming, for I could not return it. His body was transparent in its lack of excitement. His hands and mouth seemed fervid enough, and yet he remained persistently flaccid, persistently unexcited, although I could hear his breathing, jagged and fast in the dark. I could not touch him there, coax him up to it, give him anything. And for everything he gave, and I took, I felt further damned. I felt bought. And yet it was an exquisite torture. I could not have raised a finger to stop it. I was addicted: I could not wait for nightfall.

And of John? John was something yet untasted, forbidden, and all his brother gave me only whetted my appetite for what he might offer, in differences and in sameness. I wanted them both; one was not enough.

And above all this, I had a more pressing problem, a more pressing jealousy:

from whence came Jack's knowledge; whence the education behind those pleasuring fingers? Not from a woman. He did things to me he could only have done with another man. Where had he learned it, this arcane knowledge? Another jealousy, another fear. Even of some old affair, some previous lover, I was jealous. I was jealous that he may have loved and given freely of himself to another. Had that other roused him, fed off his excitement in the way I longed? I imagined so. I imagined everything, and it was all my self-destruction.

It took until the return of summer for me to realise my wish, and like my first wish, it came as easily and with as much surprise.

## TEN

It started as a slow, warm day in June. It had been sunny the day before and the heat had built up like a low-burning oven. The night had been close and we had slept with the casements thrown wide open. I had lain on my back and been licked and cajoled into one animal delight after another. I awoke in that exhausted sticky torpor that feels as if your dreams have not left you. I turned on my side and watched him in sleep. He looked damp and dishevelled, like a newborn colt. He, like me, had cast off his covers and was lying more out than in.

His beauty in that morning light was without par, soft and tumescent. I ached for him even after the exhaustion of the night. He was deeply asleep; I could see the slight movement of his eye. He groaned and muttered something incomprehensible. And there it was, stirring into life under the sheet, and surely standing?

I lifted the coverlet and took my peek. I felt the sweat start under my arms; my mouth was dry. It seemed like the snake of legend, stretching up over his russet belly. It was taut and straining, the eye winking with a pearly tear. I reached out my hand.

Oh, just let me touch, but once. Let me feel that pulsing beast, pretend it is my own. Let him not wake; let him dream of who he likes, only let me have it this once – this essence of excitement, of lust. His animal passions caged neatly, hidden, kept for someone else, let *me* have them – let me have *him*.

I saw my hand go round the shaft, close to his belly. It lifted him clear and upright, like a totem pole. I felt it pulse once under my hand. He was close to pleasure; I could see the sweat stand out on his lip. He groaned again, spoke urgently in that unknown dream language.

I searched his face and gripped him harder. "Who is it?" I hissed under my breath. I began to slide his plum-skin up and down. The feel of it was delight: shivery goose-pimple delight. I felt as if I owned him, as if I could destroy him. It was like a knife poised at his throat, waiting for his hot life's blood to gush over my hand. His head thrashed suddenly as he groaned his torment. My heart began to hammer, tripping out a lively jig. "Who is it? Tell me." I rubbed him harder. I could feel the sticky juice on my fingers, easing the passage of that moleskin covering up and down, up and down. "Who is it?" I breathed on his mouth. I ran my tongue over his lips, tasting the salt sweat.

Suddenly his eyes opened, with that immediate unblinking cat stare of his. He always went from sleep to waking without any of that drowsy confusion. My heart lurched; my hand was arrested. His tongue came out from between his lips and licked. I was transfixed by those eyes, caught with my hand in the honey pot. "Please," I said.

Please what? Please say nothing? Please tell everything? Please tell me who it is, who it was, why it isn't me?

"Please, let me." My hand began to move again, cajoling. *Don't let him stop me, not now. I'll die.* It was ridiculous, outrageous, yet real. "Please," I begged him, as if my life depended on it, rubbing him ever more ardently.

He closed his eyes and lay back. "Suck it," he said, his voice thick and slurred. "Come on, suck it." He put his hands behind his head and thrust his loins up.

I never tasted a more intoxicating brew.

## ELEVEN

He made me ask, every time. My abjection was absolute. He would come to me and entangle me and behave like a pagan, except when I wanted *his* excitement. And then I knew what made him stiff – my humiliation, my need. He fed off my abasement. He was rendered powerful by my degradation. Yet I had to have him. He rendered me more giddy in my desires than a monkey, and they could no longer be satisfied without him.

I became more insistent. We would stop on our rides, find some quilted tussock, a hidden bower, some pliant knoll, and I would plunder him inside his garments, pin him against the bark of some aged oak and urge him to spend in my hand. And yet I could not exhaust him. He was cunning and devious, managing to keep me at my distance between times, and then letting me 'catch' him by surprise, ready and able again to let me see him spurt in those copious, earth-shattering pleasures.

I suckled him in the apple store, stripped him naked and goose-pimpled by a stream only feet from the road, and watched while he spent for me. I washed him in my bath, begging him to let me suck it clean. And he conceded to it all with that peremptory detachment; always, always, *always* closing his damned, infernal secretive eyes.

I was no closer. I had gained nothing. I was enslaved, enraptured by a creature I had once treated like a dog. And I was inflamed beyond bearing at each new turn. I felt my lust had heretofore been but a toy, a pantomime. My previous tortures seemed thin, childish.

Each new 'gift' took something further away of my self, my own respect. And now I wanted to know more than ever who it was who had taught him this carnal catalogue of perversions. I was the innocent; he knew everything. And he was nothing but a boy, or at least so he had seemed. Now I know he was older than Methuselah. He made me feel as if my life had been but a slow death. Before him, I had felt nothing, and now I felt everything, like man with the sensitive sickness. I could see now for the first time what Hell might provide for me. And I was sick: sick with longing. The more I knew, the more I wanted. I wanted *all* of him, with his eyes open, wanting me. I wanted his brother, oh so much more potent than the first. I could see them both stretched out before me in a succession of degradation, and I could not wait, could not have been halted, in my desperation to taste every dreg of the bitter drug they fed me.

And so I gained John, as I had gained all things, with an ease that belied the months of waiting.

# TWELVE

It was the height of July, and the weather continued in that vein of unnatural peace. I suggested swimming, perhaps with some half-nostalgia for that last time – only a year ago? – when he would not even go in the water. I sent him to tell John to saddle the horses. As he was going out the door, I called out, "Perhaps you might ask John to accompany us."

I don't know why I did. If I had thought to do it consciously, I would have surely reined my madness in. I stood with my back to him, holding my breath.

"Of course, my lord," he answered, as if I had requested nothing more pregnant with significance than shaving water.

The path was narrow, and so John rode ahead. He wore his hair longer than his brother, and tied it back with a black ribbon. His locks were the same rich russet, and I saw tendrils escape down his neck. I noticed he was wearing a silk shirt, given, no doubt, by his brother who had as many as he could wish.

It made me feel odd to see it there, on the wrong creature, like a man who confuses the gifts between his wife and mistress. Hard on the heels of that thought, followed the other. The other which had plagued me since I had uttered the irrevocable words: would I see him naked?

*It was what you wanted, wasn't it?*

He would see me – how could I hide my lust from him?

*You don't want to hide it.*

The day was warm and my lust sweated out of me like a fever. They must have been able to smell it, like a rutting bull slavering over his herd.

When we arrived at the river, the pool was alive with the iridescence of dragonflies. The surface shimmered and scintillated, just as it had that first time.

I watched John dismount from his horse and saw with a thrill of lust that his chest was covered with silky red-gold hair. I could see his arms likewise covered beneath his rolled cuffs. What strange insidious differences these twins displayed. They were like mirror tricks of the same man.

John tethered the horses and I began to undress. I turned my back to them, let nothing distract me, arouse me. I had just pulled off my boots and straightened up when I saw John walk – deliberately? – into my vision. He hung his shirt on a tree branch. His chest was narrow and hard as his brother's, but covered in that thick reddish hair. The sun shone through it, giving him a pale glow.

I undid my straps slowly, fingers fumbling while I surreptitiously stole glances under my lashes. He pulled off his boots then straightened up and looked directly over my shoulder. He smiled.

At Jack? Who knows? It was a complete and derisive little smile, fleeting and self-contained. I hated him for it. Then he undid his britches and pulled them down.

He was the same; just the same.

I turned curiously to see Jack and discovered he had his back firmly towards us. Had he been like that all along? Why, then, the smile? If not to him, was it *at* him? He followed John into the water with a war cry.

I was last in, and was thankfully spared my blushes by the brothers' boisterous frolics.

The afternoon grew late, the sun still blazed low in the sky, and I lay watching my two water birds sporting and playing. They seemed inexhaustible in their energy, and I was enervated just watching them.

I felt like the hunter who surprises two rare animals at play. I had never seen either so animate. They ducked and dashed one another till I was heartily sick of it. When, eventually, they tired, I witnessed another of those strange gestures that I had seen before.

Jack was half-heaved from the water, crucifying himself on the bank, his back and arms spread out on the grass while his bottom half sported and kicked below the water. The bank shelved there beneath him, so it allowed him to float while resting on his arms.

John, who had been pursuing some animal at the other side of the pool, suddenly swam towards him with purposeful strokes. I watched Jack become warily alert. At first, I suspected some prank afoot, then I saw Jack lick his lips and his head went back in that half supplicating, surrendering way I had seen in the stables that day. His look perplexed me. I could see the parts but not name the whole – then I caught it. He looked anticipatory. Like a man awaiting some strange half-pleasurable, half-fearful event.

When John was but a few yards from him, he suddenly dived down, as a duck will do, with a bob and dip of his white tail. From the bank, I could see the pale rippling eel of his shape shimmering below the surface, like some huge lamprey or water snake. I frowned against the light fracturing on the surface of the pool. I longed to sit up to see better but knew that it would be a mistake. I half suspected they thought me asleep.

I saw his body flash again briefly. He seemed to be swimming under Jack's splayed legs. Then I saw Jack's head drop further back. His body seemed to sag, the tension ran out of him. I saw the creamy arch of his throat, his head thrown back, his hair haloed brilliantly against the sky. His eyes were open, staring. His lips parted as if he had let out a breath. I saw ripples move before his body. But of John, I could see nothing.

I was startled to sit up, when he flung out of the water like a seal, his whole face laughing without a sound. Jack snapped down and clamped his hands on his brother's shoulders, pushing him back under the water, screeching his revenge.

The peace, and the moment, was lost forever.

## THIRTEEN

I dreamt my death in a field of poppies. They were lit with that brilliant white summer light that makes of them a vibrant red tissue: butterfly-wing gossamer fluttering its insufferable fragility, pinned to stems like crane-fly legs. But of course I've forgotten the dream. Only the poppies remain. You forget everything eventually, if you try.

But I remember I could see poppies from my chamber window in the field that stretched beyond the rear of the house. It was a tree-encircled field, where they grazed the horses occasionally. This year it had been turned and planted with clover to be left fallow. Poppies had, as poppies will on newly-broken soil, broken in huge drifts across its clodden treacle. The field was a sea of waving red, and the hot summer had illumined it into that paper-lantern brilliance that intensifies the summer's heat.

I stood by the window, alone in the cool of the house. It was that hour before afternoon tea, when the house seems subdued with the finishing glow of the day's labour. Only the distant sound of crockery, the odd bang of door, broke the peace. The air rustled with leaves and insects.

I could, perhaps, see the stables from here, and perhaps I was filled with that vague longing, whenever I was left alone: my mind preyed upon by the desire to know where *he* was.

*With John?* I wondered how often a day I asked myself this.

John came across the field from the trees. At first, looking for Jack, as I was, I thought it was he, but the differences in his gait – head cocked, arrogant beyond his station – told me who it was. And he was whistling. I could hear the odd snatch of music. I could see his shirt billow out with the breeze. It was a startling white against those red splashes of colour. He looked up at my window. I drew back, lest I be seen, but the sun was in his face, lighting him before; he could not see me.

Jack emerged from the same entrance to the woods. I felt my heart lurch unreasonably to see them both together. Had they been together in the woods? Surely so. What had they been doing there? Why did I imagine the worst?

John climbed up the stile and sat astride it. He looked back over the field then leaned back against the post, shading his eyes with his hands. Jack made slow progress. He looked thoughtful, perhaps sad, with his head down. John, in turn, had his face held up to the sun, his mouth idly chewing a blade of grass as he waited.

Jack seemed to slow as he came to the stile. Had there been a falling out? He stopped about a yard away from where John sat and raised his head. I could see the smile spread across John's face as their eyes met. It was that same evil, enigmatic smile that perplexed me, filled as it was with hidden suggestion, a feeling of secret, private jokes: a sophistication beyond his rank or intelligence.

He said something and Jack shook his head. He said it again, perhaps, his smile sliding from his face. Jack turned his head in temper, like a man clamping words. This was another surprise to me. He had always been acquiescent to the point of obsequiousness with me. I could not quite recognise this transformation. John repeated his command. His posture became more displayed, more bantam in its strut, and Jack finally came forward and climbed onto the stile.

John's hand shot out and grabbed his hair, twisting it into a knot that bent his body like a hunchback. I could see Jack's face, set and truculent, but showing no pain, as he never showed it with me. Now I understood his stoicism.

John muttered something in his ear and let him go with a push. Jack began to stride away without looking back, and then I heard John call his name, once and clearly. Jack stopped, but did not turn or reply. "You'll remember," John called out, not so much a question as a command. Jack nodded once and walked up to the house, John and I watching him all the way.


Jack brought the afternoon tea to my room shortly after. I pulled him to me and ran my hands over his shirt. He was still warm from the sun. I could taste fruit from his mouth. "You've been eating strawberries," I said, looking at his red stained lips.

He uncovered a dish of the fruit from the tray without answering.

"Take your britches off," I said. I could hear the heat in my own voice. I sounded dry and hoarse. This sudden longing to have him was novelty, but the intensity of the urge unsettled me. I watched him undress. He was out of sorts. I could sense it was not something he wanted to do. It inflamed me. I wanted to press demands on him more than ever.

When I pulled him to me, I could taste salt, something more than sweat. He tasted as he did on those nights when I was robust and rode him twice to pleasure. But if I had not had him at all, then who had?

The scene at the stile was still fresh in my mind. I could see John's lazy cruelty. I pulled Jack's head back with sudden violence. I saw him flinch. Oh pleasure to my eyes. Rare, exotic pleasure. "Why do you let him tug your hair like he is berating the ash-shoveller?"

He almost struggled, trying to pull back, pull away. He closed his eyes, pushing the air from his chest like a man defeated, trying to prevent tears of rage.

"Do you *like* it, boy? Is that why?" I tugged again, and once more he flinched, but this time his body seemed to soften; his lips parted. I pulled his head back hard to reveal the line of his throat and licked his neck with the instant hot tongue of lust. I could feel his staff, hard against me, smell the salt sweat of someone else's lust. He licked his lips and pulled my mouth down to his.

## FOURTEEN

We were caught, finally, in the stables. Of course, it had to be in the stables. Why else would I have done it there?

I have questioned myself, justified myself endlessly, and know it to be true. I went there, to him, to be caught, to draw him in. But even then, fulfilling my dreams, my fantasy, I knew who was really snaring who. Beneath everything, as mad as I was, I doubt if I was ever a fool. May God forgive me, I did it all myself. For all their deceit, they can be blamed for nothing in God's eyes.

It was but a scant week after I had witnessed the scene at the stile. I had not again picked up the courage to goad Jack with his brother's cruelty. I deceived myself that it was from kindness. Ah yes, kindness. Kindness to me, *that* was true. For I knew, as sure as I knew my own lineage, that Jack's life's-blood came from John. Not John's cruelty or John's lust, but from John alone, and if I had used him again to stir him, my jealousy would have devoured me. I was a coward, I could not bear to touch him with John. And yet, still, disbelieve me if you will, I knew there was another lover, as yet unnamed, and I *could* not place John with this.

Did he deceive John too? Was that from whence his cruelty came? My confusion was absolute. My arguments made no sense. I was defeated.

We had gone to the stables on some odd pretext, probably manufactured on my part, for it was a day of sultry rain, thick and impenetrable as a grey blanket: the price for the weeks of intense heat. The air was clammy and oppressive. It had been raining at dawn, when we awoke, and was raining still, on the same dull, hissing note, after lunch.

Strangely, our spirits were not oppressed. There was an odd sense of suppressed excitement between us. And I remember that when I suggested we went to the stables, his eyes sparked with that rare light and caught mine briefly in that old familiar twist of satyr that was so startling in his face. I felt my heart plunge and leap simultaneously, with excited dread. We knew – we both knew it then – as if we had been born for this moment.

We ran down to the stables, laughing and breathless under that insistent downpour. The ground was a quagmire. The rain streamed off the gutterings in great gushing spouts. The trees were heavy and black with water.

The lamps had been lit inside the building and the horses seemed dozy in that warm golden shelter.

We went to the end stall. We could hear John above us, moving hay in the loft. Jack's face streamed water. His eyelashes, long and bovine, sparkled with drops. His hair, more curled by the damp, clung in wet tendrils to his face. I was always surprised by how dark it looked when wet. It needed light to bring out the red.

I smiled at him and he ran his tongue along his lips. It was as sweet an invitation as I needed. I moved against him, our wet clothes chill against our skins. His lips met mine partingly, hungrily. This was the moment we had waited for. His eyes were closed. I kissed his face, his neck. I pulled out his shirt and ran my hands over his chest. He felt feverish. Would he make me ask? Must I *always* ask?

But before I could speak, before I could utter that familiar plead, I saw his eyes open. He looked beyond me, and I knew who he saw standing there. Had I even heard him on the ladder? Surely I must have?

All he could see was our heads. Still I could move away. Nothing need be lost.

Jack's eyes came alive with some awful fascination of terror and lust. I hesitated, then slipped my hand inside his breeches. I thrilled to feel him stirring in my grip. I watched his eyes mirror his brother's movements: I could see where he stood on Jack's face. The eyes were still large and greenly afraid, water ran down his brow and dripped into his eyes. He blinked once, but his stare remained unchanged. I could feel that smile, that vicious smile, large and carnivorously white, right through my back.

"John," he whispered. It had not started as a whisper inside him, but thus it came out. Oh, and he leapt so hard into my hand, huge and hungry as he was that first night of the dream.

I turned my head to the side, as a man listening might, then half turned my body towards that unseen presence. I could not face his eyes.

"Let's have a view of it then," he said. His voice sounded commanding in that hissing silence. I finally turned and saw him silhouetted against the square of grey wet afternoon. He moved forward into our circle of light. I stepped back, unconsciously offering Jack's body to his gaze. Jack was pressed to the wall, hands spread as if for support, his britches half-undone. John was stripped to the waist. They faced each other like a nightmare reflection.

"Come on then," John said, his hands reaching out towards his twin. "Let's see what we're made of."

# FIFTEEN

He seldom touched his brother. Perhaps some natural fastidiousness? In that situation, it seemed preposterous, but perhaps some finer sensibility still lurked in him. Why then did he do it?

I began to imagine blackmail and extortion, and then realised that such things could have been had sooner, if they were wanted at all. And anyway, why blackmail a man who already gave you everything? I felt out of my depth.

I dreamt, predictably, of swimming in black seas without shore nor rest, the water always dragging me down, finally exhausted, into an appalling vortex of pleasure. My body would judder into wakefulness and I would find my belly sticky with my own spendings, Jack's hand enmeshed in the thick thatch, relishing in the feel of my emissions.

John watched and relished with detachment. He would pull his brother's britches undone and offer him to me with insolent observations. He would watch while we coupled, and caress himself, always smiling, but never venturing near our lustful bower. Nor would he let me touch him, nor even enjoy the pleasure of seeing him spend. He held his excitement in check, always turning away at some crucial point as if the sight sickened him. And yet he pushed us always together. We had never experienced such carnality as he incited in us. He was with us always, pressing and squeezing his brother, presenting him to me like a whoremaster for my delectation. And Jack, eyes cast down, or blackly sparking with that dry-lipped, wet mouthed lust, would come to me, gorged with blood, always ready to be abused, while his brother watched and watched and watched. Endlessly watched.

But all things change. Everything must. And with that inevitability that had always marked this frenzy, the change came because it was not enough. It is never enough. We could not stop. By now none of us could stop, even to save our own skins.

Perhaps it was no longer enough for John to watch, perhaps Jack was not yet humiliated deeply enough to rouse his ultimate excitement, and I? I still longed for them both, because I, simply, had never had either.

I would have conceded them anything. But I was no longer making the choices. Had I ever?

## SIXTEEN

We were drunk. Doesn't drink make everything justifiable? How many of my sins can I confess to under drink, be forgiven for not being myself? With drink we are all truly ourselves, our souls are without disguise.

Autumn was approaching and a fire had been lit in the library. We, all three, sat round its warm comforting glow, hidden from the world by the thick velvet drapes. I was well drunk, happily immersed in spiced rum, which I shared mouth for mouthful with Jack.

John sat in my armchair and watched us Ashyputtels in our hearth, sharing our bottle, much as a cat watches the ground-bird from his vantage point high in the tree. I do not know how much he had drunk, but other than an unnaturally flushed look to that milky skin, he seemed untouched, except perhaps he seemed sharper, more contemptuous than usual.

He caught my eye and smiled his obnoxious little smile. I held my glass up to him and returned his smile with what I hoped was equal contempt. He leaned his head back on the chair and, watching me from slitted eyes, began to slowly unlace his shirt. I could see the thick red hair beneath the thin silk. I despised myself for the instant quickening of my pulse, the dull betraying red I felt colour my skin. His insolence and blatancy both incited and angered me.

When he reached his belly, he pulled the shirt out, then opened his legs. From the corner of my eye, I saw Jack struggle upright. But I could not tear my gaze from John. He shifted down into the chair, letting him open his legs wider in invitation. He was stiff beneath the fabric of his breeches; they pulled tight against the resistance of the brocade chair. He began a slow thrusting of his loins.

What new game was this? My mouth was dry. I was afraid to make a move.

"Jack," his voice startled me; I turned my head to see Jack sit up with his knees contained between his arms, "why don't you let the master have his way with you?"

Ah, this I understood. Already I began to stiffen in anticipation.

Jack wavered to his feet like a newborn gosling and began to take his clothes off. I sat quietly, waiting for my command.

"Good *boy*, Jack. Now," he said, taking his hand from the chair arm and encircling his staff through his leathers, with long, slow strokes, "bend over that accommodating table and the master will see to you."

He turned his eyes to me. I think it took moments for it to penetrate my drink fumed-brain but it struck home eventually. "And you," he said, "you'll ride him well, like a good steed deserves to be ridden."

He smiled, all pike-mouthed with teeth, and unfastened his breeches, his eyes never leaving my face. "What are you waiting for?" He threw his head back and laughed. "Oh, so that's how the land lies?" He fixed me again with that underbrowed stare. "Never tupped him, eh? Too gentle, gentry. You need the whip, not the sugar lump."

He stood up and came towards me, reaching down to clasp my hand. "First, on your feet."

I looked at his filthy hand as if it might bite me. Nevertheless, I took it. It felt warm, dry and rough as bark. I saw the red hairs glint on his blunt, broad fingers.

He pulled me up with a jerk, flush against him. I could feel his breath on my face. "Needs a little warming up, methinks," and he caught my queue with his hand, as if I was his obedient brother, and pulled my head back. His lips were hard and unyielding. I felt his tongue thrust into my mouth like a rapier.

He let me go just as suddenly and I staggered. "Oh now, here we go, a-falling over," and he led me to the table, where Jack stood bent, legs akimbo. I could see his great thick length hanging down between his legs. His head lay on his hands as if he were asleep.

"Nothing but fledgling schoolboy larks, eh? Well, we'll cure you of that." He spread his brother's legs wide and spat on his hand, and his finger, then two fingers, disappeared up to the knuckle with startling suddenness.

I heard Jack's muffled groan and saw him lift his hips a little higher as if he was eager for their plunge.

"Look at you; you are in a fine way, eh? You'll give this lad a good seeing-to now. Ream him home. Ream him home."

I lifted my spicket and pulled the plum-skin down. The sight of myself, peeled back and placed between his cheeks, already made me want to spurt. I had dreamt of this. I can confess it now; never expressed and long longed for.

John pulled his cheeks apart with both hands. "In you go. Deep now. Make the young whippet cry for mercy."

I held Jack's shoulders and began to push in, slowly, *slowly*, until I was up to the hilt. I could see his head toss from side to side as he whispered some prayer of denial.

"Come *on*, lad, ride him. You're too soft." He slapped my rump a stinging blow.

I slid out and in again carefully. Not for fear of hurting him, but for fear of spending too quickly, of robbing myself of this exquisite moment.

Suddenly John slid behind me. His hands reached round and finished the unbuttoning of my britches, dropping them to my thighs. I did not halt in my rutting. I could not have stopped, supposing God himself had commanded it. Then I felt John's hand push me forward. "Bend and spread, lad. Come on, bend and spread."

Oh, the feel of those hands, the incitement of the liberties they took. I did as he said, careful to slow my charge. Not now, I sermoned myself. Slowly, slowly.

I felt his auger push at my buttocks with a thrill of lust and repugnance. I ached, *longed* to push him off and offer myself up at one and the same time.

Jack shifted beneath me. "*John.*" He whispered the name like an incantation.

"I'm here, boy. You'll feel me in a minute." And he was up me with a sharp, swift gutting pain. That ram-sized shaft was buried to the hilt. I could feel the bastard in my belly. I shouted and tried to pull up.

The punch of his hand rode cavalry over my brief insurrection. "Nay, we'll have none of that. This is a fucking, good and proper. No half-measures for the gentry." And he began to pump in and out, with long hard strokes, stopping just short, then ramming into me with a sharp thrust before he withdrew, teasingly, to plunge in again.

After the dull shock of pain, I began to feel: that incredible threading out from my stomach down through the pit into my arse, an incredible flush that spread up from my bowels with each down stroke and the curling pleasure of fear with every up stroke.

I slid my hand under Jack and felt him stiff as a ramrod. My delight was complete. I began to move as John moved. I could do nothing else.

"Good lads." And his voice was thick and coppery. "Now, let's see how you spend," and he took himself back from me only to thrust himself hard, and ever harder, into my rear.

"Come on now, we can fuck these pretty boys into a lather. There's a fine white staff riding them. Up he goes into that sweet little crack. How big are you Jack, eh?" Then he bent and breathed hot into my ear, "How big is he? Big as that maypole you gift us servants every year? Want to dance your dainty feet round that big pole? Then jig, boy, *jig!*"

And he rode me hard, thrusting into my very chest.

I felt myself spurt deep into Jack as each of John's thrusts pushed me home. I howled and bit deep into his back. I felt as if I would die in the act, as if John would burst out of my mouth and spend on his brother's back.

"Oh I'm giving it now, boy. I'm giving it now. Here it comes!" and he began to buck like a fiend, his hand twisting in my hair as he pushed me ever downwards, suffocating me in the burning snow of Jack's back.

Jack spurted into my hand. He needed no rubbing or friction, just the pain of my steel grip and his brother's wounding thrusts. Then, finally, I felt the gush of John's efforts inside me. He said nothing, only a grim grunting while he pushed me down hard into his brother – his hands on my shoulders in a grip of ecstatic revenge.

I thought I would never sit down again.

## SEVENTEEN

It was the first of many. How admirable to be able to say that was the end of it, we were satiated, finished. At last, the ultimate had been reached and we were cured of our sickness.

And what utter lies we would spew in claiming it. It was never finished. Indeed, it felt like a beginning. It felt new, pristine, something innovative we had never done before. Something irrevocable and something pre-ordained. It was my song, the song of Lazarus: I who was dead was now alive. I who had been asleep was now awake. I felt everything to the tip of my fingers, every experience intense and glowing, as if I dreamt my death in a field of poppies.

But not on this day.

It was winter, although the time was still autumn; the climate severe, as if to punish us, charge us that requisite pound of flesh for our halcyon summer. John had brought logs into the bedchamber, and I remember him kicking the door shut with his foot. I was fingering Jack, who displayed himself by my chair while I watched John struggling with the logs. His colour was high from the cold, very nearly beautiful. He dumped the logs unceremoniously by the fire and grabbed Jack with his cold hands. Jack yelled with shock and half-pleasurable annoyance. "Aha! That stirred your blood! Look how hard he's getting, the little coxcomb."

And he was. The barest touch, even... *often* a look from his brother was enough to make Jack stiff. It made me sick. Sick with envy, and sick with some nameless dread. They never really touched, not with any intent, and yet look at him.

He pushed John off with a mouthful of indecent deprecations, which only seemed to amuse his brother.

John bent to the fire and began putting logs on. Jack had retreated to the end of the bed and sat there in the half-light, still open for my pleasure and temptingly half-hard. He made my mouth water.

"Right, now we're cosy," John said, turning to roast his rump at the fire. "I think we'll have some pretty parlour games tonight."

I said nothing, but my heart began to race.

"Yes, something to tickle my Lord's fancy," and he fixed his eyes on Jack, now illumined sharply in the crackling red flames.

I turned my head to Jack and saw him hold his brother's stare; like men facing themselves in a mirror. They were so different in temperament, even in physiognomy, and yet when lust came within an inch of them, their eyes took on that same intense, almost calculating look. I saw him always, always, *always* grow hard under nothing but his brother's gaze.

"I think," and he began walking towards his twin, "we'll provide a little entertainment for our lord and master tonight," and he stood before him, blocking my view, but I could still see him lift his hand and stroke his brother's cheek, holding his chin for a moment, like that first day he performed the same gesture in the stable.

He turned to me. "On your bed," he bowed ostentatiously, adding, as ever, just a little too late, "my lord. That'll be just tasty, Jack, eh? Just tasty." He turned to me again. "Be a groundling or take your box as the fancy takes you – you don't want to miss a stroke."

I moved over to the window seat, where I could see the bed in side-view. I felt a sick, numb horror in my stomach. I wasn't sure I wanted this, and yet I would not have missed a blink of this macabre pantomime – this dumb-show of brothers coupled together in a sweating stew of sin, all heedless of me. And I *knew* they would be heedless. I knew that as soon as they touched they would be heedless of anyone. And I knew that in *that* I was facing the final unpalatable truth.

Jack lay back on the bed, fully clothed, only with his shaft exposed, stiff along his belly. He put his hands behind his head with a lazy languor, watching John undress.

His was a slow disrobing. Their gaze held steady on each other, their faces wore the same private smile. I watched them begin an intricate weaving of their very beings into one.

John stripped to the waist, leaving only his breeches on. He climbed on the bed and lay his body along the length of Jack's, swinging one leg over his. I saw him thrust himself against him. His hand ran inside Jack's shirt. I could imagine that touch, greedy for his brother's mole-soft skin. He took both hands and ripped the expensive silk shirt asunder with an undisguised glee. Jack's smile widened, but their eyes still held.

John's hand slid down and circled Jack's dirk, lifting it up, proudly displaying it, like a torch to light his way. It seemed huge with delight – had I ever really seen it so big?

"Very good, Jack. Very good." His voice was throaty, pained, as if he were speaking through a constriction.

He began to slide his brother's cockskin up and down, with powerful, slow strokes, trying to make his prick longer, harder. "Another inch, Jacky, another inch," he murmured. I saw his tongue flick his lips. He pushed his pelvis forward with every tug on his brother's scythe. "What do you need, brother? What do you need for that other inch?" His voice had become treacly, sticking to us both with its honeyed promise. His hand moved faster, slicking up and down, up and down.

Jack's smile had faded; his cheeks were flushed. I could see his chest rise and fall as he breathed. Then I saw him reply; I could not hear the words.

"I can't hear you..." John's hand slowed into long deep strokes.

"I need *you*, Johnny," he finally groaned. "I need *you*." His eyelids flickered.

John's hand dragged his cockskin down into his body, peeling his auger taut as a bowstring. Jack arched and groaned.

"Don't close your eyes. What have I told you? Eh?" He punctuated each interrogative with a punishing tug on Jack's already tortured shaft. Jack's eyes opened. I could feel the tension, like fear or lust, come bounding into the room like a rabid animal.

Jack made a noise in the back of his throat. John smiled, releasing his iron grip and once more beginning that slow, persuasive glide. "Well, you're going to get me, Jack. You're going to get me alright, but first…" and he sat up, dropping his prick, and straddled Jack's head. He sat down on his face, grinding himself as if to smother him. He unbuttoned and pulled his shaft out.

I began to fear for Jack's life under that cruel suffocation. John thrust himself forward, riding Jack's face as if it was a rock or a tree limb. He grunted twice, three times, then lifted himself clear an inch from his brother's face. I could see Jack's chest lift with the sudden intake of air, and I could see the twitching of his hair-splitter as it jumped with excitement.

John backed off a little – enough to let Jack's head surface, enough to let him see. "Time for your pap, brother." And he took his staff and pushed it between his brother's lips. "Oh he likes to suckle. Come on, to suck, babe," and he began to push himself into his brother's mouth.

The huge prong stretched the boy's mouth. I could see his cheeks move with its outrageous pressure, and yet he *was* suckling. I could hear the abominable noises. He was relishing it, drawing sustenance, taking his living from it.

John threw his head back and howled like a beast. I felt the hair stand up on my neck. He looked back down at his brother and smiled like the wolf he was. "Come on, plump up, we'll never fatten you on that nibbling," and he began thrusting his prick, holding his brother's head rigid, raping his mouth.

Jack's stretcher bobbed with each thrust. I could see it, dark, stained almost purple, gorged with blood. I could see the glistening strings from its eye to his belly, lifting like webs with every sally.

"Oh that's my lovely boy. Sup your gruel. Come on sup it up, sup." He grunted and rutted then gave a gasp and pulled his sconce out with a sudden pop. "Up."

He threw himself off and delivered his brother a short sharp blow to his face.

Jack rolled off the bed in one fluid movement. His face was flush, his hair soaked with sweat. He knew this part of the ritual. He began pulling his clothes off with haste, then climbed back on the bed. He kneeled down with his head on his hands, his legs parted, his prick angled down, peeled and pointed towards the bed.

John climbed round behind him and reached between Jack's legs. I saw his hand grab Jack's prick and pull it backwards. Jack moved his head with sudden emphasis and bit down on his arm.

"Right, lad, I've got you here." He gave the poker a vicious pull. He took his own auger with his other hand and pushed it in. I knew how easily it parted the waves. I had done it myself already so many times. I felt again that incredible spurt of envy, of hate.

"Right up snug. Now we'll rest a breath. Wouldn't want to spoil things, eh?"

Then it really began. Then I saw everything of their absorption. I read the truth in every line, every movement. *Theirs* was the lust, the only lust. I, the world, were only bystanders, witnesses to their absolute truth.

At first there was a silence, abrupt and absolute, with nothing: no grunts, no gasps of pleasure. Then he began.

"Jack?" This, in a voice different from anything I had ever heard from him. Soft, gentle, insecure. Jack did not reply.

"Jack, tell me. Tell me now." This, wheedling.

Jack still said nothing.

John's movements became slower, more languorous, like a man in love drawing out every drop of pleasure. "Jack? Are you listening?"

I could see Jack's face, turned towards me, startlingly clear, etched by the side-glance of firelight. It was wet with tears.

John groaned and held fast to his brother's shoulders, perfectly still, unmoving. He whispered, "Tell me, Jack. Tell me."

Jack lifted his head and raised himself onto his elbows, thence from there up onto his haunches. John bore his weight from beneath, his sting never emerging from its sweet honeypot.

Jack leaned back against him, seating himself on that meaty sceptre.

John's arms came snaking round, holding him tight, pressing him to his chest, and Jack began a slow ride on that most royal of staffs. I could see it pull out then sally forth again. John's face contorted in an agony of pleasure.

"For you. Only for you." He pulled Jack's head round. "*Always* for you." And their lips met with a fusion of passion that inflamed my lust beyond imagining. I was filled with a bitter, jealous hate. They were like two lovers, parted for years, coming together again.

They broke apart with groans of longing. I saw Jack's staff spring up with a final burst of energy. He moaned, "Ride me, Johnny. Ride me… ride me… *ride* me," with each juddering bounce. His sconce sputtered once, twice, fountaining a milky arc across the blemishless silk of my counterpane, as John gallantly drove his rampant steed home.

# EIGHTEEN

How blind is a man who will not see? Who but a fool, or a fool in love, looks for cuckolding behind other doors when it hides its stealthy face in his own boudoir?

There *was* no other lover. Every time he had come to me, stinking from another's bed, it was John who'd been before me. Every lust, every passion, every sigh of exhausted torpor, belonged to someone else: belonged to his brother; his own brother, his twin. They were an obscenity, an abomination in the eyes of God. I had witnessed their absolute passions. They fed on each other like vampires. Every grain of Jack's knowledge had been licked and fondled and fucked into him by John. For how many summers? For how long had they been lovers? How long their filthy incestuous longings, that had dragged me down to their level, tricked me into their caprices, stewed me in their steaming lusts?

I left them there, alone in my chamber, and walked out into the frosty October air. The world was silvered by a large white moon. I saw everything through a vaporous mist of hate. I felt as betrayed as an innocent. I felt abused, despised. I had made a fool of myself before man and beast. My servants laughed at me. The maids snickering in corridors at my cries of ecstasy; my pleadings with a peasant, begging to be loved: begging to be defamed, robbed of my manhood. I had been made vile. *Vile*.

I stood on that hard earth and stared at my chamber window. I could see the dull glow of firelight. I turned on my heel. I would throw them out. I never wanted to clap eyes on either of them again. With their gluttonous lust, their sickness, their corruption.

I climbed the stairs with a grim determination and approached my chamber when suddenly, without any reason I can yet understand, I stopped and listened. Filled with hate, I wanted to hear their private love. I wanted to know what they whispered to each other in those secret stables, those clandestine trips to the woods, their forays into every place that was withheld from me. These thieves, these liars, these cheats of their betters.

I pressed my ear to the panel.

At first, I could hear nothing but my own thumping, sickly pulse, pounding in my ears. Then I heard someone moving about, then a laugh. My heart skipped a dulled beat of anger. How dare they laugh out of my presence, in my private chambers, without my consent?

There was a murmuring, then I heard the sound of the canopy curtains, then the bed. Another laugh.

I ventured the door ajar an inch or two. They must hear me; I knew they must. Then I could see a little. I widened my spy hole a little more. Jack lay on the bed, watching John somewhere beyond my vision. He laughed then spoke: "No, not that one. The red, that ruby brocade. That's it, Monsieur Magnificent."

I could hear the rustle of clothes. He was in my closet. What in God's name was he doing with my clothes?

"The velvet britches, they hug him like a bear. You haven't his loins, Johnny." This last with a teasing laugh. I could not make out John's reply, only mutters amid the rustles.

Jack raised himself on his elbows to see better. "My God, you could pass for the brute. Put on the jacket. No, over there, on the peg. That's it."

More laughter, then his face settled into that beautiful evil angel smile. His voice crooning, "Oh Johnny, Johnny." He lay back and lifted his staff from the tip. Circling it with his fingers, he made a lascivious loop and tugged on the head. "Come here. Come let me feel."

John hove into my vision. He was dressed in my black velvet suit with white silk shirt and red brocade waistcoat. Indeed, he did bear a passing resemblance to me. But the hair was too rich, too leonine. I felt fury bend my very teeth with its buck and kick.

Jack reached out and began to rub his brother's pizzle through the thick velvet. "Kiss me."

John bent forward over the bed. They looked like some depraved diorama, an obscene Princess and the Rose; Sleeping Beauty being awakened by the prince; Narcissus kissing his own reflection. They were phantasms from a beauteous dream, and I hated them for every angle of perfect symmetry they possessed. It was not mine. No part of them was mine. They were one: one man, indivisible, striving to be complete, enraptured by their own seamless verisimilitude.

I dared not breathe. The kiss was tender, yielding. I saw John push the tendrils of hair back from his brother's face, then begin to kiss the column of his throat. Jack's hands began to rove over my waistcoat, feeling the plush, brushing it against the inner skin of his wrist. He murmured his brother's name as if he could not believe in his transformation, as if he might place him inside my skin through that incantation alone. John suddenly stopped. "Let me take off this finery."

Jack held his arm. "No, leave them be."

"Why?" John frowned down at him.

"It pleases me."

"You mean it *excites* you." The frown was deeper. "You enjoy him, don't you?"

Jack started rubbing the sleeve of his cuckoo's jacket. His fingers looked deathly white against that raven black. "I enjoy his clothes. I enjoy the way he eats and drinks. I like the way he sits on a horse." He slid his hand into the folds of the jacket. "I like the way he sits on *me*."

John grabbed his arms and pinned them back against the bed. "You're a conniving little trollop. A nancy little pickpocket. He doesn't know what he's got in bed with him, does he?" He let go his hands and backhanded him. "You're a lead-penny little whore."

Jack lay there, tight, enclosed, as indifferent as I had ever seen him. His eyes shifted like a cat's, watchful. His tongue came out, licked his lips and was gone.

John grabbed his shoulders and shook him. "Don't try and dazzle me, in your whore's Vauxhall Glass. What d'you think I am?" He dropped him. "Dance for your damn whoremaster. I don't care. Just don't expect me to jig to his tune."

Jack smiled then reached up his hand. "You're too late. He's already had you. Every night, using my mask for your face." And he mimicked my voice so close I might have been lying on that bed, taking his brother's punishment for my own: "Oh, Johnny, please come for me. I want to feel you spend, *John*. "

"Shut up," and John yanked him up by the hair and slapped him again. "Can't you shut your filthy little mouth?"

He dropped him on the bed and stalked out of my vision. I could see his shadow cross Jack's body, to and fro, as he paced by the fire. There was a trickle of blood running down from the corner of Jack's mouth.

"One of these days I'll kill you, Jack, so help me. You're nothing but a whoring little whelp."

He turned suddenly and hove back into view. His face worked as he looked down on his brother. Then he bent down.

Jack took his abject kisses, lay repeating that same lazy movement with his fingers, circling up and down, skimming the plum. His lips were stained a bloody crimson, his teeth unnaturally white, as he smiled, delivering his final valedictory command: "Leave them on, Johnny. Leave them on."

## NINETEEN

I dreamt my death in a field of poppies. Am I afraid of dying? Yes, I am. I'm afraid of living too; living to see others have what I haven't; to see others take what is mine. I'm afraid of everything.

My lineage, my wealth, my power are nothing against this compulsion to degrade myself.

How long have I held a secret passion to be used, to be abused, to be denigrated and debased? How long before a man sees himself? Does he ever?

How long might I have lived? Would I have died the sagely red-nosed squire, vicious to women, beloved of men, despised as only a despot can be by his servants?

How long? How long anything?

Or would it have been another, if not him, if not these? Which him? Why 'which'? There is only one. There has always been only one.

I dreamt my death in a field of poppies, and all I could see was red. Great sweeping swathes of red, bright, crimson, spread across the earth. Waves of bloody red, drowning me.

Why am I putting it off? What am I saving it for? Do I hope to redeem myself or spare you, in the telling?

Let me tell you. Listen to the words.

It was December. Two months after that fateful night. Yes, two months. You are counting, not I.

Two months. How many days is that? How many nights, slept together, twined together, wedged between them, a thorn in their side? A thorn in *John's* side. Perhaps. Who knows? Who knows what John thought? I could never penetrate that mind, read his eyes, judge his feelings. He was always an enigma to me.

And what was Jack to *him*? The same elusive figure. The same enigma. He was John's reflection. The real man stood before the mirror, Jack within. He was flat, a stage-maker's oilcloth, a paper puppet. And we were all besotted with him.

It was December. For two months I had witnessed their cojoining. They had lain before me, performed. I had become a passive spectator, a voyeur on their unholy alliance. At night, alone with Jack, I would take him again, spend myself on his satiated body while he lay quiescent, questioning him: "How does it feel when he does this to you?", "Do you like it when he …?" I tortured myself.

I took him again in the morning, insisting that he spend for me, always describing those feelings of love, the passion, the lust that I could only ever experience at one remove. We played games, dangerous games where often John would lose his temper and attack his brother with studied viciousness. And Jack soaked it all up: the rages, the beatings, my frustrated lust; his brother's frustrated love. All was meat and drink to him. And it was not the last time John dressed in my clothes. They would have me stripped naked while John dressed and acted my part, shafting Jack into delirious abandon while I sat boiling with unconsummated lust and anger; jealousy and rage.

We fucked everywhere. Once on the breakfast table, between courses, finishing our furtive fumblings only just in time. Always in the stables, when it rained, the three of us in the hayloft spending with loud cries that must have been heard in the servants' quarters. Outside, in the ruins of an old farm, in the dead of a November night so cold we could barely stand, and John sucking Jack to the peak, then watching his essence shoot in great spurts under the moonlight streaming through the skeleton roof. Nothing was debased enough, nothing tragic enough; nothing too low to destroy us, except love.

There was a chapel, originally my family chapel, which lay to the west of the horse pasture. In summer, when those poppies were in full bloom, the chapel could not be seen for the verdancy of the trees. But in the winter, as it stood now, its solid ecclesiastic outlines were revealed amongst the skeletal trees. I had not used it since I had come home. What would *I* do in a church, other than lust after the figure of Christ naked on his cross?

My family had been Catholics when the church was built, and for some reason the decoration had never been altered, despite the Anglican who now took service in it. Perhaps beauty had won the day. Now, it was only used for Sunday service for the estate and a handful of village worthies, but I never attended.

It was Jack who suggested it. We weren't even drunk, by the grace of God.

It excited me. I knew what he wanted and it excited me. He was goading John by petting me. Or to be rather more truthful, by allowing me to pet him. I remember he was wearing work clothes that day, rich brown moleskin breeches and a rough shirt of some heavy cream linen. He looked as if he had stepped down from some rustic painting of a lad and his lass. His rough clothes incited me further. He was playing games, always games, with such dangerously loaded weapons.

John said nothing, but threw on a heavy woollen cape. I put on my jacket and we left the house. We had to cross the poppy field to reach the church and the wind whistled stinging barbs of ice into our faces as we crossed the hard-frozen turned earth. I could feel the beginnings of snow whip around my scalding ears. I held the key in my hand. We could expect no interruption on this grey leaden afternoon, but I doubt if we would have cared.

In the event, the church was already open and quite warm. The stove had been lit but was burnt low. It was a small chapel, heavily decorated in gold with rich old stained glass. The altar was richly encrusted, and above us hung a beautiful Italian alabaster Christ. And, by God, he *did* look like him. That deathly cream skin, the red hair. Christ's eyes were shut, his bleeding hands clenched, but I could imagine his eyes green.

John stood beside me. "It looks like him."

"And you," I said, turning to look at him.

"No, there's no martyr in me." And he turned away and yelled for Jack.

He emerged from the vestry, carrying an ornate robe. There was nothing Anglican about that either. It looked papist to the last golden strand.

"Come on, Johnny, put it on."

"No, not me. Enough of your games, Jack." He plumped down on a pew and stared stonily at his brother, his mouth a fixed line.

"Well, my lord?" And he turned to me, his eyes meeting mine in that rare glimpse of lust that I had come to treasure more than anything: that small crumb of his corrupt soul.

I looked to John. He would not look at me. *Yes*, I nodded once.

He came up to me and began undressing me. I could hear the sleet hiss on the windows. The altar candles flickered at each fresh burst. I felt goose-pimples rise on my skin. I doubt if the robe had been designed to be worn naked and it was some heavy satin unpleasantly cold to the touch. In places, it had worn away. The jewelled brocading on the front hung heavily. I could feel the weight pulling on the back of my neck.

"A man of God. A veritable cardinal. An angel," Jack crooned. He parted the front just enough to expose me. "Look, John, isn't he an angel, with that strawberry hair, his fair blue eyes? Such an angel."

John only lowered from below his brows and said nothing.

"He's jealous because he's a profligate heathen and will never go to Heaven. He knows he's going to roast in Hell." Jack suddenly threw himself at my feet. "An absolution. Confess me, father. Relieve me of my sins."

"Indeed not," I said, tugging the robe away from his hands. "You are too pretty a boy to have sinned. Go away." I stalked up the aisle to the altar in mock indignation. He crawled along behind me, pleading.

He climbed the altar on his knees and hung onto my legs. "Oh hear me, father, I have sinned."

I tried to prise him loose, but he held fast. I felt half-excited, half-afraid. "Oh, very well, tell me then..."

He pulled himself up against me, holding me tight around the thighs. I laid my hand on his head.

"I have sinned, father." His head nuzzled for the opening in my gown.

"Yes," I said, "go on." I could feel the pulse begin to beat in my temple.

"I have committed onanism father, many times."

His head butted. I made a noise signifying nothing. He pushed in between the folds. The gown fell open.

"Yes," he kissed me, "many times," another kiss. "I have spent, father, copiously, on stony ground. My seed is dispersed upon barren soil, father."

"My son," I whispered. I ran a hand through his hair. Thick, soft, russet silk. I loved that hair with all my being.

"With men, father. With many men. I have committed sodomy, father." His kisses became more fervid. He ran his tongue up and down my shaft, nibbling the plum. He nuzzled my belly, pulled the hair between his teeth.

"Many?" I asked, trying to withhold my gasps.

"Oh yes... father.... many. Since I was but a child, father..."

I thought we were playing a game, enjoying yet another frisson of corrupt pleasure. He pulled me into his mouth with that quick, deep suckling that so marked him.

I pulled his head into my groin. I thrust into his mouth. "Here is your penance. You must suckle on the holy rod every day, till it runs dry, then you will attain the Kingdom of Heaven. We will attain it together." I looked up and saw John's face, deathly white, like a man who has witnessed an unbearable revelation. I had never seen him so pale, so stricken. I think I may have spoken: "What ..." but Jack was talking again.

"My first was my own father. Forgive me, lord. I was but thirteen years old and I saw his nakedness, may God forgive me."

I heard the words. I saw John's face. He had stood up. "Enough of your games, Jack." But Jack went on – his voice went on: "I'm a bastard. A craven little bastard." He bit me sharply.

"No more," I said. "You are forgiven. You have your penance." I tried to pull away.

But there was no halting him. "Lord Monsour, father, one-time lord of this manor, *my* father."

I looked down at him, up at John. The truth was written there for me, although I did not want to read it. "No," I said.

"Oh yes, father. Father of me, father of my brother, father of the present Lord Monsour. Duke of four counties. Monarch of all he surveys. Father of you, *father*, father of *you*."

"You lie."

"Oh no, father, I never lie. It's not one of my sins. Thirteen years old, soft and white as a girl. In the stables. I knew he was my father, and he knew I was his son. Taught by a master. A *loving* master."

I pushed him off and backed against the altar. I clung to it lest the weakness in my hamstrings drop me to the floor. I felt I must faint. Somewhere outside myself, I could hear the spiteful snow rattle against the casements. The sky was almost black. His face was lit by tallow light. John stood like a man etched in wax.

"And my brother, John, my *loving* brother, a little innocent foundling before, but after my father I could teach *him*. John suffers from fascination – don't you, John?" He lifted his head like a man listening.

But John made no reply.

Jack laughed. His eyes fixed on mine. I could see everything in his soul, read every depth that he had ever hidden from me. At last, when it was mine, when I held him in my hand, I discovered I no longer wanted him. Oh God, that I had thrown away my innocence so easily. His eyes were greener than the slime of corruption.

"He used to tup me in your mother's bed."

"No." I put my hands to my ears.

"Oh yes. He was like you; had a taste for young boys. I always wished I'd known him younger. Then my chance came. You arrived."

He advanced towards me.

I backed away, along the altar, as if he might destroy me with his touch.

"Look, John, he's afraid of me." John still stood immobile.

"John never really knew our father. John's always been a bit jealous. Isn't that right, John? There was a curate, a beautiful young man. He taught me to read. Every night in this chapel. And I taught him *fellatio*. A fair exchange. And the woodsman. Stocky as a tree, covered in thick foliage. He was hard to seduce, but he had the temptation of loneliness. He lived in that cottage, the one you frigged me in, remember? I only had him twice. The first time I inflamed him sufficiently to break the barriers, the second I tricked him in his cups. His was the most brutal, the most rending. John didn't know about that – did you, John? John's jealous, you see – doesn't do to tell him everything. Your father came here more and more often. Couldn't get enough, just like you. Took me to bed with him, fornicating with his own son while his wife lay awake far away down the long dark corridor. He used to cry out in ecstasy. Perhaps she thought it was the housemaid."

He laughed a wild little laugh. "He used to keep you away from here. Perhaps he didn't trust me. Oh, and I did have the miller's son, one brief summer in my fifteenth year. John didn't know that either, eh John? Eighteen, he was, and hung like a horse. And you know what his taste was? His little peccadillo? The curate's word, that. Never thought about my educated tongue, never cared about it, did you?" He grabbed the front of the robe and shoved me back against the altar, letting me go just as suddenly, with that same brilliant, unrelated smile.

"He liked to be razored with the cut-throat. I used to hold his huge dirk in one hand, slicking the blade around it while he shivered with fear and delight and got stiffer and stiffer. Then he would admire my handiwork in a little cheapjack mirror, while I pulled away on his great naked sconce as if it was made of caoutchouc. I missed him when he left. And of course your father died, didn't he?"

I could say nothing. I could not move; the candles guttered low. He slapped me sharply – left, right, left, right – as if to round up an unruly schoolboy's want of attention. I stood like a dumb animal while he pounded my face. He stopped, stroked my cheek. Tears streamed down it. "Yes, of course he did. Your father killed himself."

"He died in a fall."

He laughed like an inmate of Bedlam, full of mad delight. "An accident!" His face changed suddenly: vicious, twisted, sneering. "Your mother walked into his bedchamber one night, unannounced. Perhaps the stupid bitch thought she'd catch him with the maid. Perhaps her little quim was on fire and she wanted your father, *our* father, *my* father," his spittle sprayed in my face, "to give her a little cooling draught. Instead, she caught him peeling me. Sixteen years old, hardly a hair on me, but already sporting that long white prick you love so much. Can't you just see it? He was on his knees beneath me, begging me to spend for him. Just like you do. Like father like son. For three years he had been carnal with his own son. He made excuses to escape his wife and business in order to ream his own flesh and blood. And now here he was, caught in a web of his own devising."

He laughed that lunatic laugh again. He stopped and his face fell into a deathly pallor. He was shaking like a leaf; two hectic spots appeared on his cheeks. "I'd have given him anything. What could she offer? He hadn't mounted her since he'd laid her out with you."

He stopped as if plunged back into sudden memory, then started up again: "He pushed me away and ran out of the house. I pulled on my clothes and followed him. I could see him already almost at the stable. 'Johnny, don't give him his horse, Johnny!' I pleaded as I ran, praying, praying. But Johnny had to give him his horse – didn't you, Johnny? He was gone before I could reach him. I ran into the stable and told John to saddle me a horse. 'Quickly,' I demanded, '*Quickly*,' but he wouldn't move. Johnny was jealous, you see. Johnny was always jealous.

"He rode his horse right up to the selvage of the frozen pond. The horse wasn't stupid; it threw him, pate first, onto its stony crust, cracking the shell of ice and bleeding his brain into a fatal slumber that he might drown all the easier."

He pounced on me with a sudden frenzy, grabbing the robe, choking it against my Adam's apple. "He robbed me. *You* robbed me." Tears of anguish ran down his face. "I would that he would have *recognised* me, but it was lust, only lust. He even begged me to entice John. He wanted to watch his sons couple together. I told him who we were and all it did was make his prick hunger the harder. I hated him. Just as I hate you."

He made to press me back, choke the life out of me entirely, but I tore free and ran down the side aisle. I reached for the door, but John was there before me, grim and white-faced, standing between me and freedom. But, in truth, he faced only Jack. I had ceased to exist. I was but my father's shadow. We were all but shadows in the shade of their granite hatred.

"Jacky..." John's voice sounded leaden, pregnant with grief.

"Get out of my way." Jack pushed up against him.

John's hand snaked out and caught one of his brother's wrists against his chest. I could not see his other hand. Suddenly Jack stiffened. I saw his eyes widen in shock.

"You lied, Jacky. You *lied* to me."

Jack took a step back. He stared down at his belly. A knife hilt stuck out, as unnatural as an antler sprouted, fantastical, from his gut.

"You said you loved me. You said he *made* you. All those nights I suffered for you. All that love, wasted on lies."

Jack's face was still disbelieving, not registering his transformation into this bizarre roebuck with death thumb-printed on its skin. I could not move. I was sick-to-my-soul afraid; plague-black afraid.

"'Only you, John. Only you,' and you were lying all the time. I *loved* you. May God forgive me, I love you still."

Jack grabbed the knife with both hands and pulled. I shouted then – to stop him, to keep his guts in that dying shell for but a moment longer, to see him still breathe, his skin still blush with that wonderful rhubarb pink.

But it was too late. The knife came out like an unwilling lugworm, sucking grimly at the mouth of its torn burrow.

John's face crumpled in on itself. He watched with horror, now pressing his hand over Jack's wound, trying to stem the flow of blood. It seeped, dark and oily, down the skin of his breeches.

"Get out of my way."

"Be still, Jack. Be *still*."

"Out... of... my... *way*, brother."

John stumbled back under that dead man's shove and Jack pulled open the door. He staggered out into the night.

The snow lay thick on the ground, like a quilt of down. The moon had risen and the night was suddenly still. Jack lurched across the snow like an unwinding automaton. That trail of blood seemed to flow out of him in an ever-widening smear, our footprints spreading it as we followed his ghoulish bridal train across the field.

Jack fell halfway to nowhere. We tried to lift him, but he would not be moved, hissing and swinging like an animal when we approached him.

Suddenly he cried, "*John!*" like an ailing cat will when the light begins to fade from its eyes.

"I'm here, Jack. I'm here." The tears streamed down his face.

"Come lie with me. I'm bitter cold."

And as he lay down over his brother, I saw the blade gut upwards, like a sudden flourish of iron grass sprouting from the snow. It went deep into his stomach, with far more power than either man should have possessed, never mind the fading one. John groaned and gripped his belly, trying to hold his guts together.

"Now we can spend together." Blood welled from Jack's mouth. "Come kiss me." And he dead-weighted John's head to his mouth.

My eyes misted over then, as if my tears had frozen. All I could see was a sea of blood across that field of blinding white, like a dream of death in a field of poppies.

I walked away from them, still warm, still living. They bled to their deaths alone in that field, melancholy reflections, reflecting like two opposing mirrors, on and on into eternity.

I sold the estate. Isn't that what they always do when there's a tragedy?

Of course, this was no tragedy. Two peasants dying like frozen cattle in a winter's field in the dead of night. Two guttersnipe brothers perished in a drunken fight over dogs or whores. And me? I had the innocence of power and wealth behind me.

Always.

Three brothers died in that field that night, but only one still walks the earth. And I am he. Lazarus who was dead, but yet is risen, walking among the living, a corpse without animation, without heart or soul, waiting for God to forgive him and let him die.

For yes, I dreamt my death in that field of poppies.

And now I wait to lie down.

# Afterword by Chancery Stone

This afterword contains PLOT SPOILERS, so please don't read it till *after* reading Nothing But A Negro and The Boy With The Red Hair. I know, that should be obvious, but if you're like me you flick through books backwards. Okay, you don't do that, but I really don't want to spoil these for you, so don't read this afterword till you've read the damn book, okay?

The two stories you have just read are the origin stories not only for each other, but also for my massive magnum opus, The DANNY Quadrilogy.

The first story, Nothing But A Negro, or The True Story of Robinson Crusoe, was written in the 1980s. I never had any luck selling it round magazines because nobody had the first clue what it was about. I even went so far as to give it the (present) subtitle, so that it would give people a hint (in the nature of the bleeding obvious), and send it out all over again, but still no joy. It remained far too cryptic for magazine editors.

When I went back to re-edit it for inclusion in this book, I was expecting to read some high-fallutin' piece of obscurantism, because that's how I'd come to think of my work from back then, as difficult and obscure, since it was regularly rejected for those reasons. But I was most surprised to see that it's perfectly clear what it's about – at least with the subtitle – and what's more, it's expressed rather well, if I say so as what shouldn't.

The idea for the story came from my love of the 1964 French TV series, The Adventures of Robinson Crusoe, which was dubbed rather wonderfully into English and had a great theme tune. This had a decidedly beautiful Robert Hoffman, a very blonde Aryan Austrian, playing the Yorkshire-man, Crusoe. Friday was a rather lush Polynesian-looking actor called Fabian Cevallos (who I suspect was actually Italian), although in my story I made him ebony black.

Although I didn't recognise it at the time, it was all very sub-rosa homosexual – all male-bonding and hero-worship – and that early tingle of the forbidden stayed with me over the years. Older, wiser, and altogether more twisted, I one night decided to write the story up as I imagined it would *actually* be if an aristocrat was alone on an island with a 'servant' who not only owed him his life, but was an outcast with nowhere else to go. What if Robinson's loneliness justified the unjustifiable, and he found himself contemplating a triple-whammy of taboo-busting?: an aristocrat with a 'native', a white man with a black, and worst of all, a man with another man.

Man, if you'll pardon the pun, that was a tortured love story to die for.

And so Nothing But a Negro was born, a study in what it would be like to be trapped on a desert island, alone, with someone you wanted, and over whom you have implied authority, but no actual physical power, yet you cannot touch them because of all these deeply-ingrained social taboos, which you don't *really* need to uphold. After all, who's going to tell?

Subsequently, my Crusoe's madness plays itself out via endless plotting of poor Friday's downfall, even to the extent of planning to some day take him home and extinguish the very thing he loves about him by letting him wither away in the cold British climate. And then, of course, the necrophilia comes knocking. But that's a whole different story....

When I left London, Nothing But A Negro came with me, still unpublished, to my new tiny one up-one down cottage in the village of Crosby, West Cumbria, where, trying to write something more challenging, I turned the aristocrat and servant premise into a more classic across-the-class-divide tale, but threw in a bizarre love triangle to complicate matters. And thus the second story in this anthology, The Boy With The Red Hair, was born.

When I wrote The Boy With The Red Hair, I had no intention of writing a novel, although I was fed up with short stories and the grief they involved, trying to get magazines to take them. Ironically, I would have fared better now, with the internet and its insatiable demand for short, easy-to-read fiction. What does that say about humans? We're regressing; it's true.

I was inspired both by themes from Nothing But a Negro and my new next door neighbours, of whom I knew nothing, other than that they ran a dairy farm; 'they' being mum & dad and their family of four sons. They had a fascinating dynamic of mysterious pecking orders and hidden resentments, and, of course, a pair of rather fetching eighteen-year-old red-headed, curly-haired twins called John and Stephen.

There was also a blonde, slightly rock-starrish favourite son whose name began with R and who looked *nothing* like his brothers. So much so, I originally believed he was a cousin living with them. The last and eldest son had (too much) authority over his brothers, and shit-brown curly hair, but otherwise bore no resemblance to his fictional namesake/s, being a genial, good-natured boy, not John material at all. However, put all these elements together: the handsome blonde aristocrat from Robinson Crusoe/favoured blonde middle son, then add in the two put-upon youngest twins/coveted Man Friday from my *first* story, and bingo! A whole new cross-bred cur was born: The Boy With The Red Hair.

I started 'The Boy' on 12th June 1990. And finished it July 19th that same year: just over a month. I was so taken by its love triangle and the idea of a secret twin that I plunged straight into DANNY, without knowing I was doing it. In fact, I was so desperate to explore these new relationships that I couldn't be bothered with the historical setting and just set it contemporaneously.

Every day I churned out more and more pages, and more and more of my newfound heroes, the Jackson Moores, came pouring out of me, their secrets getting more and more complex. I literally learnt their history as I wrote it, and often it would shock and surprise even me. My Progress Logs for the time are full of "Jesus Christ, what are they doing *now*?" and similar exclamations of horror and dismay. I frequently bemoaned them changing the plot on me, doing sudden volte faces, and the *lying*? – my disgust at their mayhem knew no bounds.

I found myself giving the John & Jack characters of The Boy With The Red Hair more and more time on stage, backing the poor old aristocrat into an ever-shrinking role until he ended up, in DANNY, as a decidedly neutered cousin, Rab.

Rab was, in fact, the original leading man in DANNY. I just lifted the aristocrat role and re-inserted him as the arrogant blonde cousin, but he was soon ousted by this new, altogether more alpha-male version of John, who put him so firmly in his place I was obliged to go back and give many of Rab's scenes over to him before I could carry on. So, DANNY's central 'love story' was almost Rab and Danny. Unthinkable now.

At the end of the day, Nothing But A Negro and The Boy With The Red Hair are enjoyable stand-alone stories, effective portraits of jaded rich men and their collective downfall through sexual obsessions. They are more po-faced, lacking DANNY's black humour, although 'The Boy's' aristocrat does compensate by having a good sarcastic tongue in his head, but for me they will always be first and foremost the DANNY prototypes.

Well, that's the history, so I'll take a back seat now and let you have a glimpse into the mad, bad world these stories helped create: *Heeeeeeeeere's* DANNY……

If you have enjoyed this book please post a review to your favourite online bookstore today

67

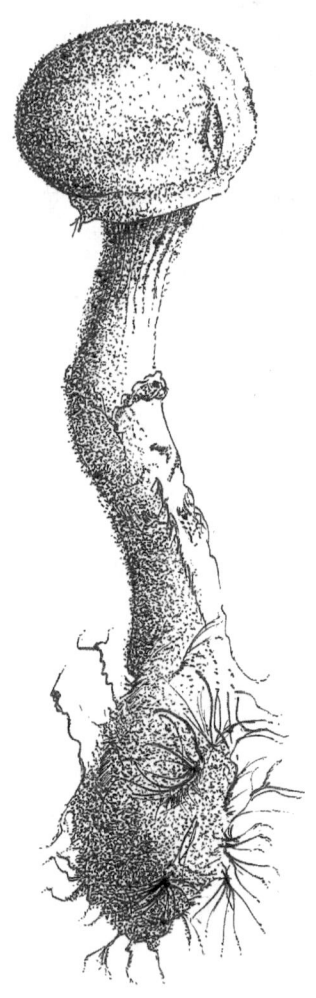

# Free Excerpt from
# DANNY 1 – Hope House

ISBN 978-0-9567154-3-2

"What of the very handsome boy, seeing himself in mirrors, hearing
people comment on his beauty?.... Like the adolescent girl who
must walk more slowly and be less, the boy must give up knowing too
consciously what his beauty buys him. How very twisted."

### Nancy Friday *The Power of Beauty*

"Research shows that when sibling bonds are intense and exert a formative
influence on the development of personality… these siblings use each other,
much as other children use their parents, in a search for personal identity.
It should not surprise us, then, that violence between siblings is more
common than violence between parent and child or violence
between spouses. Sibling violence is the most overlooked form
of domestic violence. Knives or guns are used by one sibling
toward another in three out of a hunderd cases of sibling violence."

### Jane Goldberg *The Dark Side of Love*

"If you cannot get rid of the family skeleton
you may as well make it dance."

### George Bernard Shaw

Danny was waiting for the bathroom. Danny was *always* waiting for the bathroom. He was still sitting in the kitchen when his mother came in. She passed behind his chair, pausing to look at the back of his neck. "You're peeling again."

Danny flinched away from her. He heard the fridge door open and close, the sound of a milk bottle. He did not turn. "Tell me about it."

He rubbed his stinging neck, trying to ease the stiff nettling pain, then dropped his hand in disgust and took a swig of beer from the can on the table. He didn't even know whose it was.

He heard the kitchen door open and close as his mother went out again, the television babbling briefly in the front room, playing to no-one in particular. He stood up and crossed to the dresser, picking up a piece of pie crust from the dish. It tasted unpleasantly salty. He threw it back on his plate and sat down again heavily.

The dog wandered into the kitchen and lapped noisily at his water bowl then fell into the doorway in an undignified heap, trying desperately to catch the slightest stirring of air through the open door.

The kitchen door opened yet again, with a suddenness that made Danny look up. John came in, wrapped only in a towel. His dirty brown hair, bleached with the sun, curled wetly on his neck. He looked twice as naked as anyone else would have done in similar circumstances.

Their eyes met briefly, away again. John pulled the towel tighter about his waist before saying, "Plenty of hot water left."

Danny nodded. He heard the glass cupboard door behind him open and close. He got up with a noisy scrape of his chair and went out quickly, before John could say anything else.

The bathroom window stood wide open, letting in the last of the evening light. It was a pink room and the red setting rays of the sun deepened the roseate light. The large mirror above the basin streamed with long streaks of condensation and odd sworls where the others had attempted to clear it to shave.

Danny undid his jeans and peeled them off, throwing them in the wash-basket, then his shorts. He turned on the shower and stepped under the sharp scalding spray. He could almost feel the weariness seeping out of his bones and running down into the shower tray.

He lay back against the wall and turned his face up into the spray, running his hands up slowly over his chest. He jumped guiltily when someone pounded on the door.

"Don't be all bloody night in there."

"Oh fuck off," he whispered fiercely, turning his back to the door and scrubbing water from his eyes.

"You hear me?" More pounding.

"I hear you!" he yelled back.

Nothing. Silence. He let his forehead drop against the wall and closed his eyes.

After a moment, he straightened up and took the soap and washed down, careful not to linger or rub too hard. He shampooed his hair and rinsed.

The towel was rough and dry, and he got a masochistic pleasure out of rubbing his sunburn. He could not see himself in the mirror to shave and did not try. He moved to the bathroom window, letting the air blow dully on his damp skin. It felt shivery and cool and vaguely disturbing.

The bathroom faced onto the backyard. He could see the tractors parked below, looking oddly desolate and abandoned, John's parked awry as usual.

He wondered briefly if anyone could see him up here.

He turned away abruptly, feeling that odd prickling sensation of arousal again.

He went to the sink and brushed his teeth with a punishing enthusiasm that left his mouth numb. His mother always bought the same clear bright green toothpaste that blew your mouth off. He couldn't feel his tongue afterwards. Maybe he ought to scrub his prick with it.

"Danny!" The door thumped again.

"Alright, alright. I'm coming!" He grabbed a towel and knotted it round his waist then opened the door.

"Don't know what the hell you find to do in here." His father pushed past him, slamming the door in his face before Danny could even frame a reply.

He stood there for a moment, staring blankly at the door, then stuck his tongue out with an intense childish pleasure.

He turned away and went along the hall to his room.


He pushed the sash window up a little higher and stood looking out onto the village green. The sky was noticeably darker at this side of the house, but the breeze was still poor and dull. Danny stood at the window and ran his hand through his damp hair. It always formed a thick tangle of curls when is was wet. Time-it-was-cut season again. Well they could fuck that.

He could see the vague forms of people moving about on the green below, hear the odd murmur of conversation. He felt restless and irritable. He was over-tired and his hair was wet. He hated sleeping on wet hair, but it never had a bloody chance to dry because that lot never let him have first shower, fucking...

Rab banged suddenly on his door. "Put that down and get to sleep."

He heard John's low laugh, could almost see his smug smile. "You probably woke the bugger up."

Danny gave them the finger, but did not answer them.

"'Night, Danny," Rab called. But Danny still did not answer. He heard them laughing together, then their doors closing in succession.

After a minute or two he heard the toilet flush, and then the bathroom door open, and his father shouting something down to his mother. She, too, finally came upstairs. He could hear his father's muttered replies until their door, too, clicked shut.

Danny lay down with a sigh and immediately felt his wet hair, cold and unpleasant, against his neck. He sat up with a jerk, cursing under his breath, and reached for a cigarette.

He lit it and sat watching its glow ebb and flow as he smoked. He wasn't supposed to smoke in his room.

Well she can fuck that too, he thought irritably, defiantly letting the smoke stream out of his nostrils.

After he finished the cigarette he realised he was thirsty.

He went out of his room carefully, stealing past his parents' room, wishing he'd put something on. All he needed was someone to bump into him wandering around the house like a bloody nudist.

Downstairs, the dog thumped his tail lethargically on the kitchen floor but did not bother to get up.

"Don't blame you, dog," he whispered, pouring himself a glass of cold milk and shoving the fridge door shut with his foot.

He wandered back upstairs, glass in hand. On the landing he nearly spilt the lot.

"Danny?" The figure was peering at him. It was John. "What the hell are you doing?"

"Getting something to drink. What does it look like?" They were whispering.

"Well, since you ask..."

He could feel John looking down at him. He blushed, glad of the darkness. "I didn't expect to bump into anyone, did I?"

"You say." He could see John's teeth glint in the gloom.

"Oh fuck off, John."

He made to pass him, but John was already turning away, pushing open the bathroom door. He whispered back suddenly over his shoulder, "Watch, or your mother will hear." There was no laugh.

Danny gave him the finger and slammed back into his room.

## TWO

That night Danny had the same dream.

He was wrapped deep in a pile of straw, just like usual. It was dusty, suffocating.

It was high summer, very hot and pitch black: no light at all, like he was blind.

At this stage it wasn't threatening. There was no sense of menace in the darkness, only a kind of doped paralysis. He could smell the hay, feel its weight on his body, but his breathing was easy and deep, as if at some level he knew he was safely asleep.

Abruptly he realised he was in the old hayloft at Jerrett's, and with the knowledge came a peculiar shifting of the light, as if he'd come into the darkness after being outside, his eyes slowly adjusting, becoming aware of hazy red silhouettes, of objects swimming slowly, and with a faint hint of menace, into focus. Then the weight on him shifted and he realised that someone, or something, was lying on top of him.

He tried to lift himself off the floor and couldn't, but now it was not that doped paralysis that prevented him, it was whatever was on top of him, pinning him down. Then the weight shifted again and became, unmistakably, a person. A man. He could smell fresh sweat from him, feel their skins sticking together as if they were both barechested.

"*Danny…*"

The voice seemed to call from a long distance away. He knew that voice, but he was still blinded, struggling to see.

"*Danny…*"

The man was somehow closer, hotter. He could feel breath on his face now, like a draught of hot air. He struggled again to get up, and it was as if the man suddenly came into his own body much as Danny had, as if he too had been paralysed up to that point.

He felt the unmistakable sensation of the man's face close to his, his cheek brushing against his as he turned his head. He felt a sudden and immediate panic, but now he was gripped, as if the man held his head rigid in two massive hands. He was going to kiss him. Danny knew it before the man even moved. Then his lips were there, horribly cold and wet in that heat, as if the man were dead or frozen.

The man's mouth moved off, trailing across his cheek. He felt heavy and drugged under the odd icy, burning trail of that mouth. He was aware of a bitter metallic taste on his lips, like snail-slime. He felt poisoned, slowly dying.

"Danny."

The voice was suddenly right in his ear, no longer disembodied, but breathless and urgent, close.

Danny could feel a sudden excitement. The man had not touched him, there was nothing sexual in that cold kiss, and yet Danny had gone from nowhere to the point of no return in seconds.

The man was suddenly thrusting against him. He could feel his tongue, a horribly cold, thick thing, trying to push between his lips, and yet, somehow, he was still saying Danny's name, over and over again, in that low, urgent voice.

Danny felt himself surge up as the man's tongue finally pushed into his numb mouth. It felt huge, thrusting down his throat, coated in that same thick poisonous slime. Danny gagged convulsively, body jerking up. He groaned and twitched as the man's smell seemed to engulf his head: salty, sweet, exotic – horribly familiar.

"Wake up, Danny. For Christ's sake, wake *up*."

Danny's eyes jerked open, body half upright, panting with fright, as someone shook him.

He found himself held there, staring at John, half-dressed, frowning down at his pale face.

He blinked stupidly and dropped back down onto the bed as John let him go, defensively pressing his fists to his sticky groin. "What is it?"

John's frown deepened, eyes going from Danny's glistening chest to his face before he said, "It's time to get up. What did you think, fire drill?" There was a pause that felt a hundred years old before he added, "What was all the groaning and moaning for?"

Danny blinked again, eyes suddenly somehow focusing on John's, then he blushed the dull brick red of all redheads. "Nothing, bad dream."

John smiled disbelievingly, his eyes flicking down the bed to where the unmistakable shape of an erection showed through the thin summer blanket.

Danny tugged over onto his side, curling up, face flaming. "Why don't you fuck off and let me get up?"

John smiled a small smile. "Seems to me you're up already." He stood up slowly and moved to the door. "And you've overslept half an hour."

"Alright, alright. If you'd piss off I'll get up."

"Don't worry about me." He opened the door. "I've seen it before, remember?" And he went out, closing the door behind him.

Danny lay there for a second or two, fists clenched, eyes tight shut, then he sat up and jerked the sheet back, trying to dry up the mess as best he could.

His cock was still standing to attention as if it had some kind of depressing intention of never going down. He could still feel his skin crawling with the unpleasant sensation of the man's skin against his, the crushing weight. He felt repulsed by his own arousal.

Stuffing his ill-disciplined member inside his trousers, he pulled on the rest of his clothes and went downstairs.


Rab was hanging off the tractor, passing something down to Ian in the yard. He swung round when Danny came out the kitchen door. "Well, well, look who's at the cow's tail."

Danny said nothing. John stuck his head round the kitchen door. "He got lost in a dirty dream. Couldn't tear himself away."

"Oh yeah? Who was it then? Anyone we know?" Rab climbed down off the tractor at the possibility of a new point of attack.

John came out the back door, wiping his hands. "Won't say. Obviously a big girl though, you should have seen the size of his hard-on."

Rab laughed, too loudly, but Ian only ran a hand through his lank hair. He smiled though; that twisted smirk that served him for a smile. Oh, Ian was happy enough.

"Practising for the big day maybe." John was suddenly close up behind him, making Danny spin round at his nearness.

Ian laughed sourly. "What big day? He hasn't got a cherry left to lose – unless it's with a sheep."

Danny pushed past him aggressively. "Are we going to do any work this morning or are we just going to fuck about?"

Rab winked at John over his shoulder. "Tetchy, tetchy."

"Must be love," John answered softly, no smile at all.

Danny stopped and turned. He had never realised before just how irritating his brother's face could be.

"Come on, you lot, get a *move* on." Their father came out, slamming the back door, shattering the moment.

Another day had started.


They came into the kitchen in dribs and drabs at one o'clock. The tractors were hot and creaking in the noon sun. Already Danny could feel yesterday's sunburn playing up, although he'd kept his T-shirt on for as long as possible.

Rab and Ian were already at the table. His mother was ferrying cold food over from the fridge. "Eat," she said to him. "Before it gets hot."

Danny pulled his shirt off and sat down, well away from the sun slanting in the back door.

Rab leaned back in his chair and smiled his dirty smile. "Well, Don Juan?"

Danny gave him a warning look.

His mother looked up at him from the plate of ham she was cutting. "Don Juan?"

"He's taking the piss," Danny said, trying to divert her attention.

"I've told you before about that expression." She slapped ham on his plate. "Why Don Juan? What have you been up to?"

"Nothing." He concentrated on cutting his meat, trying to hide his irritation. He didn't know why he was bothering.

Rab and Ian exchanged malicious glances.

"Leave him alone, you two," she said flatly, and went into the living-room in search of missing glasses.

Ian immediately sat forward, body bent over the table, elbows spread wide. "Think our Daniel's left his mother any dirty evidence?" He made a small noise like he was sucking his teeth.

Rab sat back again, laughing abruptly, too loudly, just like he'd done that morning in the yard.

Ian's body bent further forward – so far he had to tilt his head in order to look up into Danny's face. "Oh, he's a dark horse, our Daniel. Wouldn't know it to look at him, would you?"

He dropped his cheek suddenly onto his hands, like a small child falling asleep, then began tracing a pattern on the table with his fingertip. He whispered so softly that Danny barely heard him, "Bet I can guess who it was about…"

Danny jerked up out his seat. "Why don't you fucking shut up?" His face was scarlet.

"Here, what's the language in aid of?" His father came in, shaking out his shirt. "Well?" he demanded, looking from one to the other.

Danny was standing at the table, glaring. Ian sank back in an odd satiated boneless slump. It was Rab who answered, "He's just getting upset at nothing, as usual."

"Tell them to leave off me," Danny demanded.

His father turned to him. "Who the hell are you shouting at? You go and eat outside if you can't control your temper."

"Don't worry, I'm going." And he grabbed his plate and stalked out the door.

"You two want to…"

But Danny didn't hear the rest of his father's sentence.


Outside, the sun hit everything squarely black and white. He crossed the yard and dropped down into the shade of the henhouse and ate his second roll, not tasting a mouthful.

He saw John go into the house. He was raging thirsty, almost thirsty enough to contemplate yelling across to him to bring him out some beer, but he'd be damned if he would. This was all his fucking fault anyway. And he wasn't going back in there either. He'd die of thirst sooner. Fuck them.

He lay back against the warm, gritty paintwork of the henhouse wall and closed his eyes.

"Here." John's voice spoke suddenly out of his darkness. He opened his eyes and squinted up against the light. John was standing there, a red-rimmed silhouette above him. Danny hesitated then took the offered can from his outstretched hand.

"Look," he said, sitting down beside him, "I even brought you a glass."

Danny took it and muttered a grudging thanks. What was he, a fucking mind reader? He filled the glass slowly so it wouldn't foam up and put the can deep in the shade. He took a mouthful.

Suddenly John reached over and patted his stomach. "You'll need to watch your belly, drinking all that beer."

Danny flinched away, pushing his hand off. "Don't."

"Don't what?"

"Just don't." He could feel his face burning.

John only raised his eyebrows as if to say, Touchy, then leaned back against the shed again and closed his eyes.

Danny looked at him surreptitiously. His belly was hard and flat, his chest broad and muscular. He had definitely lost weight this summer.

Danny looked down at his own stomach. It was flat enough, but he was never going to have John's washboard muscles – or his lousy tan for that matter. "Are you saying I'm getting fat?" he demanded abruptly. He looked down at himself again. From this angle it did look a bit podgy.

"What?" John sounded dopey. He didn't move.

"Are you saying I'm getting fat?" Danny scowled at him irritably. He sat up further to flatten his stomach out. He even tried pulling it in.

John opened one eye, turning his head to him. "Mm?"

"For Christ's sake. Fat, John – me. Is that what you're saying?"

John opened both eyes, considered him. "You look alright to me." He closed his eyes again and turned his face up to the sun, adding, "So far."

Danny felt more irritated than ever. They were silent for a while, Danny taking covert glances at John's body. His jeans were so tight it kept drawing your eyes down to his crotch. That had never been his style before, but now whatever Rab did...

Suddenly he realised John was watching him through deceptively half-closed eyes. He blushed violently, just like he always did.

"Well?" John's lazy drawl.

"Well what?" Danny took another swig of beer and glared over at the house, studiously not looking in his direction.

"Have you seen enough?"

How the hell was he supposed to answer a question like that? I was only comparing sizes?

He continued to glare silently at the house, blushing harder than ever. He heard John climb to his feet, brush his hands on his jeans. His body moved level with Danny's eyes, blocking his view, but Danny didn't lift his head.

"Danny..."

He could hear the smug smile in the fat rat's voice. He lifted his eyes slowly to look up at him.

John grinned down at him for a moment then blew him a silent little kiss.

Danny turned his head away with a violent jerk. "Fuck off."

John reached out and rumpled his hair. "Only joking, Danny-boy. Only joking."

Danny could hear him chuckling all the way across the yard.


They had been baling hay all afternoon, until the tractor had finally overheated.

"No water in the fucking radiator," John said, slamming the hood back down. "Ian, you can be today's hero, go and get some. Take your time. It needs a chance to cool down."

Ian looked up at the hay wagon as if to say, Why not him? then turned abruptly and began walking towards the pick-up.

Danny dropped exhaustedly onto the hay bales and stretched out luxuriously, covering his face with his T-shirt.

After a minute or two he heard the pick-up roar off.

Almost a full minute passed before John called up to him, "Danny?"

He didn't reply. After a second or two he felt the wagon rock, followed by the rustling sound of John crawling across the hay towards him, then the weight of his body settling next to his. "Not talking?"

He said nothing. He could feel John stretching out beside him, feel his skin sticking against his bare shoulder.

Under the shelter of his T-shirt, he felt suddenly blindfolded, abruptly afraid. He wished he could take it off to see what John was up to. He lay tense and unhappy. All his nerves felt rubbed raw. An insect tickled over his chest. He jumped and brushed it away.

A second or two later he felt it on his stomach. He brushed it off again.

A second later it was worming its way under the waistband of his trousers. He threw off the T-shirt and shot upright.

John was lying beside him, lazily playing with a piece of straw. "Something biting?"

"Yeah, a six foot blonde horsefly."

"*Blonde?*" John's laugh was incredulous. "Either I'm improving or you're going blind. And that's six-*three*." John gave him an unsettling look then added, "Of course, maybe you're just mixing me up with Rab."

Danny flushed and threw himself on his stomach. After another minute the tickling started again. "Fuck off, John," he said without turning.

The tickling continued with exactly the same irritation as a fly. "I said, fuck off, John. Are you deaf?"

"Me? I'm not doing a thing. Just lying here, minding my own business, going slowly blonde."

"Like fuck you are." Danny jerked his elbow in, blocking the straw's path to his armpit. It withdrew.

After a few moments it started again. Danny saw red. He flung himself over and on top of John's body, knocking him flat and pummelling his sides with his fists before John could stop him. It took several seconds and too many hard blows before John came to his senses. But he outweighed Danny by almost two stone, and outstripped him by at least four inches. He threw his arms around him in a tight bear hug, effectively pinning his flailing arms down.

They lay breathlessly locked together for a second or two, panting heavily, stupefied by the violence of the skirmish. Danny became aware of the scent of hay and sweat, a faint hint of something else. John's soap? No, it was the stink of Rab's fucking cigarettes. And then he realised. In the dream – that was the strange exotic smell in the dream.

It *couldn't* be.

He was trapped tight in John's arms, pinned down in the hay, the stink of him invading his nostrils. Suddenly he was tired beyond all reason, emotionally exhausted. He felt himself go limp. He didn't care anymore. "Let me go," he said numbly.

"Why? So you can beat fuck out me?" John's voice was ugly with damaged ego and fright.

"I won't touch you," Danny said dismally. It was the wrong thing to say, inferring as it did that John had nothing to fear from him. It wasn't what he'd meant.

"Too fucking right you won't," John said and rolled him onto his back, pinning him down with his weight.

The smell of his sweat, with that faint hint of spice, seemed to rise out of the hay itself. Their skins were stuck together, their hair soaked with sweat. Danny felt panicked. All he could see was John's dark silhouette, outlined in red. He couldn't read his face at all. His eyes watered with staring up at him. "Let me go, you shit." He tried to push up, but his exhaustion and the soft base of hay gave him no leverage at all.

John sensed the rising panic in him and his anger fed on it. "You look like a girl, know that?"

Danny could feel tears of frustration begin to form in his eyes. "I said, let me *go*."

John rammed his shoulders down as he tried to lift himself. "Dream on."

Danny jerked his head away, feeling a drop of sweat run down into his mouth, filthily salt. He licked his lips feverishly, straining his head to one side.

John saw the tongue darting over his dry lips. They looked swollen, cracked. Another drop of sweat dripped from his forehead onto Danny's cheek. Danny scrubbed it furiously against the hay, eyes tight shut all the while. In that one movement, petulant, skittish, he really did look like a girl.

John brought his face close. "Come on then, give us a kiss."

Danny struggled violently, suddenly galvanised with something very like terror. "*Don't.*"

But John pressed his mouth down on his.

Danny tasted of salt, his lips, not cracked at all, moist and open with shock under his own.

It was all he had intended to do, humiliate him. But the thing felt surprisingly good. Danny groaned beneath him, still struggling, making things worse for himself. John kissed him again, hungrily, enjoying his struggles and, he realised dimly somewhere in his overheated brain, enjoying the kiss.

"Hello?!" A door slammed. "John?!"

"Christ." John sprung off him as if he had been stung. *Ian.* Christ, the little shit must have fucking raced it. *Shit.*

"John?!" Querulous now, full of suspicion.

"Here!" John's voice sounded shaky. His face was white.

Danny lay flat on his back, his eyes blank with shock, his face streaked with sweat and dirt.

John crammed his fist into his pocket and yanked out his handkerchief, pushing it at him. "Here, clean yourself up, for Christ's sake." He turned away, sitting up and dragging his hands through his hair.

The wagon rocked. John yelled, "Hang on, I'm coming down," and scrambled quickly over to the edge. He swung his body over then paused to check his footing. He looked up for one second, right into Danny's eyes, then whispered fiercely, "Move, Danny. No-one's fucking raped you." He looked down over his shoulder to judge his distance then back up into Danny's face. "Yet." And then disappeared from view.


That night Danny was afraid to go to bed. He stood hanging onto the chill satin of the curtains. The breeze stirred coolly through his wet hair. He hadn't eaten, just grabbed a sandwich, pleading a headache.

John had ignored him solidly for the rest of that day. At supper his mother had said he looked ill, and God knows, by then he felt ill – ill enough for Ian to let him shower before him, at any rate. Be thankful for small mercies.

He had watched John go across to the pub an hour ago, while he had been waiting on Rab finishing up in the bathroom. He'd paused at the pub door and suddenly turned and looked back up at the house, right up at Danny's bedroom window.

Danny had dived back behind the curtain, then began cursing himself. "What the hell am I doing?" he'd hissed. But his heart still pounded with fright, as if he'd been caught doing something he shouldn't.

He lay on his bed now, watching the clock, careful to keep his hair off the pillow. Half eleven.

The back door banged. Danny closed his eyes.

After a minute or two he heard them come up the stairs together, talking and laughing. So he had ordained to honour them with his holy presence tonight? Big of him.

He listened as each went into the bathroom, then their doors closed for the night. The silence was absolute.

Christ, he would never sleep tonight. He hadn't even undressed yet. He got up and went to the window again and sat by the chair.

He didn't hear the door open, only the click of the door closing. He turned, only half curious at the odd noise, not yet realising what it was.

When John spoke, his stomach plunged as if he had been handling a knife that had slipped.

"Still up?"

John was leaning back against the door, both his hands behind him, holding the door handle. His voice was quiet. To Danny, menacing.

Danny stood up. His legs felt like rubber. "No, I'm asleep. This is my astral projection. What do you want, John?"

"Only to talk." He pushed himself up off the door and came towards him, hands open, palm outwards, as if to say, Look, no tricks. "Only to talk, baby."

Danny could see the moonlight on his face, the deep-set black eyes, the wide curving mouth, the high, broad planes of his face, the oddly bleached hair, so much brighter than he ever remembered it going before. He thought his brother had never looked more thuggish, or more persuasively charming.

John stopped his advance. He'd hardly moved any distance at all, Danny realised. He stood with his hands on the headboard of Danny's old bed, unmistakably leaning on it.

Danny realised abruptly he was drunk. John, who was always so careful, so in control, was *drunk*? He felt an immense surge of gratification. His fucking great ugly lump of a brother was drop-dead drunk.

John sat down heavily on the bed then patted it like a large, clumsy uncle. "Why don't you come sit beside me?"

"I'm fine where I am."

John looked up at him. He grinned. It looked evil in the dark moonlight. Nothing drunk about his dirty rapacious grin. "Promise I won't *rape* you." The emphasis was unmistakable, the voice mocking.

"I'm fine where I am, John. Get on with it."

John got up, almost creakily, leaning on his knees. He came towards him until he was suddenly close, uncomfortably close. Danny backed away until he was pinned against the window. He wished now he had sat on the bed. He felt out-manoeuvred. John's breath was close enough to smell. He smelt of spirits, not beer. He smelt like his father.

"You stink." Danny jerked his face away. He turned back in time to see John's face tighten. He felt perversely pleased with the reaction.

He stepped to one side, intending to move round him, but John's hand shot out indecently fast and grabbed his shirtfront, jerking him up against him. "Don't get fucking smart with me. It was a joke." He shook Danny slightly for emphasis. "A *joke*."

Danny pulled out of his grip and walked towards the door. "Sure."

Suddenly he was spun round by his hair. He felt as if his scalp was being torn off.

John pushed him down on the bed then caught hold of Danny's shirtfront and lifted him again. "You started it."

Danny felt the sweat of anxiety immediately soak the armpits of his shirt. He felt suddenly soiled, as if he'd never bathed, as if he'd come straight from the hay baler to here, as if John had been with him all along, just a continuation of the same scene, the scene that had somehow started that morning, in his room.

"Lying there pretending you were asleep, your dick twitching, moaning my name."

"You fuck off, you liar." But Danny's voice was a weak whisper.

John let him go suddenly, with a little push, and he fell back.

Danny struggled up onto his elbows, staring up at him. "You liar," he said again. It had more force now.

"Keep your voice down. Christ knows, we wouldn't want your mother to hear."

"You're lying, you scumbag, I wouldn't suck your dick for mon..." Danny stopped, realising too late what he'd said. He saw John's white teeth glimmer in a carnivorous smile.

"No? Why don't you prove it?" He leaned forward and pulled Danny up against him, a sharp, aggressive tug. The smell of soap was strong on his body. It felt hot and hard, dry as a lizard. No sweat now. "You're awake now. Let's see you prove it."

Danny prised him off, succeeded in half-sliding off the bed. But John caught his legs in a tackle, grunting with effort. Danny lashed out with a stream of low hissed invective. The bed thumped against the wall. Suddenly his parents' room door opened, flooding the floor of his room with light.

"*Shit*," John's voice hissed in the dark.

Danny went limp. John had one arm round his neck, the other locking his arm behind his back. They sat there like that, a tableau, neither daring to move.

Whoever it was went into the bathroom. Slowly, John eased his stranglehold.

Whoever it was came back out and went back into their room. The light went out.

Their bodies came apart like something coming unstuck. Danny was aware of John's weight lifting off the bed. There was a silence, no sense of movement. It went on too long, too unnaturally quiet, as if he stood there in the dark, waiting. Finally the door opened, a barely perceptible click, then John's voice whispered, "Next time, baby."

## THREE

Twice Danny woke in the night, convinced he heard the door handle rattle. He woke washed in cold sweat, his chest suffocated with holding his breath, and listened.

Only the creaking silence of the house, the distant tick of the old downstairs clock.

He woke finally to his mother banging on the door. "Danny? Come on, you're late again. Shake a leg."

He mumbled a reply and struggled up into a sitting position. He felt like a limp rag. He was sticky with sweat. His face felt stiff and sore.

His mother banged on the door again. "Did you hear me, Danny?" The handle rattled irritably.

"I'm up. Just give us a bloody minute, will you?"

There was a pause, then he heard her moving off down the hall, ominously silent.

When he got down to breakfast the rest had already gone out.

His mother looked at his face. His white skin took on a bruised look when he was tired or ill. He had it now. "I take it your headache hasn't cleared up?" She cut him some bread.

He shook his head. "Couldn't sleep. Too hot or something." He didn't look up at her. It seemed to hurt his eyeballs just to move them.

She stopped what she was doing and looked directly at him, then she came right out with it. "Why was your door locked?"

Danny immediately flared up, "I'm allowed to lock the bloody door. That's what the fucking key's for."

"I will not stand for that language, Danny. I asked you a civil question."

"Well here's my civil answer..." He pushed up out of his chair, facing her furiously. "I am *nineteen* years old. I'll lock my bloody door if I want to."

She turned away sharply to the kitchen sink, her back speaking volumes. Danny glared at her, daring her to say another word, then turned and slammed out of the kitchen.


Danny spent the whole day by himself, clearing rubble down by the copse of trees that grew by the river.

Ian came down at half one and wanted to know why he hadn't been up for lunch. "You're in deep shit, little brother."

"So I'll swim." Danny hefted another boulder onto the trailer.

"You'll more likely have to eat it."

"Wouldn't be the first time."

Ian raised his eyebrows, smiling faintly, then simply turned and walked away up the hill.

Danny spent the late afternoon building up a bonfire with the cleared wood, tyres, and general flotsam that always seemed to build up down here. He arrived home late for tea. Only his father and mother were still in the kitchen.

"Where were you at lunchtime?" his father demanded without greeting.

"Down the back field, where you sent me." Danny sat down at the plate his grim-faced mother put in front of him.

"If you don't intend to come home for meals you tell your mother in future."

Danny said nothing. He began eating.

"I'm talking to you, boy."

"I heard you."

"Well you bloody well answer me then. And before you disappear upstairs, you're helping John clean out the old hayloft tomorrow, so you make sure you've got your arse in gear."

Danny stopped eating. "What? Jerrett's?"

His father scowled at him. "You heard me."

"But I haven't finished the bottom field yet. You said..."

"Well now I'm saying different. You're helping John."

"Ian could do it. Why not Ian?"

"Ian's doing fences with Rab until the weather breaks again."

"I could do the fences."

His father slapped his hand flat on the table, making them both jump. "You do what you're bloody well told." He pushed his chair back and stood up, jabbing a finger at him. "And tomorrow you be up on time. This isn't a bloody holiday camp." He left the room, slamming the door behind him.

His mother looked at him as much as to say, Now look what you've done, and started clearing up the dinner dishes. Maybe she thought he'd engineered this – went with the door being locked.

He pushed his meal away half-eaten and went up the stairs to wash.


He could not remember, could not pinpoint the precise *moment* when he realised he was crying, but somehow he found himself standing there with his face pressed to the wet tiles, water streaming down his back, and the taste of salt in his mouth. He was glad he couldn't see himself.

He turned and leaned back against the wall, hugging himself, shivering even in the hot water, and cried till he was dry, nothing else to cry.

That night he fell into bed, oblivious even to his wet hair, and plunged into a deep and dreamless sleep.

## FOUR

The alarm roused him slowly from the depths.

When he finally surfaced he wasn't sure if he had actually heard it. He peered at the clock's face. Six am. It had gone off then. He got up and dressed slowly and heavily. His fingers felt numb.

He went down the stairs, still tucking in his shirt. When he opened the kitchen door he saw John was alone in the kitchen. He lifted his head and stared at Danny with a fixed, unreadable expression, then bent his head and went on eating.

His mother came in behind him. "Made it this morning, I see."

Danny took his hand off the door handle and moved into the room. He sat down as far away from John as possible. He said nothing. It seemed there never was anything he could say. Every time someone spoke to him it was only offering him rope to hang himself.

His mother banged his plate down.

He wolfed his food like a starving man. He hadn't known he was hungry till he tasted it. His mother refilled his cup without comment.

John pushed his plate away then took out a battered cigarette, idly watching Danny mop up his plate.

"John, if you actually intend to smoke that filthy thing you can do it outside." His mother jerked her head in the direction of the door. He got up without speaking and sauntered out.

Danny looked up at her. She did not meet his eyes. "I don't know what's wrong with everyone this week. Let's hope it's the weather." And she stuck her head out into the hall. "Ian?! Where are you?!"

There was an indecipherable reply.

"You said that ten minutes ago. I'm not calling you again. You can answer to your father next time."

Danny stood up and went out.


Jerrett's Farm had been acquired, part and parcel with fifty acres of land, before Danny had even been born. There had been a time when they had actually used the old hayloft, but not now. Now they used only the ground floor level, mainly for storing surplus animal feeds and the general junk that there never seemed anywhere else to put.

Danny didn't like the hayloft. In fact, just looking up the ladder gave him the creeps.

John was already inside, wearing thick work gloves and pulling plastic feed sacks across the lower floor. He didn't turn when Danny came into the building. It was deeply shadowed inside. What little light there was shone in from the open doors; one up, one down. The tiny windows were so grimy they barely let in any light at all.

It took his eyes a moment or two to accustom themselves to the change before he could discern the white of John's T-shirt moving in the dark.

"Fucking rats. Place is overrun with them." Another came bolting and squeaking from under a sack as John pulled it free. He turned and pulled something from his pocket. "Here."

Danny caught it on reflex. John had his back to him again.

"Gloves. You'll need them."


One by one they pulled the sacks out into the yard. By eleven o'clock they were exhausted, soaked with sweat.

They went outside and sat down in the shade of the tractor, each smoking a cigarette. The sun beat down just beyond them, already fierce in its heat, although the rain had not been off twenty minutes.

They had been sitting talking for almost half an hour when John looked up at the sky and made some quip about the weather. Danny laughed. It felt almost strange, everything suddenly washed over with normality. Maybe his mother was right, maybe it was just the heat.

John stood up, stretching. "Come on. We better check out the loft before we get this lot onto the trailer."

Danny squinted up at him. "There's nothing up there, is there?"

"I don't think there's ever been anything up there, other than some hay out the ark, but we'll check just in case. You know what he's like. Come on." He offered his hand to Danny to pull him up.

Danny pretended he hadn't seen it and scrambled to his feet, hitching up his jeans.

John looked at him shrewdly. His face seemed to metamorphose from that rather perverse handsomeness he owned into something sharp and vindictive. "Don't overestimate yourself. Just because you like boys doesn't mean we're all tarred with the same brush."

"I never…"

But John cut him off, turning away as if the conversation had suddenly bored him. "Oh come on, let's get this over with."

Danny followed him with a heavy heart.


His eyes took longer to adjust this time. He could see John's bare torso going up the ladder ahead of him. He always had to strip his bloody shirt off, just to show him that real men could take a little sun. That long slope of back kept catching his eye, and the front was worse, the mat of hair on his belly tailing off into his waistband. Why not buy new jeans if he'd lost the button? Fact was, he liked flaunting it. Another bad habit he'd picked up from Rab, fucking conceited pig.

Danny followed him up the ladder, trying to concentrate on hating him, and not on the sudden paralysing fear he could feel leadening his legs.

He hoisted himself up through the hatch with weak arms and straightened up.

It was brighter up here: bigger door and skylights in the roof. The light streamed down in shafts, dancing with dust from where John had disturbed it opening the hatchway.

"John?" Danny realised he couldn't see him. He felt panic surge through him ridiculously.

"Over here."

Danny spun round, feeling the hairs stiffen all down his spine.

John was standing in a shaft of sunlight at the other side of the hayloft. The light lit his hair from within like a glowing halo. The same bright light washed his features clean, bleached him of detail. The lines of his chest seemed curiously blurred, making him look even broader, more powerful. Danny blinked.

"Over here," he said again as if Danny couldn't see him. Or was it a command?

Danny walked over to him, his skin crawling unpleasantly. It was suffocatingly warm up here. He sneezed, both hands to his face.

John smiled, that lazy sinister smile that always seemed to make his face a malcontent's. "It happened just here." He gestured at the floor with a nod of his head.

Danny stared at him, feeling his stomach slowly roll over.

"Old man Jerrett."

Danny pressed his hands to his stomach.

"This is where he finally lost it and topped himself."

Danny looked down at the floor. There was a dark stain on the floorboards, black in this light. He dragged his eyes back up to John's face. "You're kidding me."

John shook his head. "He had a weakness, liked little boys." And he looked at him in a way that Danny didn't want to understand, that could have meant anything – but definitely didn't.

Danny could hear his own breath grunt out of him as he lunged forward, hitting John straight in the gut.

John folded and went back into the drifts of mouldering hay. Danny flung himself on top, flying into him with both fists. John pushed the heel of his hand up under his chin.

Danny kept punching, kneeing, trying to gouge out his eyes. They grappled fiercely, rolling over each other.

"You little..." John grunted. He managed to twist a hand in Danny's hair and pull.

At first, Danny felt nothing, the adrenaline was too strong, then he began to feel a dreadful red-hot pain right down his neck. John was still pushing against his chin, trying to get leverage to push his weight off.

Danny suddenly went with the pull on his hair. He lay on his back where he had fallen, abruptly winded, his eyes filling with pain. Inside he felt nothing.

John sprang over him and slapped his face with a broad, flat-handed slap. Danny felt his head jar with the impact of the blow. John kneeled panting above him, his hair wild, his lip bleeding. "What the fuck is *wrong* with you?"

Danny said nothing.

John sat down heavily on the floor. "I was only telling you, for Christ's sake.

*Chat."*

Danny didn't believe him. Danny didn't trust him. He said nothing.

John felt his ribs tentatively and winced. "You stupid little cunt. I think you've broken something." He stood up shakily. "You know something? You're sick in the head."

He walked unsteadily to the hatchway and started very carefully to climb down. "I'm going to get those fucking sacks loaded. You've got two minutes."

And he disappeared.

## FIVE

"You were winding me up yesterday, weren't you?"

John looked up from rolling a cigarette. There was something awkward about it. Not clumsy, John was never clumsy, he just didn't look right doing it. He never would.

"What?"

"I said, you were winding me up yesterday, weren't you?"

John shaded his eyes with his hands, squinting up at Danny against the light. Danny had the advantage and knew it. He pressed the point. "Weren't you?"

John dropped his hands. They lay in his lap, palm upwards, the half-rolled cigarette held delicately between thumb and forefinger. "About what?"

"You knew I didn't know about Jerrett. That's why you took me up there. You weren't interested in whether there was anything up there, other than that."

John looked sideways down at the floor, then he lifted his head, licked the cigarette, and sealed it. He put it in the corner of his mouth and patted his pockets, just like Rab always did.

Danny could feel the anger as if it were changing colour. What had started as a tight blue knot of anxiety in his stomach was flowing out redly through his veins with every moment that John studiously wasted. He felt his skin come alive like a cramped limb flooded with blood. A warm flush, almost like pins and needles, began to cross his skin.

John levered himself up into a standing position and felt in his hip pockets. Still his eyes were veiled. He was thinking, much faster than his hands were moving.

Danny held on like a terrier. "Why, John? What was it all for? Just to annoy me?"

That made him smile. Danny could see the tension ease out of him. *He thinks I'm stupid.*

John found his matches and held a light to his face.

"Or were you leading up to a confession?"

The hand flinched, the flame wavered in the gloom for a second, then he lit the cigarette and threw the match in a long arc out into the concrete yard. Finally he spoke. "What d'you want me to say? Something revealing that you can go tell mummy?"

"No. Why? You got a burden you're aching to share?"

That brought him round. "I've got nothing I need to share."

"No? Then what was it about?"

"I told you. It was just idle conversation. I had forgotten all about the dirty old bastard. Being up there reminded me, that's all."

Danny moved towards him, no clear intention, other than perhaps to force some kind of reaction out of him. Any kind. "Like hell you had."

John looked out the shed door as if the conversation was suddenly boring him, but he didn't make a move to go. His face looked set, his eyes bright and evasive.

Now was Danny's moment. He said, "Maybe it's because Jerrett's not the only one who's had problems with little boys."

He got his reaction.

John swung on him, his mouth white with fury. He grabbed Danny's face, his powerful fingers digging into his cheeks. "You just shut the fuck up or I might just break your fucking neck." And he let him go with a push, as if he was an irritating insect.

The red began to flare into Danny's head. He felt as if it would burst out from behind his eyes. He could feel his face burning up with it. "Oh you'd like that, wouldn't you? You've always been dead fucking keen for me to shut up. Well not this time. I'll fucking tell her. Then what?"

John turned away with a jerk, putting distance between them. He grabbed one of the tractor's wing mirrors with both hands, as if he didn't trust himself. He spat out his cigarette and ground it underfoot, still hanging there.

Suddenly he lifted his head. The tension in him seemed to have undergone some kind of wonderful transformation, as if an unexpected light had just illumined his darkness. "You go for it, Danny-boy. After all, *what* exactly are you going to tell her? That will surprise her, I mean."

"I'll tell her about you coming into my room, for one. As it is she's just burning up to know how you got that fat lip yesterday. Maybe I'll just tell her."

John suddenly grinned. If a grin could look venomous this one did. "Go ahead, tell her that you attacked me for no reason. She'll go running off to the old man, trying to convince him you're not the sick little bastard she really knows you are. Me one, you nil. Just remember, you might have her fooled, but he isn't queuing up for your fan club."

"Don't try shoving it back on me. I'll tell her alright. You see if I don't. You just get off my fucking back, John."

They stepped towards each other, a hairsbreadth from each other's throats, when Ian's yell unexpectedly shattered the tension. "John?! You out here?! You're wanted!"

John gave him one last poisonous look then turned on his heel and left.


Danny's mother had told him about Jerrett, surprised and a little uncomfortable with the subject.

"Why do you want to know?"

He didn't see any reason to hide it. "John showed me the spot where he's supposed to have done it."

"*John?*" She managed to sound surprised and unsurprised at once.

Danny nodded. "We were working up there yesterday."

There was a silence. She turned her back to him, fiddling with something at the counter.

Danny waited a beat then cleared his throat and said, "So it *is* true?"

"Oh it's true enough." She became suddenly brisk about her work.

Danny wet his lips and pushed, "So he did? I mean, he was... messing about with kids, I mean."

"Boys," she said emphatically. Her voice was clipped. "He was even charged with it once. He couldn't have been more than forty. I think everybody liked to think he'd stopped it. Maybe some of them even believed it. He hadn't, of course. They never do."

Danny was silent. His mother slammed a cupboard door. "Right, that's enough. Finish that up, I'm waiting for the dish."

And so Danny knew the subject was closed. But he was still sure it was no coincidence. If he had compromised himself by attacking John in the hayloft, then John had at least done as much up on the hay wagon. Now it was quits. He wasn't going to become a butting post for John's frustrations. Let him use Rab if he was so fond. He could just leave him alone.

For good.

## SIX

August rode on, hot and relentless.

The weeks passed in the same endless pattern. Everybody felt burnt out with the heat. Even Ian was unduly waspish.

It was the end of one of those fortnightly cycles: two weeks of blazing sun followed by two days of muggy rain.

Danny stood in the doorway of the tractor shed, enjoying the smell of the rain, the sound of it on the galvanised roof.

John drove into the courtyard and manoeuvred the tractor, reversing it into the shed. The vehicle's windscreen wipers slapped to and fro in the silence after the engine was cut, then they too stopped. John got down from the cab and came over to where he stood.

Danny was leaning against the doorjamb, staring out into a yard mystically transformed by the grey hissing veil of water.

Theirs had been an uneasy silence. Neither caring to be in each other's company, they had avoided each other as much as possible.

Danny could smell the faint aniseed that clung to John's damp clothes as he moved to stand beside him. He felt that familiar prickling sensation of awareness and animosity he always felt with him.

John went through his already familiar parody of Rab's pocket patting. "No matches," he said finally.

Danny reached into his pocket and took out a lighter. He flicked it on for him.

John bent his head over it, steadying Danny's hand with his own. It took a massive effort of will not to flinch from those rough, dry fingers.

John took a long drag then pulled his T-shirt from his jeans, waving it to and fro to let air into his body. Danny caught the faint hayish smell of him with his familiar soap. They stood for a moment in the grey, scented silence, both soporifically relaxed by the enveloping whisper of the rain.

"I've never heard it so quiet." John's voice was soft. The tractor creaked massively behind them as it cooled.

Danny licked his lips and shifted his shoulder more comfortably against the frame. He looked down at the puddle at his foot then said, "You were bullshitting me that night in my room, weren't you?" He could feel John's instantaneous tension beside him. The air seemed to snap around him.

"When?"

He could still redeem the moment, make up something, but he said, "When you said I was saying your name."

Now it was out. What was it? A fortnight? Three weeks? Every night he was afraid to go to sleep. Every morning he woke with dread. He went over every detail obsessively. The dream, his waking, John's face. And now here he was letting John see how much it had bothered him. A monster in his brain made real.

"Come again?" John was looking at him. Not frowning, but his eyes were alert, so fucking sharp and bright. Oh *he* knew. John knew alright. John knew everything.

Danny looked at him, flushing to the roots of his hair. "You know when. The night you came to my room drunk." He gave John the chance to reply, but John was going to sweat it out of him. He was enjoying this, the motherfucking sadist. "You said I was calling out your name while I was asleep."

John threw his cigarette out into the rain, half smoked. "Yes, Danny-boy. That's your answer."

Danny's heart sank.

"Yes, I remember, and yes, I was bullshitting you."

Danny stared at him. He could see the corners of John's mouth turn up a tiny flick. His tongue kicked a strand of tobacco off his lip.

"You never uttered a single word."


Danny knew he was lying. He was lying to him when he must have known the truth was much worse. So why?

Danny hung onto the cross-spar of his window and bumped his forehead against his hands. Why? Why? *Why?*

He turned away and threw himself on his bed. He hadn't even bothered to wash tonight. He smelt of salt and his skin was sticky. He was so restless he could have smashed everything in the room. He should've been in bed an hour ago. Half of him was dog tired and the other half wide awake, going over and over it, looking for the loophole. *Why* would he lie to him? Just to torture him? He could have done that just as easily with the truth. There was always something more to John, some refinement of cruelty that Danny could never comprehend.

He sat up and reached for his jeans, yanking them on and very nearly ripping the button off. He had to get some air.

He moved out onto the landing stealthily, pulling the door shut behind him with the barest click.

He padded downstairs and into the kitchen. He looked for the dog then realised he would probably be outside on a night as hot as this. He hated the kitchen in the heat. He opened the fridge door. The white ghostly light lit up the whole room eerily. He reached for an unopened carton of orange.

"What's wrong? Can't sleep?"

He dropped the orange carton on the floor, his heart in his mouth.

"There's an open one in the door." John gestured with his glass to where the fridge was yawning wide. "I've got vodka in mine," he dipped his head to indicate the bottle on the table, "but you can keep yours healthy."

Danny bent to pick up the carton. "You might have spoken sooner. You nearly gave me a fucking heart attack."

John smiled and took another drink, his eyes watching Danny over the rim.

Danny poured himself a glass, leaving no room for vodka, and closed the fridge door. He stood a moment, accustoming himself to the dark, then walked to the table. He put the glass down and pulled out a chair. "What about you? Can't you sleep either?" He gestured to John's drink.

"Bad dreams, Daniel. Bad dreams."

Danny thought it best to leave that one alone. John was becoming clearer as his eyes grew used to the dark. He could see his black eyes staring at him unblinkingly.

John stretched his hands behind his head and pushed the chair back onto two legs. Danny could see the thick dark hair under his arms. "Do you have to spread yourself out like that?" he said irritably. "You're as bad as Rab." *Shit*. His bloody stupid tongue. He could see John smiling at him.

"I didn't know I was. Does it bother you?" The 'bother' was cut out from his reply as if it was painted in neon letters, pregnant with significance.

Danny snapped back, "Yeah, it bothers me. It bothers the hell out of me."

"In that case I'll stop it." And he dropped his arms and the chair simultaneously with a clatter.

Danny hissed, "*Shhh…* for Christ's sake. You'll wake the whole fucking household."

John poured more vodka into his glass. He did not bother to top up the orange. He held the bottle above Danny's drink with a query, but Danny put his hand over the glass.

"Ever the good virgin, my little brother." And he put the bottle down again.

Danny wished he had a cigarette. In fact, he was wishing he'd simply stayed in bed. John was still watching him with that unblinking gaze. "Have you got a cigarette?" he said, as much to break John's gaze as anything else.

John stood up and pushed his hand in his pocket. He had to breathe in to do it.

"Doesn't Rab get sick of you copying him?" Danny asked sourly.

John paused, hand jammed in his pocket, and looked at him.

"Wear them any tighter and they'll castrate you."

"Would you be sorry, baby?"

"Oh fuck off."

John pulled his hand out with a short derisive laugh and sat down again.

Danny looked away from the expression in his eyes.

John pushed the roll-up tin across to him.

Danny looked at it. "You know I can't make those fucking things up. What was wrong with your old cigarettes? Even that menthol crap was better than this shit."

"Give it here." John took the tin back and began to make up a cigarette surprisingly deftly, his big fingers moving surely in the dim light. He licked it long and slow, watching Danny all the while, his eyes blacker and blacker, more unreadable, as the moon moved slowly behind the clouds.

Danny took the offered cigarette and felt the faint touch of moisture on the paper. He pushed it between his lips with a shiver of repulsion. He could taste the liquorice almost immediately. He pulled it out again. "God, how do you smoke these things?"

"Inhale, exhale. Easy."

Danny made a contemptuous noise, but said nothing. He watched John make up another. The grandfather clock chimed. "Half twelve," he said.

John got up to get a light from the gas pilot. Danny could feel him behind his chair like a tangible force. When something brushed against his back he jumped.

"Hey, be calm, Danny-boy." John sat back down. "You are safe from mutant invasion here in your own home."

"Christ, you're a fucking cheap sadist, know that?"

"Can't afford to be anything else, baby. Have some?" He gestured with the bottle.

"Yeah, sure, why not? Go on." And he pushed his glass over. He wasn't going to give him the opportunity for any more references to virgins. Anyway, maybe it would help him sleep.

"Good man." And John sloshed it in.

"Hey, whoa."

"No point in drinking in moderation, Daniel. Won't have any effect at all. Look at me."

Danny wasn't sure if that was an argument for or against moderation so he said nothing.

They drank in silence for a moment or two, their cigarettes winking in the dark. The moon had completely disappeared behind the clouds, leaving the room in darkness. Only the dull fluorescence of the pilot light and their cigarettes lit it up.

Danny drained his glass and decided on another. He'd lost count of how many John had had. The clock struck again. He jumped as if he'd been dozing. What time was it? Had he been asleep? Christ, he should really go to bed, but he felt too heavy to move.

"Danny?" John's voice sounded different. I think I'm drunk, Danny thought.

"Mm?"

"Ever had a girl?"

Oh fuck. No-win question time. But it wasn't enough to prompt him into a fight. "None of your business," he said shortly.

John chuckled. It sounded sarcastic. "Yeah, right, stupid question."

Danny loured across at him, his expression rendered impotent by the dark. He watched John stub out a barely smoked cigarette, could see the vague movements of him making up a new one. Christ, he wasted them just the same, effort or no.

"Give us a light."

Danny drew on his cigarette then held it out to him. John took it, holding his hand an age while he lit his cigarette. Danny hated the sight of that dark curly head bent over his hand. He looked away, watching the light spreading over the shed roofs as the moon emerged again.

"Know the best part?"

"How could I?" Danny slopped more vodka into his glass, and all but spat it out again when he took a mouthful. He added more orange juice.

"When you're on the point of coming. Your dick's like a ramrod wedged up her cunt and you daren't breathe, then she lifts herself to get it in further, impaling herself on it like she's in pain, aching for more and less at the same time – she doesn't know what she wants – and you just ram it home. You can feel it, I swear, come right out from the top of your head."

There was a silence. Danny moved uncomfortably. *No sex please, I have enough trouble keeping it down as it is.*

"Danny?" John's voice came out of the dark again.

"What?"

"Ever get desperate..." he paused as if he was searching for the right word, "ever get so desperate you'd fuck a sheep or something?" He laughed and said before Danny could answer, "You know, they make jokes about farmers and sheep, but sometimes I think, when the fuck do we have time to get anything else? When do we have the energy? Grabbing a sheep between one crop and the next is probably a better idea than they realise. I've seen some pretty sexy sheep." He laughed again, that same joyless grunt, and Danny heard the bottle clink, could see the vague movements of his hand.

They were silent again.

"It's the heat I can't stand. That and the fucking monotony. Up and down, every fucking day, six till ten, dawn till dusk, seven days a week, sweating your guts out, and for what? You know, I get so raw with it I long for somewhere to shove it, just to ease that bloody nagging ache. Every night it's the same, I'm exhausted and still I can't sleep. I feel so hot and restless all the time."

Danny saw his cigarette flare deeply as he dragged on it, smelt the smoke come out rich and sweet as he exhaled. He could visualise the two thick dragon-like streams, so typical of Rab. He'd always thought it showing-off.

"I swear I'd fuck anything that moved, if only that dull, hot fucking ache would leave me alone."

The clock chimed suddenly. The fridge whirred into life. They could hear the dog scratching outside the door.

"You ever feel like that?"

Danny hesitated then gave a soft affirmative grunt. John's laugh was complicitous, like there were no secrets between them. "Yeah, like all the time."

Danny did not reply. He saw John sit forwards, leaning across the table. "What was the dream?" His voice was almost a whisper.

Danny ground out his cigarette. "You fuck off, John."

John's hand shot out and grabbed him by the wrist, holding him down as he made to stand. "No, come on, I'm serious. It's the night for confessions, can't you feel it?"

"Let go my hand."

"No problem." John let him go.

Danny sat back down slowly then said, "I'm in the old hayloft..." He stopped, dragged on his cigarette, already feeling the suffocating anxiety of the dream, then said, "There's this weight pressing down on me. I can't see, but I know where I am. I just can't move. At first I don't know why, then I realise someone's on top of me. I feel him move, that's how I know. He's heavy, really heavy." He stopped.

John urged him, "Go on."

"At first I don't realise what he's doing." Danny heard the embarrassment in his own voice and got it over with. "But he's hard, y'know?" He stopped again, searching for his drink, finding it empty.

John's voice sounded rough in the dark, uneven. "Then what?"

"Then I get turned on too. You know the way you do in dreams? Just instant, no build-up?"

John made a small noise that indicated he did know.

"Well, like that, and he's calling my name all the time like he's trying to get through to me or something, and I can't hear him. I recognise his voice, but I can't see who it is. Then I can feel his breath on my cheek, burning, really close, and he starts rubbing up hard against me. Then I come."

He delivered it flatly, trying to deaden the embarrassment of telling it.

"What does he do to you?"

Danny was thrown. "What do you mean? I just told you."

John's voice was soft, furry with drink or sleep. "No. What does he do to make you come?"

"Nothing."

"Oh come on. In real life, in dreams, there's always something that pushes you over the edge. What is it?"

"I told you, it just happens."

"Come on." John's voice lowered. "What is it?"

"Alright," Danny snapped. "He sticks his tongue in my mouth, like he's trying to fucking rape me with it, and I go off, firing on all cylinders – that satisfy you?"

"His *tongue*..."

His dirty whispering voice. Danny felt engulfed in waves of revulsion. *I hate that dirty, insinuating voice. I hate every fucking thing about him.* He pushed up from the table. "I'm going to bed."

"No, wait..."

*Something not right about that voice, and I've had too much to drink.* But Danny got up.

John was round the table and in front of the kitchen door before Danny had even thought of it.

Dimly, Danny was surprised at his agility. Still fast as a cat, even after all that drink. He was suddenly tired, burnt out of all emotion. "Don't fuck me about, John," he said wearily, without animosity.

"Danny."

Just that and no more. It could have meant anything.

Danny squinted at his face, trying to read it in the dark. He couldn't see anything at all. "Let me out."

"No way." Definite, without malice or arrogance, just absolute. Danny could hear his smile rather than see it. What the hell was going on?

"What?"

"I said, no way."

"Get out of the way, John." Danny felt no fear, not even anger, only an irritation that everything seemed to be sliding through his fingers. He didn't understand any of this. John said nothing. His smile had faded like a brief flowering.

"You're drunk, John. Now let me past, I want to get to bed." He pushed in behind him, trying to get at the door handle, but John's body blocked him.

Suddenly John was up close against him, Danny's face in his hand. "Then get to bed... with me."

Danny's stomach dropped right into his bowels in one instant liquid movement. "Oh no, don't start."

John said nothing.

"No more of your fucking jokes, John. You're really getting on my tits with this. Grow up."

"Who's joking?" The grip on his face tightened.

Danny felt himself go hot and cold like he'd heard it told. "Are you completely off your head?"

"You said it yourself once, take it where you can get it. Well you can get it here, what's the problem?"

"In your bed, I suppose?" Danny hung onto anything that made it ordinary, avoiding the realities, obsessing the detail.

"Here in the fucking kitchen if you like."

Danny jerked his head free. "No." He shook his head. "Definitely, categorically no. You're going to regret this in the morning."

"Not as much as you will if I let you go out that door."

"What the hell's that supposed to mean?"

"We all know what your bad dreams are, want to know mine?"

"No, I fucking don't." He began to cajole, fighting the first twitchings of panic. "Come on, John, let me out." He had to get out. On the heels of that thought came the realisation that there was more than one way to do it.

He slid out from under John's body like an eel from under a rock and ran for the back door, unlocking it and almost falling over the dog before John realised what he'd done.

He ran across the yard, making for the tractor shed. The milking shed would be better, it had a back door, but it was often locked, and tonight would be the night. He didn't risk it.

He dived into the darkness and ran behind the cover of the tractors. He stood there watching the doorway, breath rasping, trying to conceal it. Maybe John wouldn't follow.

But he did.

He saw John's body silhouetted in the doorway. He pressed himself back against the wall, trying to blend further into the darkness.

"Danny?" John's voice was low and carrying in the night's stillness. It sounded almost uncertain. Danny pressed himself further back. The shed was hot and airless from the day's sun pounding on its tin roof. The tractors were pungent with hot diesel.

John stepped into the dark. Danny darted behind the wheel of the nearest tractor. It was almost as tall as his head.

"Danny, you here?"

Danny held his breath. He could feel the oily dirt beneath his fingers. He pressed his face to the tractor's side, trying to become smaller.

"Come on, Danny." John sounded as if he were smiling. "Forget it. It was a bad joke anyway."

Danny didn't move. He couldn't trust him, didn't dare. He heard John's foot hit something – oil can, maybe – prowling.

When he spoke next Danny jumped, his skin breaking out into a cold sweat. He was closer, much closer, and moving this way. "Come on, baby. I'm sorry."

Danny panicked and darted forward. He heard John's grunt behind him and turned, desperately trying to place him, and ran full tilt into the wing mirror. It knocked him back, clutching his head, hissing, "*Shit.*"

John grabbed him round the neck, hauling him back towards the tractor. Danny gurgled like a baby, scrabbling at John's hands. He couldn't breathe. He was thrown hard against the back wheel. The wind came out of him in a grunt.

"Don't ever try that again." John's breath was sour from too many cigarettes.

Danny tried to squeeze out a reply, but nothing would come.

John grabbed his chin, jerking it up, banging his head against the wheel. "Don't you ever run away from me again."

"John..." he croaked. But John was up against him and suddenly he could feel his hands on his bare chest, his thumbs, rough and callused, deliberately insistent, brushing purposefully over his nipples.

His head came forward, equally deliberately, but Danny yanked his face away and the kiss landed on his cheek. But the contact was enough. John pressed against him, forcing him back against the hub of the wheel. Danny lost his footing, tried to regain it. John's mouth hovered over his ear. He kept whispering his name, as if he was trying to somehow make the whole thing more real, more normal. He took Danny's hand and pressed it against the front of his jeans. "Feel that?"

Danny pulled his hand back as if it had been burnt. "*John*, don't, for fuck's sake."

But he might never have spoken. John's hands slid down Danny's body and began working at his belt.

Danny grunted, "*Don't.*" But John undid his trousers, dragging them down to his thighs. Danny had no underpants on. He felt John's hand grip him tight then unmistakably begin to masturbate him.

Danny tried pleading, begging. He didn't even know what he was saying. He wasn't listening. "John, don't. Don't do this, John... please." Incoherent, useless.

John whispered against his face, "What's this I feel?" He was pressing himself hard against Danny's side, tugging Danny's cock as if it was made of rubber. "Christ, you *have* got an itch, haven't you?"

Danny tried not to listen, but John's mouth was against his ear, the words burning right inside his head. And he was right. Danny had an itch alright, an itch he couldn't scratch, was desperate to scratch. God, he'd never wanted to satisfy an itch so bad in all his life. John's hand was pulling, teasing, drawing him out.

Danny didn't answer. Instead every muscle in his body suddenly went limp. He let his head roll back against the wheel. He closed his eyes. He didn't need to answer. He was no longer resisting. Danny had said yes. He wanted it.

The relief of it was immense.

"Oh boy..." There was elation in John's voice now. His weight eased off him, knowing that he was captive, pathetic, enslaved to his own need.

Danny spread his arms out wide against the wheel, pressing himself up towards him, thrusting towards the relief of John's hand. John moved off him just long enough to pull his own belt out of the buckle and drag his clothes down, then the feel of his erection pressed hard against Danny's thigh, hot and sticky, long and hard, already humping against him, spreading his legs for better leverage. He groaned, "Christ..." then he began to keep time, his body moving to the rhythm of his hand. Masturbation in synchronisation. "Christ..."

Danny trembled, hovered there, already, already. "Don't. I'm going to... *John*."

John's hand gripped his shoulder, slid round his neck. Danny lifted his hands bonelessly to fend him off. John pulled him to him, humping harder, fiercer, hurting him and kissed him full on the mouth, pushing his tongue in deep.

Danny grunted, hands grabbing at John's blindly, sucking on his tongue like a starving infant and felt it all come up. It was like vomiting. He could no more have stopped it once it started than become God.

He came, John's semen spurting hot over his leg, lubricating his thrusts, his own boiling over John's fingers.

That was all it took. It was over in seconds. Like a bomb going off. And after that there was only their ragged breathing, and the slow drip of semen on the shed floor.

## SEVEN

There is always a day after. There always has to be.

Conveniently, Danny could not remember getting to bed. Inconveniently, he could remember everything else. Everything around him seemed to trigger images: the dog scratching, a glass of orange juice, the smell of Rab's cigarettes. Worst of all was the shed. As soon as he went in, the smell of hot diesel brought everything up in glowing Technicolor. He was spared only one thing: his father had gone out early in the morning, taking John with him, and they would not be back for lunch. That meant he would not have to face him till tea-time.

By four o'clock he had burnt himself out, working twice as hard, trying to distance himself from his own thoughts and the knowledge that he would have to face John shortly. By five he was chain-smoking cigarettes and feeling emotionally and physically exhausted.

At six o'clock they went home, Danny delaying until the last. But his mother was alone in the kitchen, no John, and he wasn't going to ask. "Where's John?" he heard himself say with a kind of horrified disbelief.

"I told you, out with your dad somewhere. They won't be back till late."

She'd omitted that part earlier. If it was possible to be elated and miserable at once, he was it.

After dinner he went up to bed and lay on the covers. His mind turned everything over endlessly. He felt hot and restless.

He threw himself on his stomach, punching the pillow up with his fist.

This was worse, pressed against the bed. He threw himself on his back again. He tried to go limp. *Relax*, Danny.

He slid nervelessly back into his thoughts. His brain, suddenly unfettered, ran everything through like a film, but this time he didn't fight it. John kissing him on the hay wagon, John's thumbs rubbing his nipples, John unzipping, pushing himself on his leg.

The touch of his own fingers electrified him. He looked down at himself, and felt the tight coil of excitement in his belly. He suddenly felt huge with his own potency, dying to show it off, full of strutting macho.

The idea came to him to do it at the window. A thrill of excitement at the possibility of being caught made his cock charge up harder. He could see the head of it, peeled back, massively distended. He got up and went to the window "Look," he urged under his breath.

He pressed the shaft down into his body, making it longer, harder. "There's a big one for you, girls. How would you like a bit of that?" And he frigged it hard, grunting, watching himself.

He came immediately, his knees buckling as his penis jerked under his hand. He arched his body out, trying to shoot it as far as possible. He saw it splat against the window like thick white phlegm. He moaned in ecstasy at his own marvellousness as he pulled his orgasm out harder, making it last, milking himself dry.

When it was finished he dropped down onto the seat by the window, his legs like jelly, breathless. The come slid down the glass. "What the fuck...?" he said, incredulous at his own madness.

He wiped himself with shaking hands and zipped up, then did the best he could with the window. It was on the fucking curtains. Christ, that was going to be a neat one to explain. What if someone had seen him? Anyone could have looked up and seen him. What had possessed him?

As soon as he had his breath back he went along to the bathroom and got a wet facecloth and wiped the window. He tried ineffectually to dab it off the curtains. "Oh boy..." he whispered.

He went back to the bathroom to rinse the cloth out and heard the bang of the back door. He heard his father's voice. His stomach dropped.

He ran back to the bedroom and closed the door, locking it, heart pounding.

He lay listening for a lifetime. The time dragged by like two nights, three. He heard Ian come up the stairs, Rab, his mother and father, and then, finally, John. Did he pause at his door? No. He passed by and went on to his room.

Danny lay on his bed, heart thumping.

When half an hour had passed and the house had begun to tick with its midnight cooling he knew John wasn't going to come.

He got up and stripped off his clothes. He climbed under the single sheet and watched images of himself in the shed. When his cock came up he ignored it. "Let it burst," he whispered. And he fell into a tearful and hallucinatory sleep.

## EIGHT

Danny woke the next morning with a kind of heavy dread – nameless, indefinable. Ian knocked him up. "Come on, beautiful, rise and shine."

Danny mumbled something incoherent and swung out of bed. His usual morning erection repulsed him, sticking out of his groin like some obscenity. He felt like a dirty old man.

He pulled his shorts and jeans on quickly to hide it and caught himself on the zip. "Fucking hell," he hissed.

It made his day.


The kitchen was full, everybody there at once. John was at the end of the table wearing jeans and a white singlet. His hair might almost have passed for dark blonde. Danny caught his steady, expressionless eyes once, then looked away quickly, colouring up.

Everybody grunted at each other, a ritual that passed for good morning. He ate his breakfast, keeping his head down. His father handed out his instructions. "You finish up that bottom field," he said to Danny. "John, you help him out. I want that dead tree down. Take the chain-saw and see and make a good job of it."

John nodded and looked at Danny. Danny pushed up out of his seat and went out to the shed.

He drove the tractor out into the yard and was coupling up the trailer when John came out and climbed into his own vehicle.

He was already revving up the saw when Danny got down there.


They could say nothing over the sound of the saw. Danny was secretly relieved, but it didn't make him any less aware of him. He found himself staring when John pulled off his singlet. The dark hair under his arms was slick with sweat.

John wiped the singlet over his chest and under his arms. "Fucking hot, Daniel, old son." He squinted up at the sky. "Take five minutes out, shall we?" He looked at Danny for the first time. "Underneath the spreading chestnut tree, where I fucked you and you fucked me." Something very like a smile quirked at the corner of his mouth.

Danny turned away angrily and moved off towards the tree. Carefully he lowered his back against the bark. His sunburn just kept peeling and burning, peeling and burning. It never seemed to stop hurting.

John sat down beside him, mopping his face with his shirt. He lifted his hair up to let the air under. Out of the corner of his eye, Danny was aware of those dark spikes of hair in his armpit again, and the heavy sweet smell of fresh sweat from him.

John leant his head back against the tree and closed his eyes. Thick dark lashes like Danny's own, remarkably similar in colour.

"Penny for them, Danny-boy." John's eyes had opened and were watching him slant-wise.

Danny blushed immediately and then hated himself for his transparency.

"Oho, dirty thoughts?"

Danny turned his head away.

John sat up a little and began rolling a cigarette. "Want one?"

Danny barely shook his head.

John lit his cigarette and inhaled deeply. He turned to Danny and leaned over him, smiling. "Here, share mine," and he covered Danny's mouth with his own.

Danny, taken completely by surprise, did nothing except grunt with shock, allowing the smoke to invade his mouth. He tasted the strong aniseed of the rich sweet tobacco, and then John himself, that wide, curving Cheshire cat mouth, hot and searching, pushing his tongue in deep.

Danny broke away, coughing and pink. "You dirty bastard."

John laughed. "Do you good. Stop you growing too big." He leaned back against the tree again as if nothing had happened.

Danny glared at him.

John closed his eyes. "No good glaring, Daniel. I refuse to kiss you again."

Danny was flustered, outraged. He scrambled to his feet. "You fucking..."

But words failed him.


The rest of the afternoon passed in a frigid silence on Danny's part, and an incredibly irritating amused one on John's. How could he be so relaxed? Did nothing ever worry him? It was all one big fucking joke to him.

Danny sat on the back of the trailer, watching him dismantle the chain saw. All that talk about desperation. He'd been drunk and horny and seen a way of getting his rocks off. The fucking hypocritical... Danny watched him with mounting fury.

John finished up and picked up his T-shirt, clambering over the cut logs to the trailer. "That's us, lad." Then he looked up at him. "God, look at its face. What's wrong with you?"

Danny jumped down from the trailer and turned his back on him. "Why don't you fuck off?"

"Just going to," John said, climbing into the cab, and did precisely that.


Danny got into the house last. He was at the end of the queue for the shower again.

He slammed around the kitchen, collecting cold meat and some salad that had been left for him. He ate his meal rigidly, as if he could barely open his teeth to let it in.

Rab came in and spoke to him, but was chased by his grim expression. Ian took one look at him and didn't even bother.

Finally John appeared, wrapped only in a towel as usual, and had the gall to smile at him. "Your turn, Daniel."

Danny glared at him.

Suddenly John whipped his towel open like a stage magician. He laughed, the funny that isn't funny, then pulled it shut again, saying, "Now you can toss off in the shower." But he couldn't seem to hold his gaze. He turned abruptly and went out.

Danny looked down at his hand. He'd crushed the piece of bread he was holding. He threw it on his plate and went up to the shower.


Danny tried to watch television, but couldn't concentrate. He went over for a quick drink before closing time only to find John secreted in the back with a couple of girls.

He left the drink half-finished and went home.

He felt as if he could hardly get his feet up the stairs. He unbuttoned his shirt and dropped it on the chair. He peered through the gap in the curtains. No sign of him. Probably poking one of the stupid cows out the back of the pub. He dragged the curtains shut.

He pulled his clothes off and climbed under the sheet. For the first time in his life he wished he could cry.

The back door slammed. Danny held his breath. But it was only Rab. He recognised the whistling as he came upstairs.

He must have dozed, although he could not comprehend how he managed it. He was startled to hear the toilet flush and the bathroom door bang. His mother? No, whoever it was came down the hall and went into John's room, banging the door again. Pissed, by the sound of it.

Danny peered at his clock. 12:34. Where the hell had he been till this hour? Christ, he *had*. The dirty bastard had been fucking some bitch behind the pub. Where was 'desperation' now?

Danny punched the pillow and buried his face in it. Finally he was crying, tears of humiliation and rage.

Carried away with his own melodrama, he cried till he hiccupped and then hiccupped till he was sore. "Shit," he hicced again and swung upright, scrubbing at his itchy face. Christ, what a dickhead. He needed a drink.

He crossed the floor, opening the door carefully, and was shoved back into the room. He didn't even grunt. He staggered back and sat down plump in the chair by the window.

John closed the door quietly. His white shirt was unfastened to his waist, but still tucked in. He was barefoot. He looked as if he had been disturbed undressing. "Hello, baby."

Danny stood up, then sat down again, realising he was stark naked.

"Ready for me, I see." John began to pull his shirt out from his trousers.

Danny stared at him in disbelief. He had to be joking.

John began to unbuckle the heavy belt on his jeans.

"You've got to be kidding," Danny finally blurted out. "You go off fucking some bitch behind the pub and then come up here..."

"Quiet, Danny. Mum's next door, sleeping but lightly."

Danny glared at him and went on in a low voice, "You come up here expecting... expecting..." But he couldn't say it, couldn't put it into words.

John raised his eyebrows. "Go on, expecting what?"

Danny clamped his lips shut, would say nothing more. John finished unbuckling his trousers, undid the button, and then stopped. "Expecting to fuck you too? Oh, baby, have *some* faith. I can manage two in one evening. No sweat."

Danny was immediately furious. "Don't you dare..."

John laughed suddenly, richly, as if he were genuinely amused. "Just like his mother, listen to him." He mimicked, "Don't you *dare*." He laughed again. "I'd like to see you stop me."

Danny hurled himself at him, head down, knocking him flat onto the bed, pummelling him with his fists. The bed thumped against the wall.

John grunted with surprise. Every fucking time this little bastard caught him on the hop. He got a hand free and punched Danny in the kidneys – once, twice, three times, with low, short, hard jabs.

Danny flinched away, trying to avoid the blows, and at that moment John pushed him. He fell onto the floor, flat on his back, the impact knocking all the wind out of him.

John scrambled off the bed and knelt on his chest, pulling his head round by the hair, and hissed, "That's it, wake the whole fucking house, then we can be rolling around the floor naked, at one in the morning, with plenty of explanations, and every one a winner." He pressed down sharply with his knee. Danny winced, gasping for air, then lay quiet, exhausted of everything.

John got up and sat on the edge of the bed. He started searching his pockets for a cigarette. Danny lay on the floor, unmoving.

"Get up." John nudged him with his foot.

Danny remained immobile.

"I said, get *up*." He reached down and yanked Danny up by the hair, dragging him up onto the bed.

Danny wouldn't cry, not again, not in front of him.

"Here." John thrust the cigarette into his mouth. Danny took it between numb lips. "Inhale," John said. "You know, suck."

Danny lifted a shaking hand and inhaled the cigarette, passing it back to him.

"Good boy." John fell back abruptly on the bed. "Now I want you to see something."

Danny turned his face away.

"You're going to look, whether you like it or not. Now turn around."

Danny half turned, glancing over at him. He jerked his face away again.

John yanked him round by the arm. He was lying there, jeans undone, crammed down tight under his balls, squeezing them up fatly, his cock red and angry, sticking up his belly.

He grabbed Danny's hand, wrapping his fingers round the sticky head, pushing himself up into it, squeezing the fingers tight round himself, thrusting into it. "Feel how stiff that is? Know how it gets that stiff?"

He gave Danny's arm a yank, pulling him down onto his lap as he fell back. He grabbed Danny's hair and shoved his face into his groin, levering his hips up into his face. "Think this is what I want?" And he laughed unpleasantly, grinding Danny's face against his erection. "*You* want this."

And he pressed his fingers into Danny's jaw, and forced his mouth wide open.

## NINE

It was September.

Where had August gone? Flamed and incandescent, as ephemeral as a match.

They had started refencing the fields to be in good time for the winter. They had all gone out in a group: Ian, Rab, John and him. They had been working down the back pasture for the entire morning, even eating their lunch down there. It was the first time he had worked with John in a fortnight.

Come 2 p.m. they had run out of fence wire. Danny had been sitting watching John work, with something close to hate. It felt odd and flat inside, as if something within him had died. He felt at that moment as if he had hated him all his life.

Occasionally John would wink at Rab as if they shared some great joke. Maybe they did. Maybe he was saying, 'Guess what I got Danny to do last time I was pissed?'

And he'd flex that thick right arm of his – John's powerful wanking arm; bring you off in four seconds, that arm, he'd timed him – and they'd laugh some more and wink some more, just like they were doing now.

"Well, we're out of it then, aren't we?" John ran a hand through his hair, exasperated. Ian waited patiently for instructions.

John turned to Rab "You're no fucking use with that hand. You stay here with boy-beautiful." He didn't even look at Danny when he said it. "Ian, you can come with me." He looked at Rab again. "Give you a good excuse to fart about, Hardman."

Rab laughed, giving him the finger. Oh, they loved each other, these two.

Ian and John drove off. Rab turned and smiled at him. It looked almost sheepish. He was picking at the bandage on his left hand. He'd cut it yesterday on the wire cutters. "Might as well sit down."

They sat down on the empty bobbins and lit up cigarettes.

"Hot?" Danny asked him unexpectedly. Rab looked at him, but Danny was looking out over the fields disinterestedly. Rab uh-huhed cautiously, aware of something tenuous hiding in the question.

"Me too." And Danny gave him an odd look, odd enough to make Rab colour up. He'd been doing this for the past two weeks, a million dirty little hints just like this one. He'd tried to read nothing into it, but the tone of Danny's voice said different. Rab realised he was holding his breath. His heart was thumping uncomfortably in his chest.

Danny threw his cigarette down and trod it into the grass as if he'd come to a decision, then he looked away again as if his mind had detached itself once more, off at yet another tangent. "Want to do it then?" he said abruptly, standing up.

"What?" Rab blinked up at him, shading his eyes against the sun.

Danny shrugged one shoulder as if to say, I don't know, then said, "Whatever you want."

Rab still wasn't grasping. "I don't get you…"

"Sex. Whatever you want. And don't say you don't know what I'm talking about, I've seen you watching me." Danny looked at him steadily. It was almost challenging.

Rab wet his lips then managed to croak, "Here?" then realised what he was saying. "Are you nuts?" he added, infusing more annoyance into his tone, then he spoiled it again by saying, "They'll be back in a minute."

Danny smiled for the first time. It was soft, secretive. It was a beautiful smile, seductive. It made you understand just why he was considered one of the best looking boys in the village – if you'd been dense enough to miss it in the first place.

"I may not last a minute, so who's sweating?" The smile slid away. His eyes seemed to grow darker, like John's did when he was angry. "Come on, Rab, don't make me beg." He cocked his head and said very softly, "You never know how long you'll have to wait till next time."

Rab looked away, his face flaming. "Christ, I thought I was imagining this. I never really believed... not you. Anyway, I wasn't looking at you. Why should I have been looking at you?"

"Last chance, Rab."

Rab looked up at him.

Danny smiled.

Rab stood up quickly, not looking him in the eye. "If you tell anyone..." He was mortified by Danny's cold-bloodedness, his own willingness.

"Up on the lorry," Danny commanded

Rab climbed up and sat on the edge.

Danny smiled up at him, shaking his head. "Over there." He hoisted himself up and stood beside Rab, reaching out his hand. "Up against the cab."

Rab took it and let himself be pulled up. "What? Standing up?" He looked around him. "But we can be seen up here. It's like being on a fucking stage."

Danny came up against him, edging him backwards with his body until he was up against the back of the cab. "That's the whole idea." He watched Rab's face intently. "It's supposed to be a turn-on. Exhibitionism, you know?" And his smile had something malevolent about it. His hand was at Rab's belt, undoing his clothes.

Rab caught at his hands. "But what if they come back?"

Danny tugged his hands away. "Well, you'll have to be fast, won't you, baby?"

Rab could feel his hand slide inside his jeans, then he was squeezing, groping. "What, not stiff?" He sounded as if he was amused, not irritated.

"What d'you fucking expect, stuck up here?" Rab looked round him nervously.

"Maybe you don't want it then?"

Rab felt suddenly angry. "Yeah, maybe I don't." And he tried to re-fasten his trousers, but Danny yanked them down with a sudden jerk, pulling his T-shirt up into a bunch under his chin.

He stood exposed to all the world, naked from neck to thigh, his cock flaccidly white in the bright light. "What the fuck...?" He tried to cover himself with his hands, but Danny pushed his body in the way.

"Very nice." It was breathy, excited. "I don't think I've ever seen you naked before. Correct me if I'm wrong."

Rab followed the direction of his eyes. He looked back up into his face, flushed and almost vindictive, and felt the sudden volte-face of lust. Abruptly his cock fattened, lengthened. He felt his face grow hot with shame.

Danny stood back, still holding his bunched-up shirt. "I see you've changed your mind."

Rab's cock stood out straight from his body. He said nothing.

"Oh well, maybe not." And Danny let his shirt go and turned from him.

Rab called, "Danny, wait..." before he could think.

Danny turned slowly. Rab slowly lifted his T-shirt in offering, but Danny stood where he was, hands in his pockets. Suddenly Rab wanted this more than he had ever wanted anything in his life.

"Ask nicely," Danny said.

"Please."

"Please what? "

Rab groaned and closed his eyes. "For pity's sake, Danny, just do it, will you?"

Danny stepped forward and touched his cock lightly. His hand felt outrageously cool. "You only had to ask, baby." And then, incredibly, Danny kissed him, slowly, poisonously, like a drug.

Rab felt himself liquefy underneath the feel of his mouth. His lips travelled down Rab's neck, onto his chest. Danny got down on his knees.

Rab felt himself tauten with excitement. For two weeks Danny had been dangling the possibility of this before him, waiting until they were alone, then shamelessly flirting with him until Rab couldn't believe he was actually seeing it. Not Danny. Never in a million years. For years he'd secretly nurtured this fantasy. Only now could he confess it to himself. He still couldn't believe it. Yet here he was, kneeling before him, his white skin pale and cool against Rab's brown belly.

Danny spread his hands against the cab at either side of Rab's body and kissed the head of his cock. Rab closed his eyes, unable to bear the sight of him nuzzling him.

Danny sucked the head in slowly, using only his mouth, keeping his hands firmly pressed to the cab. Rab thought he would die. He made no noise, his eyes opening with the unbearable tension of it. In the dark, he was alone with him, and he couldn't stand that. But it was no good. He couldn't see the fields, feel anything, register anything but that intensive suckling. He wanted to come, now, but it was too soft, too pulling. He needed friction.

*Harder, harder, for Christ's sake.*

But Danny just kept gently mouthing his glans, teasing it right out to the tip, letting it come out of his mouth, then softly sucking it right in again.

Rab thrust into his mouth, trying to move it faster, but Danny simply pulled his head away, letting him fall out every time he attempted it. So he stood still. It was torture to stand still, just as Danny intended it to be, but he stood like a statue, his knuckles whitely gripping his T-shirt, the metal brace bar digging into his back. He watched Danny's mouth, full and lascivious, wrapped around his cockhead, his eyes half-closed, and knew he was going to die. He wasn't going to come, he was going to die. He could see faint lights popping at the corners of his vision.

"Please, Danny..." He tried to thrust again. Danny let him go, then used his teeth to gently pull him back into his mouth.

"*Harder*..." Rab whispered.

He could feel a dull ache right round from his anus to his shaft. He felt as if his bowels were being sucked right out of his cock. Then he saw the van, the little green jolly-van, flashing through the hedgerows before it came to the gate. How long till it came to the gate? His heart stopped beating.

"Oh no, shit, Jesus..." He jerked forwards.

Danny's hands shoved him back, teeth closing on his cock like a vice, only there was no pain at all. Instead, Rab felt it go through him like a match in a bale of hay. He grabbed Danny's head to him as the van nosed through the gate.

This time Danny let him thrust his cock deep in his mouth, urging his head forwards as if his throat had opened right up and he intended to swallow him right down it.

Rab watched the pick-up bump over the cattle grid as he impaled Danny's head on his body. "Oh no, oh God, oh no..." and he came just as John looked up and saw them standing there.


"How often?" John demanded.

"What's it to you?"

John grabbed his shirt front and lifted him bodily off the bed. "You watch your lip, you little fuck, or I might just march into her room right now and drop you right in it. If you think I'm going to spend all my fucking life fishing a squalid little faggot like you out the shit..."

Danny ripped his hand off, dropping back onto the bed with a jolt. "*I'm* a faggot? It's not me who's re-enacting some fucking gay-boy fantasy out a wank mag." Danny scrabbled back, hissing at him, "Still hide them under the bed, John? Still..."

But he didn't get to finish it. John was on the bed and had backhanded him savagely before Danny could move. John's hand was round his neck, gripping, choking him. Danny scratched at it feebly.

"Touch him again and I'll fucking kill you."

Danny managed to whimper something, a noise.

Slowly, so slowly, John's hand loosened.

Danny fell back against the wall, trapped under John's crouched body, their faces inches apart, and everything in the room suddenly seemed to go slow, become languorous: the soft whirr of the clock, their breathing, life itself.

John backed off, got up. He looked odd, unsettled. When he spoke next he wouldn't meet his eyes. "I'll be watching you."

Danny just stared up at him, trying to understand, watching John leave.

The door shut. Danny let himself slide down the wall onto his back. He stared up at the ceiling, letting his arms drop above his head. He hummed suddenly, softly, "Every step you take, every move you make..." He paused for a long moment, then whispered, "Yeah, but who knows what you're going to see, John?"

## TEN

John did watch him. As Danny's elder and better he maintained an absolute authority over him, outside his father's jurisdiction, and he used it to make sure he never worked alone with Rab. If anyone noticed they put it down to diplomacy. After all, Rab and Danny had never got on. It was typical of John to act as a buffer between them, nothing unusual in that.

September had settled into rain, weeks of it at a stretch, as if it was trying to make up for the long, hot summer. But it was a warm, sweaty rain, making everything wet and uncomfortable and changing the landscape into a perpetual grey. It was as bleak and unrelieved as Danny felt.

On the twentieth, his father woke with toothache. He was irritable and pig-headed because he would have to go to the dentist and they would be short-handed. He appointed Danny to mucking out with Rab and it was more than John could do to cross him in this mood. Nevertheless, he stood behind his father in the kitchen while he was giving out his orders and stared at Danny over his shoulder. His face was a lecture, full of implied threats.

Danny ignored them all.

Rab closed the byre doors and turned to him. It was intensely dark inside, just as it always was on wet days, and it smelled pungently of cattle. They did not put on the lights.

"He *did* see." Rab looked at the remains of the bruise on his cheek.

Danny nodded.

"Warned off?" he asked, then laughed softly, a small huff of sound. "Who am I kidding? Of course you were." He barked another laugh, joyless, heavy with cynicism, then began patting his pockets. "And we all know why."

Danny stared at him.

Rab looked up at him from rolling a cigarette. Even in the dark he managed it elegantly. "Nothing to say?"

Danny was silent, his mind racing. His stomach felt like lead. A cold sweat began to prickle down his spine.

Rab smiled, watching him. The end of his cigarette glowed faintly in the dim light. He laughed sourly and scratched his chest through his T-shirt. Danny watched him uneasily. "You're not in any rush to contradict me, Danny."

"It's bullshit," Danny said flatly.

Rab laughed then reached forward with a quick nervous movement and pulled Danny's T-shirt up, sliding his hand up inside, watching his face for a reaction.

Danny grabbed his hand. "What's Ian been saying?"

Rab laughed again. Relief, nerves, it was difficult to say. "The usual crap. You and John, joined at the hip, blah-de-blah-de-blah. He's been saying it as long as I can remember." Rab looked at him. "Okay, so he's a dipstick, but it had you going, didn't it?"

Danny dropped his hand. His stomach seemed to slowly thaw inside him. He felt as if his guts were melting.

Rab moved up closer, boldly pulling Danny's shirt out, pushing his hands down the front of his jeans. He breathed heavily in his ear, "I can, can't I? This is what you meant, isn't it?"

Danny nodded. "But don't piss me off with any more of Ian's crap, okay?"

Rab said, "Okay", but his mind was already on other things. He let it go because he didn't care, because he didn't believe it. He never had, and he never would.

Predictably, John came to his room that night, but he found the door locked.

Danny stood at the window and listened to him outside. John's voice was whispering and urgent. "Danny…? Open the door."

Danny did not answer.

"Danny... open the bloody *door*." His voice was full of repressed anger.

Danny said nothing.

John rattled the doorknob. "Open this door, you little cunt, or I'll..." But he got no further. They both heard his father's steps on the stairs, his heavy tread carrying clearly in the silence of the hall.

John must have moved away from the door. When Danny heard him next he sounded as if he was standing outside the bathroom. He was talking to his father.

After a while the conversation died. John did not come back.

## ELEVEN

It was three days after that before John finally caught up with him. He bumped into him, literally, working alone in the milking shed at seven in the evening. Danny involuntarily took a step back.

John's eyes immediately narrowed. Danny smiled with a tight mouth and tried to push past him.

"Oh no, you don't." John's hand shot out, grabbing his shoulder and pulling him half round. Danny looked at the hand, then at John's face. It was transformed by anger into something ugly.

"What did you do with him?" It had all the vehemence of a long speech whittled away by time into one all-consuming question.

"Who?"

Danny was spun round to face him. "Don't give me that."

Danny jerked his shoulder free. "You've got a one-track mind, John."

John shoved him back against the corrugated iron wall with a thump. The pail he was carrying clanked against it. "What did you do with him? And don't bother to lie to me. You were practically licking your lips, you little queer." John shouldered him back again.

Danny's ribs felt as if they cracked with the impact. He hissed with pain. "You want me to tell you?" He saw John's lips compress furiously, but he went on, hating him so intensely he no longer cared what he said, "I know what you want, John. I know what this whole fucking thing has been about right from the start." He felt John's body jerk back off him like a kicked dog.

Danny looked into his face, utterly thrown by the reaction. John was still furious, but there was something else darting in his eyes now, and Danny had known too much of it in his life to mistake it. With some barely understood need to twist the knife he said, "Funny that what's one big fucking joke with me becomes deadly serious when he's involved. What exactly *is* your problem? So I sucked his root. I've sucked yours. Where's the difference? Tasted the same to me."

John lunged at him, running him back against the wall with a ferocity that made Danny slump. His hand clamped tight over Danny's mouth, covering the whole lower half of his face. Already he was struggling for air. "You want to die?"

He clawed at John's hand, but it was like an octopus smothering his face.

"You *want* to die?"

He began to see coloured spots, areas of grey faded in and out of his vision. He felt himself grow weak. His hands seemed to pull at John's like empty gloves, without force. He could hear John saying it again and again, like an incantation, a man in shock. "You want to die?" His eyes were dilated, unseeing.

Danny slid away, thinking vaguely that it was a fucking crappy thing to die for.

It was the third such injury in so many weeks. Black eyes, fat lips, swollen jaws, and now this.

"What the hell is *wrong* with you?" Danny's father glared at him across the table.

Danny said nothing.

"Right," his father said, getting up, pushing the chair back. "This is the last. One more fight, one more, 'I walked into the tractor, Dad', and I'll expect explanations from the lot of you." He pointed at Danny as though he bore the singular blame. "This is the last, I mean it." And he slammed out the door.

Danny looked at the back door sullenly. He felt a dull diffuse resentment well up in him. This was John's fault. Where was *his* lecture? John had nearly fucking killed him for Christ's sake. Danny battered his eggshell to a pulp with his spoon. When Ian spoke to him he jumped.

"Nice collection of bruises. Gives you that well-worn look." He moved over to the toaster and pushed in two slices of bread. He turned and leaned against the counter, letting his eyes travel over Danny's body: the long slim legs, the narrow hips, the white skin emphasised by the dark T-shirt, his hair so long it was curling down over his collar, the sheer abundance of it intensifying the outrageous colour, a deep unearthly red. Danny had everything, was everything that Ian wasn't.

He realised abruptly he was staring. He straightened up and crossed the room.

Danny glowered up at him blackly as he pulled out a chair.

"What's this? Fear and loathing in Hope House Farm?" Ian sat down and began buttering his toast. "'Twas not I that marred that beauty." His gaze swept over Danny's face, taking in his fine etched brows, the thick dark lashes, his wide sensuous mouth. Poor used Danny.

Danny enunciated slowly and clearly, voice heavy with dislike, "Go *fuck* yourself."

Ian laughed uproariously, as if he had cracked an amazingly funny joke. He slapped his thighs, he choked, he coughed. "Oh boy..." He laughed some more. "Oh boy, that's rich..." He sobered abruptly, as if he had never laughed at all. His face looked thin and pinched, like a mask. "Really rich, coming from someone like you. It's all you know, isn't it? Fucking yourself."

Danny jumped up angrily and grabbed the front of his shirt. "Don't you fucking start. I've had you right up to here."

"Take your hands off me."

Danny bunched his fist up tighter.

Suddenly the door opened. John came in, stopping short when he saw them. Ian looked over at him. "Boy thinks he's had me up to here, John." He looked back slowly into Danny's eyes. "You haven't had *me* up anywhere, baby. *Way* too crowded for me."

And he moved easily out of Danny's grip and went out the door.

## TWELVE

October moved in and with it came the first tinglings of cold. Rab felt it close in around him with a depressing sense of suffocation.

He had barely spoken to Danny since the day of his uncle's toothache. Past a fortnight now. Christ, it felt as if the entire year had moved in fortnights.

The enforced distance between them had produced a raging unmitigated ache in him that he blankly refused to name. He couldn't eat, he couldn't sleep. His only comfort was that John at least seemed to be suffering as much as he was.

It wasn't his imagination that John had lost more weight. Nor was it his imagination that the old man was determinedly keeping the three of them apart. He always seemed to be watching them from a distance, as if they were potentially dangerous animals.

Only Danny seemed to remain somehow untouched, isolated in that detachment of his. He found himself constantly drawn to him, watching him till it felt like a parasite living inside him, feeding off him. At mealtimes he would push his plate away, his meal barely tasted, unable to concentrate with Danny sitting so close, John taciturn beside him, eyes ever watchful, refusing food without explanation.

On the evening of the fourth, Rab went into the living-room and found Danny sitting alone in the dark, watching TV. It felt like an act of God.

Danny looked round briefly, then smiled and looked back at the TV, saying, "Ill met by moonlight proud Titania."

Rab closed the door and leaned against it. He felt as if his entire hunger grew in his chest. *God, I feel like a wolfman, a monster. I feel like ripping him apart.*

He looked at Danny smiling there, his face planed into dark shadows and sharp blue angles by the shifting light, and croaked hoarsely, "I could eat you. You look so fucking..." Words failed him.

"Try sexy." Danny smiled some more then opened his legs, sliding down the settee to spread them wide. He gestured with his head. "Come on then, what're you waiting for?"

Rab swallowed. His voice when it came out sounded strangled, barely above a whisper. "Here?"

Danny looked around him then spread his arms along the back of the sofa. "Looks good to me."

Rab licked his lips. He could feel his hard-on pounding like it had a heart of its own. "The door..." He was still leaning against it. It was a glass door, frosted with leaves.

"No-one can see."

"They might... I mean anyone might..."

"They won't, trust me."

Rab let go the door's support like a man launching himself off a pier. He reached out a hand to Danny's hair just as the door opened.

"Did I leave my knitting in here?"

His aunt came in and began lifting cushions off her armchair. The colour swept into Rab's face like a tidal wave. Guilt and relief both. He was never more glad of the dark in his life.

Danny remained exactly where he was, sprawled indecently across the settee. His aunt looked at them both, aware suddenly of the unnatural silence. Her eyes swept over Danny's splayed body. Rab saw him look at her, his eyes half-closed, sleepy, lecherous with intent. His aunt looked away abruptly, talking to herself.

Rab thought, He did that deliberately. He embarrassed her deliberately. And he knew Danny had done it before, knew with a sudden intuitive knowledge that his aunt's thoughts were not as wholly pure and innocent as she would have them believe, and that Danny knew it and played on it.

"Ah, at last, found it." And she went from the room, not looking at either of them. The door closed with a bang.

Rab stood looking down at him, wondering what went on in his head. He was like an iceberg, always three-quarters under the water.

Danny reached over and lifted a packet of cigarettes from the chair arm and put one in his mouth. He lit it with one hand and placed the other back on the back of the sofa. "Come on, sit down."

Rab hesitated. He had had a bad fright, and something about Danny's performance made him wary, but the very act of standing there watching him smoke, his cheekbones in stark relief every time he drew on the cigarette, was acting like an aphrodisiac.

Danny grinned, "She won't be back, relax." He sounded like he could guarantee it.

Rab licked his lips, glanced at the door. Danny said, "Come on, Rab, you want, you don't want, which is it to be?"

Rab sat down beside him and put his hand flat on Danny's stomach all in one gesture. As a statement of how he felt and what he wanted it couldn't have been more explicit.

Danny looked down at his hand then up into his eyes. "You got something in mind?"

Rab shook his head. His mouth was watering indecently. He swallowed convulsively.

"Well then, how about taking your clothes off?"

To Rab, who had been thinking more in terms of a quick hand-job out the fly of his jeans, it acted like a douse of cold water. He withdrew his hand. "Are you nuts? Your mother's upstairs. Ian's..."

Danny interrupted with a smile. "Who cares? What's the worst that can happen? Anyway, she's on her way out."

As if on cue they heard the back door slam. Danny said, "See?"

Rab shook his head.

Danny smiled and slid a little closer. He lifted a hand and slid it round the back of Rab's neck, under his ponytail. "You're never chickenshit?" His voice was low and insidious.

"Ian..." Rab began.

Danny laughed. "Ian? The cat's a bigger threat."

Rab looked at him, frowning. Was he serious? But he seemed to be.

Danny's other hand was undoing his trouser button, pulling the zip down. "Come on, take your clothes off. I want to see you."

It acted like the mythic Magic Words. Danny wanted to see him. Oh, no problem then, Rab would simply have to oblige. And he did, scrambling out of his clothes with indecent haste until he stood before him naked, cock up like a peg.

Danny lay there, still sprawled, looking up at him. "All that platinum and tan." He looked up into his eyes. "Blonde all over, eh?" He smiled almost unpleasantly. Rab realised dimly somewhere inside that this surreptitious nasty streak in Danny was part of what excited him.

Danny stood up and walked round him like a buyer inspecting a carcass. He stopped behind him and said, "Kneel on the couch then."

Rab hesitated then got on the couch. Danny corrected him as he made to kneel sideways. "No, hands on the back. Look at the wall, back to me."

Rab did it, feeling a prickle of apprehension. The room was warm enough, but his skin was still covered in gooseflesh.

He jumped when Danny touched his thighs murmuring, "Spread them then." Rab did it, looking down at his own cock, the head a few inches away from the back of the sofa.

He grunted with surprise when something warm and soft tickled his anus. Warm, soft and wet. A tongue. Oh God, Danny was licking him out. He spread his legs wide, sticking his arse out, moaning softly. Danny pulled his buttocks apart with his hands, tongue pushing in deeper.

Rab grabbed his cock and began masturbating, squirming on the couch as Danny's tongue worked into his anus.

Abruptly it stopped. Rab hung there on the point of orgasm, quivering with closeness, part relieved because it had been too fast and part pissed off because he had been so close to the big one.

His head was resting on the back of the sofa. He lay there limply, heart pounding, and dimly heard Danny's zip then felt his legs against the backs of his knees. What was he doing?

It didn't take long to find out.

Rab felt the blunt unmistakable nudge of something at his anus, very hard and very insistent. Danny's knuckles dug into his balls while his other hand tugged at his right buttock as he tried to force it in.

Rab jerked his head up. "What are you doing?" He tried to see over his shoulder.

Danny pushed him down, none too gently. "Fucking you." It was flat, emphatic.

"What?"

Danny didn't answer.

"I don't want to..."

Danny cut him short. "Don't fuck me about. Where did you think this shit was leading if it wasn't leading here?"

Rab didn't answer.

"If you think I'm playing kids' wank games forever think again."

Rab tried to struggle round as it pushed painfully at his anus, nosing in. "No, wait, don't."

Then Danny did something odd, suddenly spreading his hands round Rab's chest and jolting him back. The head of his penis went in, lodged an inch inside Rab's sphincter, effectively impaling him. Rab swore.

"Good?" Danny whispered in his ear. He lay down over his back, but there was nothing slack or relaxed about it, rather the opposite, as if he was poised for resistance, anticipating it.

"No, don't."

But Danny jolted in again. He followed it immediately with another, and Rab realised he must already have about half his length up there, although it felt like more. The little bastard was raping him.

Danny began to fuck him, a steady rhythm, cock sinking in deeper with every thrust. It was deep, intrusive agony. Rab's erection had long since disappeared.

"Now we'll see..." Danny grunted, "what all the fucking magic is about."

Rab dropped his forehead against the sofa, clutching the back of it. Danny was slamming uncomfortably into his body. Rab could hear his thighs slapping against the back of his legs. Every jolt pushed him further upright, closer to the back of the settee.

Danny was in deep now, hardly withdrawing, just making small jerking movements, getting more and more rapid. Rab could feel him close in on his own orgasm. He felt an abrupt excitement at the idea of Danny coming inside him. That, combined with the fact that his movements were now less aggressive, brought his erection back with a bang. He looked down at it then realised suddenly that Danny was pacing himself, as if he knew.

Rab began to masturbate himself furiously. He was there, out of nowhere, and he'd never felt anything so intense. He tried to spread his legs, urging Danny to push up harder. "God..." he cried out. "*God.*" And he pulled his foreskin back tight and rammed his engorged glans against the stiff velvet of the sofa, smearing his come over the fabric as Danny helped jolt him into it, forking his body up into his.

And saying nothing at all.

## THIRTEEN

"Hello, Rab."

Rab's head shot up, banging himself on the engine hood. "What the...?"

Ian smiled at him, unobtrusively, like a good librarian. Rab rubbed the top of his head with his arm. "Fucking creeping about..." His eyes took in the dry clothes. It was pouring outside. "Where the hell have you come from?"

"In here."

Rab looked at him. "Since when?"

But Ian only smiled, offered no information.

Rab picked up a rag and wiped his hands. He shoved the rag in his pocket saying, "You know, I've never told you this before, Ian, but I'll let you into a secret. You fucking bug me." Ian smiled some more and pushed his hands into his pockets. "And for the last two weeks you've really been fucking bugging me. What gives?"

Ian looked out into the yard. The rain was growing faint, drizzling. Soon it would be over. The light shone on everything with a sharpening glare. He answered without looking at him. "And I thought we were allies too."

"Did you now?" Rab's voice was sarcastic. He pulled a dog-end of cigarette out his pocket and began patting for matches. "Allies in what precisely?"

"The war against Danny." Ian looked at him steadily.

Rab managed to tear his eyes away, aware that his colour was betrayingly high. He struck a match and lit his cigarette, taking a deep drag and letting it out slowly down his nose.

Ian continued to look at him steadily, then he moved a little closer and said in a low voice, like one imparting a birthday secret, "I know about you and Danny."

Rab stared at him, waiting for what came next, because there *was* a next. It was written all over his face in capital letters.

But Ian said nothing, simply smiled that irritating little smile of his. What a grudging little spastic he was. That suety little face, like John without the strength or beauty.

"Well, Ian, what's next? Am I supposed to give you a badge of merit or something?"

Ian laughed. "What a comedian."

Rab grew impatient. "You've waited a long time for this. You should get a badge for perseverance at any rate." He took another drag on his cigarette then looked out at the rain. This was beginning to bore him. Let the little git spit it out. "What do you want?"

Ian looked at him. He was still smiling. That is, an eighth of an inch of his teeth showed in a thin yellow line. It was the most of his smile the stifling little creep ever spared anyone. Rab saw it and thought, I've never realised before just how much this little bastard hates me.

"You."

Rab's surprise came out of him in a sort of soft grunt, then he laughed. "What exactly? My head on a platter?"

Ian was still smiling, as if the damn thing was painted on. "What the hell would I want with your head?"

He paused just long enough for the insult to sink in. "What I want out of you won't even fill a teaspoon." And Rab saw his eyes move over his face hungrily.

"Mealy-mouthed to the last. Why don't you just say it? You want to suck my dick."

"No, you're going to suck mine."

Rab turned his face away from him, pinching out his cigarette and tossing it out into the dying rain. "You stupid little prick." He turned back to him. "I wouldn't look at you if I had been blind for half a century. You seriously think I'd give you anything, you grudging little fart?" He suddenly pushed Ian's shoulder, making his smile falter for the first time. A dull, angry colour crept into his face.

"My mother isn't going to like finding some queer mauling her favourite son, especially when, after all this time, it turns out to be you."

"Some queer? She doesn't have to look far for queers in this family. Besides, she wouldn't listen to you if you told her the barn was on fire. As far as she's concerned you're somewhere below the fucking dog. But don't let me stop you. You go tell her. I don't get many laughs around here." He turned away from him again. "Now fuck off, your face gives me a headache."

Ian smiled again, suddenly, like a peach bursting under the sun. The ugly, nail-paring little grin split his pasty face in half. He reached up his hand and brushed his thumb over Rab's cheekbone. Rab flinched away angrily, grabbing his hand and throwing it away from him. "Keep your fucking hands off me."

Ian shook his head. "No. I've paid years of lip service for this and now it's reward-time. You see, I know a little something else about you, and it's wicked not to share."

Rab's face stilled, his last fleeting expression held there like a snapshot. Ian played his trump card. "I know all about the *girls*." He watched the tan pale, become yellowish. "I know exactly where you went and what you did..."

Rab moved his head robotically. He looked out the door without seeing. Ian could see his mind racing. *Think you've got life stitched up Rab? Well, just you watch it come undone.*

Rab lit a cigarette. He put it in his mouth, going straight to his matches without preamble. It was curious to see how like John he looked when he did it. He spoke to Ian without looking at him. "You're full of little surprises, aren't you?"

Ian simply smiled.

Rab played his own trump card, knowing it was expected of him, knowing it was a losing card anyway, doomed to failure. It pleased Ian to see it there, held out to him. "Why should she care? It's nothing to do with her."

"Who says I'm taking it to her?"

Rab turned and looked at him slowly, his eyes black, his mouth white. "Is that meant to scare me?"

Ian smiled, and for the very first time it looked genuine, as if there was a tiny hint of pity there. "You tell me."

Rab turned away. Ian watched him take another cigarette out then throw it away unsmoked. He watched him rub his palms on his shirt, hugging his body as if he was suddenly cold. He waited, everything on one throw of the dice. Rab was skewered between his needs and his wants. On the one hand Danny, on the other John. But John was old news, Danny was here and now. Still, he was quite capable of throwing everything away on some desperate and pointless act of vanity.

Ian gave one final jerk on the wire. "Of course," he added, "I haven't told him yet about what I heard in the living-room last night."

Rab's body went limp. He said wearily, "What do you want?"

Very slowly, and with infinite care, Ian said, "Just what the rest get."

Rab looked at him.

Ian smiled his sickly smile. "And now seems as good a time as any." And he reached up again to stroke the contour of Rab's cheek.

## FOURTEEN

It was going to be a solid gunmetal day, grey and heavy. Danny lay on his bed wide-awake. Ten minutes more and he would have to climb out into the cold.

His alarm went off unexpectedly, causing a reaction in him not unlike a bomb going off. He beat the clock senseless, then lay there for a second or two, trying to regain his composure. He took a deep steadying breath, then climbed out of bed and into his work clothes.

In the hall he bumped into John coming out of his room. Danny nodded curtly, but John only looked him up and down and did not reply. Fuck you, Danny thought.

Downstairs, the others ate their breakfasts in sullen silence. Only Rab, his hair a bright white under the fluorescent light, surprised him by winking at him over his spoon. Danny was equally surprised to find himself smiling back. Outside the rain began to fall in heavy, greasy drops.

"Well, that settles that," his father said, staring out the window in irritable resignation. "John, Ian, you come with me." He turned to Rab. "You take him and finish that whitewashing. Christ knows, it isn't fit for anything else today."

Rab smiled slowly at Danny. Danny felt his own smile answer back. John looked at them with something indecipherable in his expression. Only Ian's gaze was easy to read. Unfortunately no-one was looking.


The tool shed was the original stone barn attached to the house, laughably small now. Every couple of years they whitewashed the interior. They tended to do the job piecemeal between other jobs so, since May, it had been sitting half-painted, the tools piled on the floor, aggravating anyone who attempted to find anything in the shambles.

They went in, leaving the door open for light; there was no electricity in here.

"Now or later?" Rab asked, beyond being able to pretend.

"Have they gone?" Danny asked, already tugging his shirt out.

Rab managed to nod.

"Then now," Danny said, pulling his shirt over his head.

Rab looked at him, standing there half-naked. Where had Danny the boy gone, the one he'd fought a cold war with for years? He felt abruptly afraid. It was too much too soon. He wanted to ask him, Why are you doing this? As if that made any difference. As if Danny would tell him the truth. As if he really wanted to know. He didn't. He wanted this too much to risk anything that might stop it.

He felt Danny's hard chest move up against his, the feel of his mouth, surprisingly cool and aggressive, pressed to his throat. How had he come to be in this situation? To find this so heady? So intoxicating? How long had it been? Two weeks, three? When had he stepped over the line from expediency into want and then into need? He'd let him rape him for Christ's sake. Not even a murmur. How could it have happened so quickly?

Danny slid his hand down the front of Rab's jeans. He was quiet and determined, but his breathing was ragged and shallow. He was pushing against him, silently asking for relief. But Rab did not touch him, too taken with the sensation of Danny's hand groping inside his pants.

Danny pushed again, insistently. He kissed Rab's mouth, obviously trying to incite him. Let him wait, Rab thought. He wanted to savour this. He never knew when he would have him next. Even if there would be a next.

"*Rab.*" Danny's voice was irritable, demanding.

Rab opened his eyes, watching Danny's deep russet hair as he bent his head to his chest. Danny took a nipple between his teeth, hand gripping Rab's penis fiercely. Everything he did was charged with that same threat.

Rab groaned, dropping his head back against the wall, letting his eyes roll open blankly, seeing nothing, and there was John, standing in the doorway, watching them.

He clutched Danny's head to his chest with a jerk of fright, some dimly understood need to hide him.

"Rab," Danny demanded, breaking free and squashing Rab's thigh between his legs to grind against it. "Will you fucking *do* me?"

Rab stared at John, standing there stock still, utterly unmoving, and suddenly knew he wasn't going to do anything. He was just going to stand there and let it happen.

He wanted to scream at him, Making you stiff, you pervert? Turning you on, you fucking freak? But instead he grabbed Danny's head and kissed him deeply, sliding his hand down inside his trousers.

Danny broke free, like a child held against his will, and demanded, "Are we having sex or what?" And he undid his own jeans, yanking them down, shoving Rab's hand on his penis. "Now *do* it."

He felt Danny's hand pull on him fiercely, urging him to get on with it. He saw John still standing there, immobilized, like a great stupid animal. He wanted to yank Danny round and masturbate him in front of him, let him see his precious baby brother's prick jerking and twitching like a marionette. But he held him tight, crushing him against him, letting his eyes do the talking, making John feel it.

"I love you," he said, eyes holding John's. And out of nowhere he came, while John just stood there and watched.


John was waiting for him in his room after dinner that evening. Danny didn't even close the door. "Forget it John – out."

"I just want to talk. Can't a man even talk to his own brother?"

Danny looked at him, surprised at his quiet, level tone. Even the sarcasm hardly passed muster. But John was against the window, hiding his face, so how could you be sure what you were really seeing, or hearing? He closed the door sighing, "Okay, so talk."

"Let's go out for a drive."

"Are you nuts? It's pissing down. Besides, it's past half ten and I'm shagged. Anything you've got to say, say it now or get out."

John turned his head to the window, showing a different profile against the dark streaming glass. "Come on, Danny, a favour. When do I ever ask you for a favour?"

"You're *asking*?" Danny didn't even bother to keep the incredulity out his voice. "I'm asking."

"Oh wow." Danny looked at him a moment longer. John turned to face him fully as if to show he had nothing to hide. Danny said impulsively, "Okay. Why the hell not?"

They went downstairs, Danny leading, John following, always in shadow, like something elusive. They stole out of the back door like thieves and took the pickup.

John pulled out into the road and drove in silence. The windscreen wipers snicked to and fro. Only the lights from the dashboard showed.

Danny looked at his profile staring straight ahead. There was something odd about his face. He looked... he groped for the word ...feverish, that was it, like he was coming down with flu or something.

"Where are we going?" he asked, taking a packet of cigarettes from the glove compartment.

"You'll see." John clicked the indicators on and the pick-up swung right across the oncoming traffic and onto a dirt track.

Danny had been watching John, not where they were going. He peered out the window now, cupping his hands to see better, but the rain was torrential and he could make nothing out.

They swung onto gravel, obviously some kind of a yard. It looked momentarily familiar, but John cut the lights before he could make out where he was. Danny rolled down the window as John cut the engine. He could hear nothing but the rain singing. Suddenly he recognised something about the squat building up ahead. He rolled up the window. He looked calmer than he felt. "Why have you brought me here?"

"Something I want to show you." And now Danny realised there was something odd about his voice too.

"Forget it. I've seen it already, remember? What is this? Some kind of pilgrimage to cure my sickness? Bring me to the scene of the crime, show me how I'm going to end up if I don't mend my ways? Well maybe you've got a hold of the wrong person, John. Maybe you should take yourself for a walk round the grounds. I'm going home."

Danny made a move for the door handle, but John stopped him. "When was the last time I touched you?"

Danny turned to look at him. "What?"

"I said, when was the last time I touched you?"

Danny looked at him blankly, hand sliding off the handle.

"More than a month ago, Danny. I can tell you the exact date. Now can we go into the house and talk?"

Danny gave him a look, irritation, confusion, then said, "Oh for Christ's sake..." and slammed out the door. He darted across the yard to shelter under the stupid little corrugated plastic porch. He pressed back against the door – a futile move in this rain – and watched John locking up the van and crossing towards him. He turned to face the door as John drew close.

John took a key out his pocket and unlocked the door then pushed it open. Danny did not move. He was still thinking about John bothering to lock the van.

"Get in then," John said, nodding his head at the open doorway.

Danny hesitated, searching his face for a moment, then stepped over the threshold.

It felt as if he was instantly plunged into subterranean darkness. The door slammed to and the black became impenetrable. "John?" he said uncertainly. The silence was absolute.

"Right here." His voice was very soft behind him. "Upstairs."

Danny immediately balked. "No."

"Danny..." John began.

"I am not going upstairs."

"And why not? Believe me, Danny, the only thing you have to fear up there is your own black soul. Now get upstairs."

Danny let out a sigh of irritation then stepped through the stair doorway. A faint light showed through it. The stairs themselves proved to be horrifically narrow, boxed in on both sides with wood panelling. They creaked badly.

There was a window on the tiny landing, which at least let in enough light to see by. Danny's heart was pounding uncomfortably. He felt claustrophobic and anxious in a way he could hardly identify.

When they turned off the landing Danny stopped dead, something huge paralysing his legs. John said softly behind him, "Don't worry, it's locked," and gave him a gentle push down the hallway and into the first door.

Danny went in thinking, *What's* locked? He was aware that he could hear his own breathing. He looked round the room nervously.

When the door slammed he jumped, swinging round in time to see John latch it then lean against it. The moon came out abruptly and John's face became almost daylight clear after the intense darkness.

Danny backed away to the double bed that stood under the dormer window and sat down.

John said, "Good." Which could have meant anything, but seemed only to indicate he was satisfied with the arrangements thus far. He settled himself more comfortably against the door before saying, "I saw you in the tool shed this morning. Quite a performance."

Danny looked up at him belligerently. No surprise, no confusion. "So that's why I'm here. So you can beat fuck out me without anyone interfering."

"Quite possibly." It was completely flat, unemotional, and somehow much more worrying because of that.

"What I do is my business," Danny asserted angrily.

"I don't think so."

Danny jumped to his feet. "Look, John, don't bother threatening me again, I don't give a fuck any more."

"Sit down." It was perfectly level.

"Fuck you," Danny said sharply.

John was across the room and had shoved him flat on the bed before Danny could even move. He stood above him, waiting for Danny to struggle upright before he said, "You sit when you're told to sit."

Danny said nothing, just stared up at him, panting with fright. Suddenly he realised what it was he'd been seeing in him all evening and had not been able to identify. Rage. A huge icy rage that had all but eaten him up. John's superficial calm was a tiny tinfoil lid on a huge furnace of rage.

And John proved it. He moved away from him and went to stand back against the door again, as if he did not want to be within striking distance. It was such an uncharacteristic move Danny sat there utterly intimidated by it, waiting for whatever it was he had to say.

"I've been waiting for this a long time." John looked at him. "No surprise? Not even a 'What the fuck are you talking about, John?'" He smiled. "Well, that doesn't surprise me. Nothing about you surprises me. Do you remember the day we went swimming?"

Danny took a while to shake his head.

"Well, I take it all back, now you do surprise me. Let me refresh your memory. We went swimming. I've been thinking about this, it has to have been a Saturday. And let's be more accurate while we're about it, me and Rab decided to go swimming, you invited yourself along. Then, for a reason that could only be apparent to your oversexed little brain, you decided to skinny-dip. Ring any bells?"

This time Danny nodded.

John smiled again, just barely. "And you remember what happened?"

"You got in a fight."

John lifted a brow. "And?"

"You thrashed the living daylights out of me."

There was another pause and then he said, "That's odd. You know, I don't remember that."

Danny pressed his palms to his cheeks.

John folded his arms and said, "It's a funny thing how memory cheats you. I can remember things about you and me that would probably surprise you. At least surprise you."

Danny said nothing, although John paused to let him.

John went on, "I even have a distant memory that we were friends once."

Danny laughed sourly. "Oh *yeah*."

John let his arms drop. They hung loosely against the door. "Maybe you're right. Maybe friend's not the right word."

Danny said nothing.

John sighed then said, "It seems pointless to warn you off again, you haven't listened so far. What if I make a deal with you instead?"

Danny frowned angrily. "You're forgetting something, John. I don't have to do what you say any more. I'm no longer your little brother."

John threw his head back. A soft dry laugh escaped his mouth. "Wrong, Danny. You are very much my little brother and ne'er the twain shall part. Didn't your near death experience teach you anything?" His voice, soft as it was, still managed to drop further when he said, "Believe me, if you don't leave him alone, next time it *will* be death."

Danny sat there breathing through his mouth, aware of all the hairs standing up on his arms at the sure, cold conviction in his voice. "I'm not scared of you," he managed and was surprised at how well it came out.

John laughed, a little soft thing. "Oh we know that, we've seen that. Trouble is, I'm not trying to scare you. You're not fucking Rab and that's that."

"Oh *right*," Danny said furiously. "Nobody fucks Saint Rab but you. That's what's wrong, isn't it? You're just aching to get it up him yourself."

John laughed again, more genuinely this time. "I fucked Rab senseless for six years. Been there, done that, I think."

Danny stared at him.

"Come on, Danny, I don't believe Ian would have let that one slip by."

"Six *years...*?"

"You heard me."

"You shit."

John laughed again. "Ian would be proud of you."

"You dirty shit."

"I think maybe he's the dirty shit. He started it."

"I don't believe that."

"Why? Because your big brother told you different? Well, let me disinform you. I was fifteen, he was twelve. He came into the toilet one day while I was in the bath and we were fixed for mutual masturbation for life. Only it didn't last that long, although it did get more inventive."

"I don't believe you."

"You don't want to believe me."

"You dirty bastard."

"Consider this good advice. Leave him alone."

"I'll do what I damn well like."

"Fine, but just bear this in mind – I can do the same."

"Meaning what?"

"Use your imagination."

Danny looked at him just long enough then shook his head, shook it again more violently, getting to his feet and crossing the room away from him. This time John did not stop him. Danny stood with his back to him, facing the far wall, arms braced against it, palms flat, head down. John crossed silently to stand behind him and whispered in his ear, "You can stop it any time."

Danny swung round to face him, dropping back against the wall as if he was exhausted. "What am I, John, some kind of toy you don't really want but can't stand to share?"

John looked at him for a long moment, his face subtly changing. He moved closer, putting a palm on the wall at either side of Danny's head, fencing him in. He said softly, "What d'you want to hear? That you're important to me?"

Danny flushed bright red and turned his face away, but John brought him back round, forcing him to look at him again. "The big admission, is that what you're waiting for?"

Danny said nothing, closed his eyes against the expression in his gaze, closed his ears to that tenderness in his voice – oh so convincing.

John suddenly moved close, his body lightly touching his, his cheek barely skin to skin with his, and whispered, "What if it was true? Have you looked at yourself recently? You're barely human. There isn't a man, woman or child in the district who wouldn't do it with you if you asked. You're a god in human form. What else could possibly have lured Rab off the straight and narrow? What more reason could I need?"

Danny shook his head.

"Is that a refusal, disagreement, what?"

"I don't believe this, I just don't."

"Why not?"

Danny pushed him off, warnings forgotten. "Because I'm your fucking brother, John, remember that?"

"And he's your ruddy cousin. You've got a fucking weird set of distinctions."

"All my life you've drummed into me..."

"That it's not right. Yeah, and all my life I've worked on this lousy farm, but that doesn't mean they weren't both mistakes. I love you, Danny."

He said it so easily, so casually, just tacked on the end like he hadn't said anything at all. Danny simply slid down the wall and sat down.

John hesitated a moment then carefully hunkered down beside him as if he was afraid of startling him. He reached out a hand and gently lifted Danny's face, cupping his chin in his palm. "You don't believe me, do you?"

"Don't *believe* you?" Danny could hardly get the words out. He slapped his hand away. "You want some kind of exclusive rights to... to..." he racked his brain for a way of saying it and only came up with, "to use me any time you're drunk enough, to shove me in between one cunt and the next, like some kind of light relief, and for that I'm supposed to be grateful or something, supposed to cut out what little life or free will I have left and hand it over to you, and all you can think about is whether I believe some crap you dredge up about loving me."

"It's not crap," John said flatly. "But even if it was it wouldn't matter. And don't harbour any notions of your free will either. You haven't got any free will. You haven't had any free will since you were six years old. You gave it away and you don't get it back, not from me. I don't care about what you think, or feel, or want. I don't care about anything except keeping your dick in your pants. It's not public property, and that includes Rab. He isn't even properly related."

"Jesus *Christ*, and that makes it *better*? Suddenly you being my brother makes it *better*?"

"Me being your brother makes it the only thing there is. Me being your brother makes it blood, not just something you lift and leave. A brother is for life, not just for Christmas. Me being your brother is all there is."

Danny struggled up onto his feet. "Cut it short, John. What does all this mean?"

"It means I want you to leave him alone, and that my reasons are none of your business. You feel free to believe what you like, but believe this, if you're going to be sucking anyone's dick it isn't going to be his."

"It'll be yours?"

"I can oblige, baby."

"What? Sober?"

John slapped him. It made a huge crack in the room. It hurt like hell. John shoved his body up against his. "Sober, drunk, any way I like. You're so fucking keen to get down on your knees then fine, but you can fucking forget him."

"And the deal?"

"We just made it. Weren't you listening?"

Danny said, "Right, sure. Till the next time you're drunk enough then." And he pushed past him and went out the room.


When they came into the kitchen Rab was waiting for them, sitting in the dark, only the tip of his cigarette glowing.

John closed the door silently, trying to keep it quiet. Danny stood like an animal waiting to be moved. He was numb with emotional exhaustion.

"The wanderers return."

"*Shit.*" John dropped the key, slamming the door on reflex.

"Rab," Danny said dully, without inflection.

"The very same." An empty bottle sat on the table in front of him. It looked like there were things Rab needed to get drunk to do too.

"What are you doing here?" John demanded. "Why aren't you in bed?" His voice was sharply aggressive, the same old John of old.

"I might ask you the same question, more even, like where the fuck have you been?"

John looked at him sharply. "None of your fucking business."

"Oh but it is, John-boy," Danny saw him push back his chair, saw the difficulty he had getting to his feet, "because that's my property you've got there and I don't recall giving you permission to take it anywhere."

"*Your* property?" The words came out as if something had choked all the power out of them. "Let's hope you're drunk, Rab. Let's hope you're really, really drunk."

"Not drunk enough."

"I don't know. Right now it's saving your neck."

"Bet it didn't save his arsehole..."

Danny heard the impact, Rab grunting like a poleaxed animal. There was a rumbling crash as the heavy kitchen table was knocked back under their combined weight.

He walked to the kitchen door and left the room.

## FIFTEEN

Ian stood in the dark again, like Ian had so many times before. Ian had learned to be neither seen nor heard and it had given him just rewards.

They had been fighting over Danny again last night. He had not been able to catch much of it, but it had definitely been about Danny. When was it not?

The door slammed suddenly. Ian straightened up.

The front light flickered on, then the wall heater. He peered round from behind the trailer. Rab was struggling into a blue boiler suit, a cigarette hanging out the corner of his mouth. He didn't fasten it. Once, in the height of summer, he'd worn it with only his underpants underneath. He'd fastened it then, to just below his navel, decent and no more.

Ian closed his eyes, seeing the image again. The thick pale hair coming up his hard flat belly, the golden skin strongly reminiscent of John's.

He squeezed himself briefly through the lining of his pocket then opened his eyes again. Rab had rolled himself under the jacked-up car.

He walked over noiselessly. "Hello."

Rab's hand slipped, skinning his knuckles. He cursed and turned to see Ian's unmistakable boots, oddly laced, tight as corsets. He pushed himself back out. Ian leaned against the side of the car, looking down at him.

Rab got up to his feet slowly. "Well, if it isn't Mickey fucking Mouse. This is a surprise."

Ian flushed. "I'm getting tired of the way you talk to me."

"Like I'm getting tired of your face."

"I've come for what you owe me."

"You think I'm paying you anything for that fiasco last night?"

Ian stared at him for a long moment. "Well, I suppose even Danny can stand a few more truths before disillusionment sets in."

"What's that supposed to mean?"

"He was out with John last night. I doubt if they were discussing farming."

Rab grabbed the front of his jacket. "You don't know anything, you stirring little bastard."

"No? It was enough for you to start a fight with him last night."

Rab glared at him then pushed him away.

Ian went on, voice soft, curiously placating, "Come on. You think Danny likes to hear himself discussed as property, even if he knows damn well he is? Then there's all that unfaithfulness," he clucked, "and with John."

"That was long before he was around."

"Of course, and I'm sure he'll forgive you in the fullness of time, but he still has illusions about you. It would be a shame to shatter them now."

"Christ, I ought to wring your scrawny little neck."

Ian laughed. "You know you should really drop the macho shit. Living with John doesn't make you him. If it did you wouldn't be having any problems with

Danny, believe me."

He stood watching Rab fume silently under the insult then said, "I think maybe you should start to think in terms of long term pleasure. After all, you never know what I might be able to push your way – when John's not looking." He smiled at him, just enough promise, just enough threat, so that Rab could not be sure which was uppermost, then slid his hand inside Rab's shirt.

Ian could feel the instant flush of revulsion goosepimpling his skin, but he bore his touching stoically, his head averted.

"Now, if you were to take off all your clothes and put the boiler suit back on I think I could have a very nice time, considering."

Rab spat out his cigarette and stood on it. After a moment he began to unfasten his shirt.


Danny was afraid.

He sat up, his heart hammering, and listened. There it was again. That same low insistent sound. Someone knocking at his door. He climbed up onto his knees and looked at it. The handle turned slowly. First one way, then the other.

Silence.

He looked at the clock. 3:36 am. Somehow that made the fright worse.

The knock sounded again, a little louder, then a whisper, as if whoever it was had their mouth pressed to the crack of the door. "Danny..."

Danny got up, wetting his lips nervously. He stood against the door frame and whispered back, "Who is it?"

"Rab."

Rab? What the hell did he want? A hundred things went through Danny's head as he reached down and unlocked the door. "Hold on."

He opened it a fraction. Rab pushed in and rolled him back against the wall, slapping a hand over his mouth as if he expected him to scream. The door was closed and locked all in seconds.

Danny smelt him before he actually realised. He knew that smell better than his own.

It was John's eyes that met his own over his hand, John's bulk that leant against him. "I'm going to take my hand away. No screaming hysterics, okay?"

Danny managed a tiny nod. John took his hand away.

"What the hell do you want?" Danny demanded immediately.

John jerked him up against him and kissed him hard on the mouth, pushing his tongue in deep. Danny struggled violently, but only succeeded in freeing his mouth. John's grip was iron-fast on his upper arms.

"What can you taste?" John was whispering against his mouth as if he intended to kiss him again.

"What?"

"I said, what can you taste? Want me to do it again?"

Danny pulled his head back sharply. "What d'you mean, what can I taste? Have you gone nuts?"

John yanked him forwards and kissed him again, harder this time, hurting his mouth. Danny didn't break away this time, John let him go. He stood there breathless, disorientated, blinking stupidly. John still gripped his arms. It felt as if he was being held by a machine.

"Well? What do I taste of? How drunk am I?"

Danny looked into his eyes. It was a slow thing, a dawning understanding. John tasted of a hundred half-smoked cigarettes, nothing more. He heard himself whisper, "You're not."

"That's right, I'm not."

Danny swallowed, wet his lips, and said in a low voice that sounded very young, "What do you want, John?"

"You."

There was a long silence then John said, "I'm admitting it, alright? I want sex with you. Here, right now, stone cold sober. Is that good enough? Do I finally earn you?"

Danny shook his head gently. It wasn't meant to be gentle, it just came out that way because he was stupid with broken sleep, pure incomprehension.

John said, "What?" as if he couldn't believe what he was seeing, and that made everything clear.

"I said no, John, because there's just one little snag – I don't want to have sex with you."

It was John's turn to shake his head. "I don't believe you."

"Too bad."

John shook him violently. "I don't believe you, you little shit."

Danny looked at him levelly. He felt completely calm. More than calm; he felt dead. "It's true."

"What is this, some pathetic punishment because I took without asking? Because I wouldn't let you indulge your adolescent itch with Rab? Christ, I'm giving you what you want. I'm sick of hiding it. I'll deal with it. You've got my word."

Danny laughed. He heard himself with a kind of wonder. "What a spoilt, conceited bastard you are. How could I ever have imagined I felt anything for you, even as a stupid little kid?"

John stared at him then said in a voice so low it sounded barely there, "And you don't now? Think you don't need me any more?" John pulled him to him again, that same remorseless grip on his upper arms. "Kiss me. Let's see you keep the self-delusion going."

Danny shook his head.

John barked a small laugh. "What's wrong, think you can't get through it?" He suddenly let go his arms. "Look, I'm not even holding you. You kiss me, Danny, and let me hear that you never loved me, that you don't love me still. You can't do it. You know you can't." John shoved his face in his. "You can't fucking do it because you're a pathetic little faggot that can't resist a bit of rough, not even your own fucking brother."

Danny slapped him as hard and viciously as he could. John grabbed him and kissed him savagely, pushing him back against the wall.

They broke apart again. John seized his head in both hands as if he intended to kiss him again. Suddenly he kneed him hard in the groin.

Danny went down with a grunt, and was slammed back against the wall. John immediately dropped forward at the knees, pinning him there by the shoulders. He jerked Danny's head back by the hair and hooked his fingers into his open mouth, pulling it wide, his free hand scrabbling at his zip. He tugged his penis out into his hand and shoved it into his stretched mouth like someone cramming forcemeat into a body cavity, all the time hissing, "…Kiss this, baby. See what this does for you. Give me the best blow job of my life. Do it like only a little brother can. Take me right back there. Cry, plead, make it real. Suck the life right out of me. That's what you want, isn't it? What you've always wanted? You *loved* it. You loved every crumb I ever… oh God, shit, *fuck*… you *love* me."

And John came.

## SIXTEEN

Danny packed his bag with one eye on the clock. It was 5:35. He had barely half an hour left. At the outside. He closed his bedroom door quietly and went down the stairs. He lifted his jacket from the hall and shrugged into it. The leather felt cold and clammy to the touch. In the kitchen he lifted his mother's bills money from the dresser drawer and her agency money from behind the clock. The dog whuffed at him softly. He shushed it, bending down to stroke its head. It lay down again, its tail thumping gently in the dark.

Danny lifted his bag from the floor and crossed to the door, unlatching it quietly. He took the Fiat's keys from their hook and slid out, letting the latch fall to gently behind him.

There was no moon, but the sky was beginning to lighten in a false dawn. That meant it was going to be a nice day.

He crossed the yard and went into the tractor shed. His money was stashed under the seat of his tractor. An adolescent leftover. His 'getaway fund' he'd always called it. His security blanket in case he ever got too bored. He laughed mirthlessly, his breath puffing out before him. *Bored.*

He swung up onto the tractor and opened the door. The corpse was sitting bolt upright in the seat, staring at him. "Hello, Danny."

Danny all but fell back out, only managing to pull himself upright by hanging onto the door.

"Going somewhere?"

Danny climbed back down unsteadily, feeling his knees buckle slightly as he reached the ground.

"Gave John a good time tonight. You should've known better than to open the door." Ian climbed down from the tractor, forcing Danny back a step.

Danny stared at him. "You heard," he said stupidly.

"I was listening."

I was listening, Danny thought, like it was entertainment. He pushed him. "Get out of my way."

He clambered into the tractor and jacked up the seat. He ferreted around inside. His heart dropped. Where was it?

"It's not there." Ian's voice came out of the dark, lazily full of Ian's inimitable brand of self-certainty.

Danny jumped down and grabbed him. "What have you done with it?"

"How beautiful you are when you're angry."

Danny hit him with both hands. A push that was intended to floor him. A spontaneous outburst of frustrated rage. Instead Ian flew back across the short space and folded up against the side of the other tractor. The blow knocked the wind from him, badly jarring his back. It was not something he had accounted for.

Danny pulled him up, sending pain jolting through him. "Where is it?" He shook him in desperation, aware of time sliding through his hands.

Ian hissed through his teeth, feeling icy-sharp jabs shoot out from his spine into his ribs, "Where you can't get at it."

Danny grabbed his hair with both hands, shaking his head like you might a dog by its ears. "I'll fucking kill you, Ian, where is it?"

"In John's room." Even breathless as he was, a deaf man could have heard the gloat in his voice.

Danny repeated it stupidly. "In John's room?"

Ian said nothing. He could save his breath. He didn't need to verify it. Danny didn't even have the strength to accuse him of lying. He knew it was the truth. After all, where else would Ian pick to put it? It was the safest bank in the world against Danny.

He made his decision. He had no time. Screw it. He had enough money. He turned and moved quickly through the shed. Ian's shout cut through the air. "Where are you going?"

Danny ignored him. He opened the door and passed out. He crossed the yard quickly and opened the car. The door caught as he pulled it shut behind him; Ian was hanging onto it.

"Fuck off," Danny snarled at him, pulling the door to.

Ian tugged it back and pushed himself between it and the car. "You can't leave." His face was almost afraid now. This wasn't in the script.

"Just watch me."

"I'll tell him you took the car."

"I doubt if you'll need to."

"She'll send the police after you."

Danny laughed. "I said, fuck off, Ian." And he kicked out at him with both feet. But Ian threw himself on top of him, knocking him back, half onto the passenger seat. They lay trapped by their own weight under the steering wheel. Danny squirmed underneath him, filled with sudden anxiety. He could see the time blinking on the dashboard, ticking away. "Get off, you stupid bastard."

He tried to get leverage with his feet and found they didn't reach the ground. Nor could he raise his legs sufficiently to get them into the car. Ian's body was like a log across them.

Then he felt Ian's hands pawing at his chest. Perhaps it was something about their snuffling movements, or the sound of his breathing, but he felt a sudden claustrophobic revulsion. He doubled his efforts, grasped Ian's hands and held them off. They squirmed in his hands like oiled snakes, sweaty and elusive. He pulled free and began pawing again. His head was buried in Danny's chest, but he was slowly inching himself up Danny's body. His head moved up onto Danny's neck. Danny felt his mouth clamp onto his skin.

He jerked away, pulling at Ian's hair. He felt as if he was caught in some outrageous nightmare. He almost laughed.

Ian said nothing. He pulled frantically to get back. Danny could feel the insistent rubbing against his hip. He could smell the feverish sweat come off him in waves. Ian had succeeded in worming a hand inside Danny's shirt. His silence was dreadful, intense. There was no passion in him. He was like a dog over-excited by the scent of a bitch in heat. He panted in Danny's ear, his breath hoarse and raw. Danny felt his stomach heave.

Suddenly there was a shout across the yard, feet running, and then Ian was being dragged off. There was a noise that could have been a slap.

Danny lay there a moment then levered himself up onto his elbows.

"Get back into the house." His mother's voice was angry, but Danny could hear no shock in it. He could see her dressing gown, pale in the feeble light.

He sensed Ian's reluctance, but it was impossible to see his face from down here. They were just two headless bodies. He struggled up. His mother's face appeared in the doorway. Her eyes ran over his face, searching. He heard the kitchen door slam shut.

"You were taking my car," she said. It wasn't a question.

Danny nodded, letting his eyes slide away from hers. But she didn't ask him why. She didn't ask him anything. She turned away for a moment, then back, as if she had made a decision. She reached across him and picked up his bag, throwing it in the back, then she looked him in the eye. "Give me the money."

Danny reached into his pocket and reluctantly returned it to her.

"Stay here. I'll be ten minutes, no longer. Promise me you'll wait here."

Promise? What the hell did he have to lose now? "I'll wait," he said.

She turned and went back across the yard and into the house.


Danny timed her. She was back in exactly eight minutes. She was dressed and carrying her shoulder bag.

She climbed into the passenger seat and handed Danny the ignition key. "You drive."

She turned in her seat and put her bag in the back next to his.

Danny hadn't even noticed that she had taken the key, to make sure he wouldn't go anyway.

He turned on the ignition and pulled down into the access road. It was exactly 5:58. There was no traffic. He didn't have to wait long for his mother to speak.

"This is about John, isn't it?"

Danny slowed the car, aware of the way his foot had pressed down on the accelerator, but he didn't have time to frame a reply before she said, "If you expect me to help I expect some answers."

He said tightly, "It's about getting out of here. Period."

"And away from John."

Danny turned to her. "Listen, I was leaving. No clear ideas, no burning ambitions, just getting out – before you and Ian decided to rewrite the script, that is. And I don't expect your help. I don't expect anything from you. This was your idea."

"You were stealing my money."

"He stole mine."

"Is that why you were fighting?"

"I was fighting, he was doing something quite different."

She chose not to hear that. "How much was it?"

He shrugged. "Four hundred pounds maybe."

She clucked at the sum then said, "And what's he done with it?"

"Who knows?"

"Didn't you ask him?"

"Of course I bloody asked him, this is Ian."

His mother looked away abruptly. "Slow down, we're turning next right."

Danny slowed, frowning at the road ahead. "Jerrett's?"

"That's right."

Danny braked to a standstill. "No way."

"And why not?"

"I'm not going to Jerrett's."

"Then where are you going?"

Danny didn't answer her.

"Well, if I was you I'd consider going there now."

"No."

"Fine. Then perhaps you'd like to go back home and we can ask John what this is about?"

Danny said nothing.

"Look," his mother's voice had changed gear, gone into what Ian called her cruel-to-be-kind mode, "you've got no money, no job and nowhere to go. I'm prepared to offer you free accommodation until you sort yourself out."

"Sort myself out?" Danny turned on her furiously. "Maybe you ought to give that speech to John."

As always he realised too late what he'd said. He could see the self-satisfaction on her mouth. She was the one person in the family where you could see a real resemblance to Ian. That tight unforgiving mouth, something manipulative about it.

"So it is about John?"

"What if it is?" he demanded belligerently.

"It's not news to me, you know. Think I don't know what's been going on?"

"Oh give it a rest." He ran a hand through his hair, turning away from her angrily.

"Danny, I am trying to help you."

Danny swung on her. "Then give me the money."

She took a breath, let it out again, mouth already a disapproving line. "Running away from him isn't the solution."

"Oh isn't it? You'd know I suppose?"

A dull colour crept into her face. She retorted more sharply than normal, "More than you'd think. You're not unique in his obsessions."

Danny tore his eyes away from hers to look at the sill, then the dashboard, then the steering wheel and, finally, out of the side window so that he needn't see any part of her at all. He said quickly, "So I go to Jerrett's, then what? What if one of them turns up?"

"They won't. That's why you were sent to clean out the hayloft. I've finally managed to talk your father into letting it as a holiday home. And I've changed the locks, so John won't be paying it any more nocturnal visits either, I can assure you."

Danny looked at her. Did she know about John dragging him up there the night before? But she offered no further explanations so he asked, "How do I live?"

"I'll take care of that."

Danny stared at her. "Why are you doing this?"

"Because it's long overdue. John should have been sent packing long ago."

"You'll have a job convincing Dad of that."

"I won't need to convince anyone, John will leave."

"John? You're joking. You couldn't winkle him out of there with a crowbar. He's in for life."

"John will leave," she said again, emphatically.

Danny looked at her for a long moment then turned away. "So what about me? It still doesn't account for my day. Am I to stay there forever, being kept by you as the mysterious holiday lodger?"

"You can come back home."

Danny looked at her. "After John's left?"

"That's right."

"You're nuts."

His mother coloured up. Danny spoke quickly, before she could. "What makes you think I'd want to? I was leaving, remember?"

"With no money?"

Danny stared at her. She went back into her persuasive headmistress mode. "You can come home, establish your savings again, then do as you see fit, only this time there will be no John..." She stopped. Danny was unsure whether she was looking for some elusive word or had stopped herself short of saying something she shouldn't. He couldn't resist it.

"No John prowling around the house looking for somewhere to shove it?" he offered.

His mother looked at him. She was hot-faced, but there was something hard and uncharacteristically unflinching in her eyes. "That doesn't shock me, Danny. I'm just surprised you want to talk about it – now."

Danny turned his face away. "I don't."

"Fine. Then I suggest we get to Jerrett's before one of your brothers comes down this road and catches us."

Danny glanced at the dashboard clock, then at his mother, then started the car.


Danny followed his mother into the living-room. She pulled open the thick curtains with a grating scrape of metal on metal. Danny could see the clouds of dust boiling through the air. "That's probably the first time they've been open in fifteen years," she said.

He looked around the room. It was bare except for an ugly old sideboard and a rusty red sofa that matched the curtains. The grate was full of soot and the ash of burnt paper.

Danny had never even seen into this room from the outside. The exterior of the building had always presented that same blank, closed-up face. All its curtains shut. Nobody home.

"Well?" his mother asked.

Danny pushed his hands in his pockets. "What can I say?"

"There's a Calor gas heater upstairs. You can use that until I get the chimney swept."

Danny nodded.

"And you'll find the bed in the room upstairs is made up. You can thank your brother for that too." His mother's voice was full of distaste, her John-tone as Ian called it.

Danny turned to look at her, but she had moved off into the kitchen saying, "The back bedroom's locked – I seem to have lost the key – but as I recall it's a poky little hole anyway. You're better off in the big room." He heard cupboard doors bang. "We'll need to get some food in for you."

She went on, but Danny wasn't listening. His mind was still struggling with the made-up bed, the heater.

His mother came back into the living-room. "...I'll get it this afternoon, that'll be safer."

Danny wanted to ask, 'Than what?' but didn't.

"Right, I'm off." She smiled her rare tight smile. "I must be at the breakfast post, keep everything normal."

"What are you going to tell them?"

"Just the truth, that you've left."

Danny shook his head. "They won't just accept that."

They both knew he meant John wouldn't accept it, but neither said so.

"I have my persuasive side too, Danny."

She turned away and picked up the car keys. "Fine, I'll see you about three then. There's a brush and so forth in the kitchen – should you wish to start clearing up." And she almost smiled at him again, then was gone.


She had an hour till they came in for lunch. She had decided on a slight change of plan and had gone shopping for Danny that morning. She'd left her purchases locked in the boot of the car.

She began making the meal, tidying the wreckage from the kitchen, evidence of her absence. She could read the confusion and disruption in the half-eaten bits of toast, the half-drunk teacups. What had Ian told them? Not that he had been caught clambering over Danny like a randy dog, of that she was sure. But he had unmistakably been trying to stop him. It surprised her. Ian had no love for Danny, despite their years of plotting in corners, so why go so far as to take his money away from him? Assuming, of course, that it was actually intended to stop him and wasn't just spite.

And there was still John to deal with. There was always John, like a second shadow, dangerous, unpredictable, pregnant with ugly possibilities, repellent and seductive at once, utterly incomprehensible to her. Her heart sank at the thought of the ensuing battle.

And Robbie, how would he take it? Time was she could have been sure of that. Robbie and Danny were enemies, it was that simple. But new images niggled at her mind. That evening in the living-room. Another when she'd walked into the kitchen and caught them standing close together, something about Robbie's stance giving everything away. Only she wasn't sure what it was he had given away.

"Where is he?" The door slammed just as she was taking the pie from the oven, startling her into burning her hand. She wheeled, sucking her injured wrist. John Jackson Moore, her husband, stood there.

"Well, where is he?"

"Who?" she said stupidly.

"Danny, who the hell else?"

"He's gone." She turned back to the oven, picking up the dish and placing it carefully on a raffia mat on the table.

"Once again." He shook out his jacket irritably and hung it up. Was it raining? She looked out the window.

"So where has he gone this time?" He pulled out a chair and sat down.

She began dishing up his meal. "I don't know."

"So where have you been then?"

"Shopping."

He looked at her. "Is this to be one of his twenty-four hour jobs?"

"I wouldn't know."

"Is that right?" He pulled his plate across to himself, looking up at her. "I'm short-handed now, you realise that?"

"I'm sure he didn't mean to inconvenience you."

"Didn't mean doesn't get the work done." He took a mouthful of pie. "So what's his excuse this time?" He was no longer looking at her, as if Danny's reasons were an afterthought, not as relevant as his actual absence.

"You make it sound like he does this every day of the week."

He ignored that.

She said, "I should imagine he was fed up."

That made him jerk his head up. "Fed up? When I've got a hundred acres just sitting there waiting for him to grace them with his royal presence? He picks the times."

"I can't imagine being fed up goes by the clock."

"Nothing about him goes by the clock, or ever has."

He began eating again, fiercely, seemingly absorbed in what he was doing. "That bloody face of his will get him into serious trouble one of these days."

She looked at him. He looked back at her, lifting his head in exactly the same way as John, Danny too, if she was forced to admit it. It was an unnerving gesture in all of them.

"All his life that face of his has been getting him into trouble. And it isn't going to get any better. Not until somebody rearranges it for him, or he loses his looks altogether."

"Are you saying he's to blame for the way other people see him? That's nonsense." She got up out of her seat on the pretext of moving a pot off the ring.

"Is it?" His hand was arrested, fork pointing at her. "Looks like his are as much trouble in a boy as they are in a girl. More. There's no-one to settle them down. No-one to come along and knock them up and knock it out of them. You never can knock it out of the likes of him."

She looked at him, the disgust evident on her face.

"Call it all the names you like," he said sharply, "all that one's suffering from is the two minutes boredom he has to endure catching his breath after he diddles with himself. He's being led by his prick, and he always will be, because the whole world's feeding it, wanting their hands about him. Christ knows, I've tried to control him, give him some discipline, but you've undermined every effort I've ever made with him. You'd change your tune if you'd seen what I've seen. He's bad, rotten. It's in his blood."

He didn't seem to see anything incongruous in the statement. She wondered exactly whose blood he had in mind, resisted the temptation to tell him that whoever's it was, at least it wasn't hers.

He had fallen silent. She dropped down onto the chair opposite him, caught by the arresting sight of his hand. It was trembling.

"You know," he said abruptly, "when Robbie first came here I thought, He's going to be exactly the same. But he's not the same breed, even though there were days I saw him just as restless, not minding his work. It never went anywhere. It always passed. But that dirty little brat is a different class of animal. It's beyond his looks, it's something rotten in his blood."

The door banged suddenly, making Margaret jump. Ian came in. His face looked tight, as if his skin hurt, or he had an ache about him that was just waiting to turn vicious.

"Your brother has disappeared." His father began eating again. "And don't waste your breath asking where he is. We don't know. Man of bloody mystery."

Margaret served Ian without looking at him. He, in turn, seemed jumpy with her, looking at her edgily, like a child afraid he is to be reprimanded later after company has gone.

John and Rab came in together. John was silent, tense, eyes immediately fixed on hers.

"He's gone," his father said, shovelling food in. "And we've no idea where, only that the fragile soul was fed-up."

"You don't know where?" John asked his mother directly, as if his father hadn't spoken. There were deep grey shadows under his eyes.

"No. Man of bloody mystery," his father answered before she could speak.

"Did you take him?"

His father looked up. Rab looked up. Everyone looked up.

"I gave him a lift to the station," she admitted. She got more food from the stove, began putting it out.

"The station?" His father was staring at her. "I thought you said you'd been shopping?"

"I was, after I took him to the station."

"You took him," he said flatly.

"He wanted to go."

"So you took him. Jesus Christ." He pushed his plate away and got up from the table, striding across the kitchen. He snatched his jacket off the peg. "Jesus Christ," he said again, yanking it on. "He always could wheedle his fucking way round you."

He yanked the door open savagely. "You lot. Out in half an hour. We're short-handed now, thanks to your bloody mother."

And he went out, slamming the door hard enough to rattle the crockery.


The rest of the meal was eaten in uncomfortable silence. Margaret felt as if every man in the room would have spoken volumes if they had been alone with her. Only Rab seemed comfortable, or at least simply bemused.

Their father's restriction on thirty minutes seemed to have dampened any possibility for conversation. They ate like prisoners, silent and tense.

They got up and left in the same tense silence they had come in. John was the last to go. "I'll see you later," he said. His voice seemed inflectionless, without any special meaning or significance, but somehow it still sounded like a threat.


John came into her room that evening. She had escaped briefly to think, to organise, but she didn't get a chance. He came in without knocking.

"You might knock first." She watched him close the door carefully, stand against it.

"I might," he agreed.

She closed her wardrobe door. John continued to watch her, unspeaking, unmoving, except for his hand inserting and removing a cigarette – you couldn't call it smoking.

She felt as if her skin became itchy under his gaze. She sat at her dressing table and studied him in the mirror. "Well?" she said finally.

He took the cigarette out again. "I might ask you the same thing."

"What do you want, John?"

"What are you offering?"

She banged down a jar that she had only lifted to cover her nervousness. "Don't play stupid games. What d'you want?"

He pushed off the door and crossed to the foot of the bed. He sat down and studied her face at closer range in the mirror. "Tell me where he is."

"I don't know where he is. You heard me at lunchtime." She began rummaging in a drawer. She tried to inject anger into her voice, but it sounded shallow, almost apologetic.

"Like fuck you don't." His voice was brittle, without humour or good-nature. She looked up at him, stupidly startled at the abrupt change.

"Why do you want to know?" She stared at him.

He stared back. "Why do you want to hide it?"

"I thought you'd be glad to be rid of him. Now you've got no reason to stay in a place you so obviously despise."

"Well you thought wrong. Where is he?"

"I told you, I don't know," she repeated, this time with more conviction.

It gave her a strange pleasurable sense of power to cross him. Not for a long time had she actually held anything he might value.

Slowly, purposefully, he dropped his cigarette onto the carpet and ground it in. Her mouth opened in protest, a dull flush of anger stained her skin. "Of all the dirty..." But she could go no further.

He was smiling again, unperturbed. "I'll wait, Margaret, I'll be patience itself, because sooner or later you're going to let it slip."

He stood up and walked to the door then he turned back. "But let's hope it's sooner rather than later because waiting bores me, and you know how destructive I can get when I'm bored."

She glared at his retreating back in the mirror, willing him to trip and break his neck, but he simply shut the door quite quietly, without any sign of temper, leaving Margaret and her reflection completely alone.

## SEVENTEEN

Danny prowled around the house irritably. He must have been mad to agree to this. The place gave him the creeps. Besides, he wasn't used to sitting around idle.

He heard a car drive into the yard and looked out the window. At last, the cavalry. His mother climbed out of the car with two large cans of paint. He went out to meet her. "What the hell's all this?" he asked.

"What does it look like? Here." She handed him the keys. "The other stuff's in the boot, bring it in."

"Other stuff?" he asked her retreating back, but she didn't answer. Danny sighed and crossed to the car and began relaying the strippers and fillers, papers and pastes, into the living-room.

"Sweep's coming tomorrow," she said, pushing the front door shut behind him as he brought the last lot in. She followed him into the living-room.

"Listen," he said as he dropped the rolls of paper on the floor, "I can't stay here, I'll go off my head. I need to get my money."

She looked at him, eyes familiarly flinty. "Suggestions?"

"For what?" Danny said blankly.

"Your money."

"Ian's got it."

"You think."

"No. I know where it is."

"And?"

"Well, I need you to get it for me, don't I?"

"So where is it?"

"John's room."

"*John's* room?" She stared at him.

Danny nodded, keeping his eyes on hers.

"Why in goodness' name would he put it in John's room?"

"Because he's Ian."

She looked at him for a long moment then turned away. "And you expect me to search John's room, on an off-chance?"

"You know when he's out. It's safe enough."

She turned her head to him. "It's obvious you haven't seen him recently."

"Why?"

His mother turned back to him, looking at him so long Danny coloured up, saying aggressively, "So I want to know he's suffering. I think I'm entitled to a little revenge."

She said nothing to that, saying instead, "So I find it, supposing your premise is correct, then what?"

"I go."

"Where?"

"That's my business."

His mother looked at him. "And if I refuse?"

"I'll go back and get it myself."

She nodded, still watching him, then said, "Well, I suppose I don't have any option. As I have no intention of standing back and letting you endanger your life, I might as well endanger mine."

Danny laughed. "Oh come on..."

His mother didn't smile.

He said, "He's hardly likely to..." his smile sliding away. He never finished it.

"He's unbalanced and totally unpredictable. He always was, even as a small boy. He was overindulged and self-seeking as a child and as an adult he's forty times worse. He's completely ungovernable, thanks to your father. He thinks he can do anything he likes. Well, he's about to find out that he can't."

Danny wanted to say, Can't he? But he said nothing.

His mother turned away and became suddenly brisk. "Right, in the meantime you can start earning your keep. This place needs redecorated and you've nothing else to do."

"Fine," he said, relieved somehow at the change of subject.

"And you can unpack the groceries."

"Okay." Danny took them through to the kitchen, putting on the light. Christ, this place was dingy. He would start the decorating in here. Not that it mattered, he wasn't staying that long.

His mother came through, carrying cleaning materials.

"When will you look for it?" he asked, packing tea and coffee into a cupboard he'd just brushed free of mouse droppings.

"What?"

"The money." Danny glanced over his shoulder at her.

"In a day or two."

"What?" Danny turned to her.

"Danny," she put down the large blue bottle she was holding, "do you want John to find you?"

It took him a minute to answer. He shook his head, colouring up. "What the hell are you saying that for?"

"Because you seem to have some foolish notion that since you've walked out the door you're out of sight, out of mind as far as he's concerned. He's practically checking the cupboards for you. He's grilled me, your brother, even Robbie, although he has no suspicions whatsoever about them. He knows it's me. He's already threatened me. And what do you think he'll do if he finds me searching his room, or even suspects that I've searched it, or is *told* that I've searched it?"

Danny shrugged and looked away.

"Exactly. In short, John's deeply suspicious and Ian's happily feeding that suspicion. Now will you let me handle this my way?"

Danny nodded and turned away.

They went on unpacking in silence for a little while longer then his mother banged the cupboard door under the sink and straightened up. "Right, I need to get back. You're on your own until tomorrow. I'm not sure when I'll be round, but you've got plenty to do."

Danny nodded, feeling a sinking of the heart at the prospect of a night alone in the place.

He followed his mother out to the hall and stood at the open door with her. "It's in a Golden Virginia tin," he reminded her, "the money."

She nodded and zipped up her jacket, pulling her shoulder bag on. "Tomorrow then."

Danny nodded.

His mother left.



Rab could feel him standing there in the dark. He switched on the front light and pulled the door closed. He hung up his jacket. Maybe he ought to take out his dick and wiggle it around a bit like live bait for a worm.

He shrugged into his boiler suit. "Come on out, Ian. I don't plan on jerking off for at least an hour. You'll get rheumatics hanging around that long." He sat down on the tractor step and began the process of rolling up.

Ian emerged silently from the shadows. Rab didn't look up until he was on the point of sealing his cigarette. When he did, Ian was watching his tongue lick along the paper with a grim-faced avidity.

"Looks even better now, Ian, doesn't it? When you can't have it any more."

"I could still tell," Ian said with a barely resigned hostility.

"Sure you could," Rab began patting, standing up to reach down inside the boiler suit into his jeans' pocket. Ian watched his hand like a dog expecting to be presented with a biscuit. Rab withdrew his hand, lit his cigarette and sat down again. "Only what would be the point? Nothing to gain, everything to lose."

"You conceited bastard. D'you think I'd give a fuck if I never saw you again?"

Rab inhaled deeply and released the smoke through his nose. "What's wrong? Doesn't it feel so good this way round?"

"What makes you think it felt good at all?"

"Oh don't make me laugh. You'd take it any fucking way you can get it, just like the rest of your stinking family."

Abruptly Ian smiled. "What's wrong? Ditched you, has he?"

"Fucking shut up."

"What a shame. You'll just have to stick to screwing his big brother then. He's the only one who even remotely resembles him."

Rab smacked him. Hard. Full in the face. Ian stumbled back into the workbench, caught the small of his back and went down with an almost comic abruptness.

Rab stood back, shocked at himself, listening to Ian's hoarse breathing.

When he spoke it was rough, as if talking hurt him. "I kissed him before he went, and you know..." he stopped, taking a careful breath, "I'd have done a lot worse if he'd let me."

He looked up at Rab, his face a pasty white. He was neither gloating nor smug, just stating facts. "First time I think I ever truly understood the fascination. He even smells good."

"Oh Christ," Rab said running his hands through his hair, "I don't believe I'm hearing this."

Ian dropped his head back wearily, looked up at the ceiling. "Poor Rab. You know, I think confession must be in the air, I've heard that expression a lot recently."

He looked at Rab again, suddenly intent on him. "I didn't have the slightest intention of doing it. I don't think I could even call it a snatched opportunity, that's what makes it so weird. At best it was what my mother would call 'inappropriate behaviour'."

"Shut up, you're making me sick."

Ian looked at him and smiled. It was the first time in as long Rab had seen his natural smile. Perversely, it looked worse than his usual imitation. "But it's true. Just because it makes you sick doesn't mean it isn't true."

He was thoughtful for a minute or two then he pushed himself up more carefully against the bench. He held his back as if it was fragile.

Rab sat down heavily, dropping his head onto his hands.

"He was horrified, completely panic-stricken, but you know..." He stopped, listening to his mind sorting words. Rab was still, expectant, knowing what he was going to say before he said it. "I think he was enjoying it somewhere inside, just like he enjoys it with John. He can't help enjoying..."

"I think you should shut the fuck up, before I knock your teeth down your throat." Rab fixed him with a tight stare. "And I think you should get out while you can still walk."

Ian smiled again. Rab could see the old Ian surfacing: sly, destructive. He got up slowly, as if he was made of glass, and walked over to the door, then he stopped and looked back at Rab thoughtfully. "You know, I think you've suspected it all along. Even when you first took him on you knew nothing had really changed, only you were so desperate for it you didn't care."

Rab jerked upright in one convulsive movement. "Get out, before I wring your poisonous little neck."

And that made Ian smile some more, before he turned and went out the door.


Margaret closed the door carefully, wondering why she felt like tiptoeing. She was quite alone in the house and in no danger of being surprised.

She stood in John's room, feeling how unfamiliar it was. She came in here once a week to pick up dirty linen, and deliver clean, and that was it. Sometimes John beat her to it and she didn't even do that much. John didn't like anyone in his room and that suited her fine.

She began with the chest of drawers. She was filled with a sense of urgency. She must find the money before Ian tried to recover it, or worse still, John came across it by accident. The money was Danny's sole means of escape and she could not afford to let it fall into the hands of a third party, or to alert John to the possibility that Danny had not gone far.

Where would Ian put such a thing? She tried to see the place as Ian saw it, but she shared nothing in common with him. After all, who was Ian? She was his mother and she didn't know.

She opened the wardrobe and felt in John's jacket pockets. No, too risky, he would never put it there.

She stood back, closing the doors quietly, and peered up onto the top of the wardrobe. Nothing.

She got down on her knees and peered under the bed. A pile of pornographic magazines lay there, thick with dust. She stood up and dusted herself down with distaste.

She heard the back door slam. She stood still for a moment then crossed to the door and slid out into the hall. The door slammed again. She held her breath, listening. She heard the pick-up start up in the yard and let her breath out. One of them back for keys, that's all. She went back into the room, still alert to the slightest sound, but the house was completely still and silent.

She crossed the floor to the small cupboard under the sink. Not enough room to hide a measle in here, but nevertheless...

She looked inside. There was something, curled around the waste pipe. She pulled it out gingerly and carefully uncurled it. More pornography. But there was something different about these magazines. There were two of them, and they both featured young men on the covers.

She began leafing through them, studying each page almost minutely, her stomach clenched and nauseous, like a betrayed woman finally finding her husband's love letters, the damning evidence, far too important and long-imagined to be dealt with summarily. They were hardcore, filthily erect, everything red and hard and slavering like so much meat.

It was when she got to the centrefold that the photos fell out. She let them fall to the ground barely noticed because she was still staring at the boy spread widely across the pages. He was Danny's double, his doppelganger. She turned the page. There were maybe a half dozen more images of him, all equally obscene. She couldn't believe her eyes. Never in her wildest imaginings had John sunk this low. This was proof.

The boy was older, she could see that now, and his hair was dyed, and there was something both harder and more effeminate about him, but he was unmistakably some kind of attempt at recreating Danny. It was then her brain registered the photographs lying at her feet. She bent down and picked them up, turning them over.

They were poorly exposed, as if they had been taken in inadequate light, but they were still clear enough. Three Polaroid photographs of a young man asleep in bed. Genuinely, deeply asleep, like a child sleeps. The blankets had been pulled down off his body to his thighs, just far enough to show him off. He was indescribably beautiful and, like the boy in the magazine, very busily erect. He was also unmistakably Danny. The real Danny.

The door clicked shut with a dreadful finality. "Find what you were looking for?"

Margaret stood open-mouthed, the photographs clutched convulsively in her hands, her face ashen.

John looked at her, at the two hectic spots of colour on her cheeks, back to her hands again, rapidly adding up. "You shouldn't have been looking." He made it sound like a threat, like Bluebeard and his little room.

"I..." I what? she thought hysterically, "I wasn't looking for this."

"No? Well you found it all the same." He waited like a headmaster, as if she was the one guilty of the crime. She felt a sudden fury at the cheek of him.

"And what have I found exactly?"

He laughed. A short, sharp bark more like a shout of derision. "What do you think?"

"Did you take these?"

He simply looked at her, head cocked to one side, waiting for her to catch up with him. Waiting for the inevitability of her conclusions.

"Why?" she demanded.

He looked at the ceiling, then licked his lips as if he were considering. Then he studied the carpet thoughtfully. Finally he said, "How about for a practical joke?" His head came up again, studying her, challenging her.

She shook her head without answering.

"Then you tell me."

"Because you're a filthy..." but she couldn't control the words. They stopped, stifled by the possibility of what she might say. He was looking away from her, smiling contemptuously, like a roué amused by a virgin's gaucherie. She found herself saying, "They've been taken at different times."

"One this year, two last summer." Then he smiled at her, an ugly smile. "And there's more, going further back. Would you like to see those too?"

"How did you get them?" she demanded.

"You don't really want to hear the answer to that. What you really want to hear is an excuse, something that shows a proper shame, a proper remorse." He shook his head as if *she* sickened *him*. "Well that's too bad, because I don't feel any remorse. I don't feel any shame. Sad, isn't it?"

"Have you been interfering with him?" It sounded preposterous even as she said it, like something some dodgy old family uncle might do, not John.

This time his smile was genuine. It looked somehow worse than anything else that had gone before. "Have I been *interfering* with him? Do you mean did I touch him up, feel his private parts?"

She grew hotter, angrier, under his sarcasm.

"Not as much as I would have liked, believe me. Not nearly as much as I would have liked."

"You're disgusting. How could you? Your own brother..." She petered out, lost in her own revulsion.

"Believe me it was easy. I doubt if even Jesus Christ himself could have resisted it. Danny is a very special taste."

"What did you do to him?"

"Why do you want to know?" The question felt loaded, his eyes narrowed with suspicion.

"I'm his mother, if I needed a reason. And don't think I won't take these to your

151

father. Maybe now he'll believe me."

His eyes seemed to suddenly accuse her, as if he could see things beyond what she could see herself. She felt as if Danny's image burned into her fingers. He said softly, almost consideringly, "No, I don't think you will."

"I'm going to your father," she asserted.

John reached out and pulled the photographs from her hand as easily as if she had no power in her fingers at all. He looked at them carefully, fanning them out like a card sharper, then pulled one out and offered it back to her. "Here, have this one. I'm keeping the others." He looked at her insolently. "Since I no longer have the real thing these will have to do." His mouth smiled, but it did not reach his eyes.

She yanked it out of his hand and marched to the door. "I'm going to show this to your father right now." She pulled the door open. She sounded as if she was trying to convince herself, not him.

"No," he said again, making no attempt to stop her, "I don't think you will."

Her heart was suddenly racing, full of air, feeling in the pit of her stomach exactly what he was about to say, knowing the truth of it before she even heard the words.

He moved close beside her, and whispered in her ear, "You wouldn't want to share him with anyone else, would you?"

She slapped him. Hard. A huge satisfying smack that brought weals up on his face. He grabbed her hand, crushingly tight around the wrist, his face an ugly mask of anger – and then his expression changed, softened, almost like some saintly possession, some religious extreme of forgiveness, and he bent his head and lingeringly kissed the palm of her hand. "Poor Margaret, you probably want him more than all the rest of us put together."

His mother wrenched her hand free and slammed out the room.

## EIGHTEEN

It was eight o'clock, and already it looked like a winter's evening. It was going to be a long, cold winter. She could feel it in her bones. No autumn, just straight into cold and damp and howling winds.

The rain began to spit viciously, almost like sleet, just as she turned up the road to Jerrett's. She felt as if she was escaping. The house had become impossible, charged with an oppressive atmosphere of suspense. Everyone seemed to be watching her, waiting for her to make a mistake. At first she'd been confident that only Ian suspected she knew where Danny was, but now she felt as if they all did, despite the fact that Ian almost certainly hadn't passed his knowledge on. If he had she'd have known about it, John would have made sure of that.

The house was all lit up, looking curiously festive. Smoke was swirling in the damp air as she climbed from the car. It was like coming home.

Danny opened the door and grinned impulsively. "Welcome, fair damsel, to my palatial mansion." It felt like years since she'd seen him smile like that. The house smelt of paint, fruity and heady with fumes.

"I've had the windows open all day, but it still stinks."

"Doesn't matter, it smells fresh and clean."

"Come and see the living-room." Danny pulled her arm.

He had finished the walls and was working on the woodwork. The fire was sharp and hot, roaring away in the grate.

Danny followed her eyes. "I feel as though that's the first heat I've had in ten years. I feel almost human again."

She looked at him. "Well, I'll make your day then." She held up the bag she was carrying. "Chinese take-away."

"Hey, great." His enthusiasm was infectious. "I'll get plates. I only had beans on toast for tea." He turned and grinned at her. "Not used to cooking for myself." And he laughed as he disappeared into the kitchen.

He brought plates back and they pulled the sofa closer to the fire. Danny sat on the floor and dished up. Margaret had brought a bottle of wine in from the car saying, "To celebrate your freedom." And Danny had smiled easily and gone to get glasses.

Now they sat before the fire and listened to the rain beating against the windows. The paint fumes were heavy in the heat and conspired with the wine to make them sleepier.

Danny stretched out beside her on the carpet and closed his eyes. She had moved down onto the floor at his suggestion and was leaning back now against the sofa. Such relaxed behaviour felt hugely unfamiliar to her. She shifted her weight, looking down into his face, and said, "We must get you some furniture."

"Mm." No protests, but then he didn't really seem to be listening.

Margaret looked down at him again and realised he looked just like he did in the photograph: half-asleep, drifting.

She looked away. How could she have forgotten the photograph? For that matter why had she remembered?

She looked back down at him. It was no use. Now that the image had leapt into her head it was going to sit there, leering at her. She studied his face, thrown into half-shadow by the firelight, his hair turned molten red in the golden light, the long stretched length of his body. His breathing was regular, heavy. He'd fallen asleep.

She felt the quickening of an impulse, only dimly understood, and which she did not stop to examine. She reached out a hand and stroked his hair.

He didn't move. His breathing was still deep. His body looked slack and relaxed, his lips very slightly parted. She ran a fingertip over his mouth.

He folded his lips as if they itched. She held her breath, but he still did not wake. She smiled, but it was an edgy thing, full of anxiety and tension. There was something compelling in this urge to touch him. She was not a tactile person, she disliked being touched herself, but Danny had always provoked this odd response in her. He was like some kind of beautiful but dangerous animal that you stroked at your peril. It was still alien enough to make her heart thump and her skin crawl, even after all these years.

He had his shirt open, as if he'd taken it off at some point and just carelessly pulled it back on, stuffing it inside his trousers rather than bother fastening it. She slid her hand inside. Her head thumped as if she had a headache coming on. The fire shifted suddenly in the grate, dropping ash. Her hand jerked, but Danny slept on. She pushed her hand more purposefully inside. His chest felt solid with young muscle, like his father's had once been. Her face flushed. She pulled her hand out.

His skin was beautiful, soft and plush, like a peach. How could anyone looking at her, dark and earthbound as she was, possibly believe that she had borne this boy? He was like a stranger to her, as if someone had stolen her child and replaced him. She felt robbed of her motherhood. She couldn't connect herself with him. She felt no protectiveness, no tenderness. He was alien flesh.

She let her hand pull the shirt out from his trousers. Gently. He had his hands behind his head and the shirt fell immediately in soft folds at the sides of his body, exposing his chest. She could see the fine hair seam running up to his belly button from below the waistband of his trousers. He looked older than he did in the photograph. She supposed he was, although surely not enough to make a difference? His nipples were very small and brown. She pressed her hand flat on his belly. She left it there, surprised at the warmth of him, the tautness, the odd blankness of his beauty.

She slid the tips of her fingers under the waistband of his jeans. He was stretched out; it was an easy thing to do. She felt the narrow seam of hair, thicker, glossier, but not that sickening mat of his father's. This was somehow childish, not threatening. It lay sleek on his belly, like a soft pelt. Her hand was squeezed slightly with every breath he took. She slid it in further and felt the waistband of his shorts. It stopped her as effectively as barbed wire. She did not have the conviction of her innocence to pass that elastic, no matter how much she'd had to drink.

She let her hand lie there, unmoving. Danny breathed in and out easily, without effort. His face was completely relaxed. She watched it, hypnotically running her eyes over its contours again and again. Gradually her hand did what it wanted to do without her knowing anything about it. It eased her neat short nails under the waistband. Past the knuckles it could reach in quickly and easily to the hot, slightly damp darkness. The hair here was thick but still not wiry, and deep in its coils lay a sleeping snake. Her hand brushed it. She moved her head slightly but still watched Danny's face. Her fingers walked it into her palm, wrapping around it, holding it there. Her heart thudded dully, as if it was slowed by an excess of drink.

She felt it stir.

It felt like a dream, an imagining. You wanted it to happen, were afraid it might happen, and so you thought it did happen. But this wasn't a dream, it did move in her hand, slowly at first, and then with sickening speed.

It grew corpulently fat. As it emerged from inside its skin she could feel the sticky touch of its swollenness adhere to her fingers.

Within seconds he was erect. To her he felt hugely erect. She saw his eyes move behind their lids as if he were dreaming. She let go, pulling her hand out slowly, rigidly, like someone withdrawing from a scorpion poised to strike.

She freed her hand and looked down at him. Her breathing was rapid. She could see it, large and hard beneath the fabric of his jeans. She wiped her hand on her sweater and turned her head away. She began buttoning his shirt, carefully, from the neck down, not looking lower than his navel, but she knew it was still there, lurking just outside her vision, like a summonsed demon that would not return to its resting place without the taste of blood.

She wanted to tuck in his shirt, but she couldn't bring herself to put her hand back in there again. She sat there staring at his face.

If she was to unzip his trousers right now she'd see him just as he looked in the photograph, just as John had seen him.

Her hand reached out and pulled at his zip.

Danny's hand wrapped itself around her wrist. His eyes were open, looking at her from under his lashes. "What are you doing?" His voice was thick, heavy with sleep or drink.

"I..." She didn't know. She didn't have a clue what she was going to say because she didn't know what she had been doing. She'd forgotten as clearly as a waker from a dream forgets everything that has passed before.

Danny didn't move. He still held her hand, eyes half-closed, watching her like a drugged cat: half-dangerous, half-indifferent.

She looked at him, held by his eyes, hand clamped to his belly, barely touching the head of his erection. She could feel the slight swell of it under her pinkie.

He moved her hand down over it with a slight firm pressure, as if he was guiding her over its contours. She looked at him and didn't know him. She recognised the features, but couldn't recognise the face. He was hard and masculine, years older than his body, filled with indefinable urges and longings. She was feeling the erection of a strange man. I'm drunk, she thought wildly. She felt his penis jump beneath her hand. It was rock-hard, straining.

"You shouldn't have touched me," he said. "Now it won't go away."

"Don't talk nonsense." But her voice was tremulous. I sound afraid, she thought.

He shook his head, tiny shakes, barely perceptible. His eyes closed like a man drifting back into sleep. "Do it," he said. His voice was a whispered command. He lifted his hand from hers, freeing it. There was no uncertainty in him.

She snatched her hand back convulsively. She held it to her chest as if imprisoning it.

"Finish it," he whispered. She wasn't sure if he had actually spoken. He lay still, seemingly asleep, except his breathing was wrong.

She wasn't even sure what he meant, could only assume he meant she should finish what she had started, and what she had started was a desire to see him as John had, to be his equal, to see him naked.

She undid his belt, slowly, uncertainly. When she had done that she wiped her hands on her skirt as if to rub off the feel of the thick leather, the heavy warmth of it. She lifted the zip and pulled it down. It seemed to drag like a ton weight, resisting her. She pulled his trousers open and saw the huge ugly shape of it under the loose cotton of his shorts. She could smell the rich, salty smell of him, like juicy meat. She felt her mouth water and felt sick.

She pulled the waistband of his shorts up and away from his body then tugged it down. His erection sprung out, peeled back and obscene. The colour was all wrong. He was as red and hard as his father was dark and swarthy. An image of John flashed through her head.

"Touch me."

She shook her head. She *wouldn't* touch him, not in that state, not with that filthy thing... she wouldn't even say it.

"It hurts me." Danny's voice was whispery, without substance. "Touch me."

She lifted her hand – she could see it shaking – and pressed it gently along the length of him.

He groaned. A low, soft groan like a man easing a cramped leg, massaging an aching muscle.

She jerked her hand away, suddenly understanding what he was doing. But he caught her hand, horrifically fast, totally at odds with the incredible languor in his body. He pressed her fingers around his penis, holding them there, applying a subtle pressure to the swollen head as if he was trying to squeeze some of the blood back out, ease his distress.

"No," she whispered, trying to pull it back. But he began to masturbate in her hand, easing it up and down slowly, tightly. She could see the tension spread out into his body. She saw lines like pain form on his face. His free hand dug into the carpet. His erection became slick, sliding easily inside her hand, although the head grew harder, rounder, fatter, with every stroke.

He pushed his head and shoulders back down into the carpet as if he was trying to lever his hips further up. He started pumping her hand faster, reaching his other hand down between his own legs and gripping his testicles, pulling them down, making the skin drag against her palm so that she could feel the little string of flesh on the underside of his penis catch and pull on her fingertips like the raised underside of a tongue.

His eyes shot open suddenly. "Make me..." But he never finished it. He threw his head forward with a jolt, eyes riveted on her hand.

She watched, fascinated, as the milky fluid spurted out of him, splashing down the back of her hand, hot and gelatinous, pumping under her fingers like an animal's cut throat.

He watched it with glazed eyes, fascinated with his own performance, desperate for his own relief.

He slumped back as suddenly as he had come, letting her go, arms falling to his sides, his erection still huge and dripping, his face flushed.

She looked at her hand in horror, the trail of slime running and dripping down the side of his belly, then squirmed backwards like a crab and bolted from the room.

## NINETEEN

She did not go back the next day, or the next. She could not face him. She could barely face herself. It was as if the simple act of being given that one photograph had poisoned her very thinking. Which was exactly what John had intended. He was trying to prove to her that she was as prey to the perversity and depravity he'd cultivated in Danny as all the rest of them. Well, he was wrong. And it was now imperative that she found the money.

They were all working long hours, trying to cover Danny's work. In spite of their father's speeches he had not attempted to hire anyone to replace him. Perhaps John had had a hand in that too, no doubt sure that Danny would be back. Well he was going to be wrong this time.

She worked as hard as they did, her time consumed with the myriad extra chores which now fell to her. But she made time to search John's room. Fifteen minutes here, half an hour there. She could find nothing.

She decided to try Ian's room. No longer needing to hide it from Danny, and suspecting that Danny had told her where it was, he'd make sure she would not be able to find it. That much was Ian, she was at least sure of that.

His room was tidy, familiar. She searched drawers, wardrobe. No tin, no pornography, no surprises. Ian's room was like Ian himself, meticulously unrevealing, giving nothing away.

On impulse she looked under his pillow – for years he'd kept a diary under here – and there it was: one Golden Virginia tin, one packet of liquorice cigarette papers. The papers threw her. She opened the tin nervously, half fearing it would contain tobacco, but it didn't. It contained forty-two £20 notes. She stared at it. More than eight hundred pounds. Twice what he'd said. She counted it again. No mistake. How had he...?

This time she heard no warning click. She just knew he was there. She turned slowly, not bothering to hurry, and found herself smiling. Maybe it was the only option left to her. "I wouldn't make much of a burglar, would I?"

But Ian didn't smile back. "I've been waiting for you to find it. I expected you sooner actually. After all, you've ransacked John's room. There can't be anything secret left to him."

She lifted her head, ready to deny it, face him down, but he smiled at her.

"You had him over a barrel. No money, no car, of course he'd tell you. He had to, because that's the only way you'd give him the money to get away. Only now you had to find that to stop John realising you must know." He nodded his head at the tin in her hand. "And sooner or later you put two and two together and realised I'd have to move it because I couldn't afford to let John know either." And he smiled at her again, a revolting little smile that she must have seen before only she couldn't remember it. Who is this man? she thought. Where have my sons gone? The house is full of strange men and I don't know any of them.

"...I want you to tell me."

She looked at him blankly, realising she hadn't heard what he'd said.

He repeated it. "You know where he is and I want you to tell me."

"What?" She tried that without conviction.

"Oh come on."

"I can't tell you."

"I think you better, otherwise I could start telling tales out of school. Danny, John, so *good* looking. I wonder what happened to me?"

"What?"

"Pretty, alike. Pretty alike even." He smiled at his own joke.

"Shut up." She said it without conviction. She just didn't want to be sick. She didn't want to throw up on the carpet because she'd only have to clean it up. There wasn't anyone else to clean up sick. That was her job, end of the line.

"Even I wasn't allowed that." His hand snaked out and clutched at her breast, squeezing it viciously. "What about them?"

She slapped his hand away. "Don't touch me."

He laughed, a sniggering little sound. "Famous last words in this house. Everyone says them, but who means them?"

"What do you want?" She stared at him angrily, suddenly back inside herself, jolted out of her shock.

"I told you, all I want to know is where he is."

"Why?"

"Let's call it peace of mind."

"You're going to tell John."

He smiled again, ingratiatingly. "I'm not going to tell anyone, least of all John. The further Danny stays from here the better, as far as I'm concerned." He smiled again. "Don't you find John's much more tractable when he's not around?"

He watched her swaying, wanting an ally, wanting to protect herself. He swung it the way he swung everything, by lying through his teeth. "Come on, you can trust me." He got high on the words, felt horny just saying them. He looked at her, all pretences dropping. "Where is he?"

"At Jerrett's." Her eyes were on his, very intent.

His eyes widened, his mouth twitched. "You're joking."

She shook her head, mouth a thin line.

He laughed suddenly, genuinely. "Oh Jesus, that's perfect." His amusement dropped away. He looked suddenly angry, vindictive. "What are you going to do, fuck him in John's leftovers? Think it'll get a better performance out of him?"

She slapped him, but it was weak, diffused by shame and guilt.

He suddenly gripped her breast again. "Maybe you've already been there. Well, Mother, got into Danny's pants yet? Seen the queue?"

She slapped his hand away again, more violently this time. Her face was flaming. "Don't you *dare*. Don't you forget who I am, Ian, and don't you forget that maybe your father has no idea about your shenanigans with John, but *I* do. Don't you *ever* threaten me." And she gave him a long furious look then slammed out the door.

John came into the kitchen last, tired and aching in his bones. She looked at him properly for the first time in days. He looked drawn, his face sharp. Already his tan was fading. He looked yellowish in the grey light of the kitchen. She smiled at him. She didn't know where she dredged it up from. Some genuine warmth? Some half-remembered tenderness? No, there never had been any.

John did not smile back.

"I have to talk to you," she said.

"Then talk." He took off his jacket, hanging it over the back of his chair.

"Ian knows something. I mean about..." She stopped, aware of the ridiculous melodrama in what she was saying, but she still couldn't bring herself to actually voice it.

He looked at her for a long moment, to be sure he understood her, but there was no surprise in him, only perhaps a quickening of his interest. "So?"

"What do you mean, So? Don't you realise what this means?"

John sat down and began searching in his pockets. "It means he spends too much time listening at keyholes."

She dropped down beside him. "You don't seem to care."

"Why should I?"

He tapped a cigarette on the table. She realised it was one of the old type he used to smoke. She tore her eyes off it as if it meant something. "What if he tells Danny?"

John laughed. "Don't be so fucking stupid, he's not going to tell Danny." He looked at her. "Besides, he'd have to find him first, wouldn't he?"

She ignored that, flushing angrily at the way he casually insulted her. "What makes you so sure? Danny believes everything he tells him."

John laughed. "Much as Danny reveres the ground his brother walks on, he'd see Ian in Hell first before he believed anything as far-fetched as that particular fairy-tale. It's a fucking soap opera." He inhaled deeply. "Talk sense."

She looked at him, realising the truth of what he said with a strange sinking defeat.

He smiled lazily. "Now, hadn't you better tell me what you told him?"

"What?" She was buying time again, pathetically.

"Don't 'What?' me. I've been patient with you, very polite, then Ian comes along with a story so thin you could glaze windows with it and you tell him everything."

"I've told you, I don't know where Danny is. How many times do I have to repeat myself?" She sounded hysterical, even to herself.

John leant across the table as if he were about to tell her something in confidence and slapped her hard across the mouth. She flew back against the chair, her teeth jarring, her eyes wide with shock.

"Where is he?"

"What do you want with him?" Her lips felt numb.

"Where *is* he?

"Tell me what you want with him!" she yelled, holding her hands to her face, warding off blows, hiding her face. She didn't know herself.

John smiled. He looked down at the table then back up at her. "Just the same as you – his long life and happiness."

"You're lying."

"Well, you tell me then. You're the one with the theory."

She said nothing. Her face burned. Anger, the slap – she didn't care. Her mouth set stubbornly.

"You know, your suspicions are beginning to bore me. It's none of your business anyway. It never was. Now where is he?"

"I'm not telling you."

He slapped her again, so suddenly that she would have sworn he never moved.

She cried out on reflex. He was up out his seat, holding the front of her sweater. "Your face could be an awful mess at this rate. *Where?*"

Her temper flared up, instantly unleashed. "You want sex with him, don't you?" Her face was white with fury. The handprint stood clear against it, red on white. She couldn't see his face; she could see nothing but her own blinding rage. "It was you I heard in his room. The same old bullying and threats. He's been running away from you all his life. Well, he doesn't need to run anymore. He's safe now, where you can't get him."

"*I* want sex with him? *I* do? Who practically had to have it explained who he was until he was twelve years old – and who hasn't been able to keep her hands off him since?"

"That's a dirty lie."

"Oh no, it isn't. It's absolutely spot on."

"You're the one who can't keep his hands to himself. I heard you in his room."

"Doing what?"

She looked at him blankly.

"Well? Doing what? You obviously have some idea."

"I know what you were doing, he told me so himself."

John laughed. "What? That I was bullying him? Is that what we're calling it today? Let's get this ugly fuck out into the open once and for all. I was *screwing* him. There, how does it feel to finally hear it?"

"I don't believe you."

"Oh that's nice. After all these years it's a comfort to know you've never really believed bad of me."

She stood shaking her head. "You've been forcing him to have sex? All this time you've been forcing...?"

John laughed again. "Oh Christ, let's drop this routine, shall we? You know and I know the reason he's not half a mile from here right now is Danny *likes* it. In fact, Danny *needs* it, that's why he keeps that stiff little cock of his permanently in both hands. That masturbatory grip on himself is the only kind of grip he can keep on reality at all – and you know damn well that's the truth."

"I'm not listening to this." And she covered her ears with her hands.

But he pulled them off, holding her arms down. "He needs it, and I, poor besotted bastard that I am, am just obliged to see that he gets it. It's the least a brother can do. I'm the victim here, and all I get is the blame. But what the hell, I love him, so I just go on sacrificing myself. That's my role in life. He wants me to find him, you know he does, so why don't you help him out?"

"I won't tell you." She tried to wrench free.

"I'll just have to go to Ian then. I'm sure he'll tell me everything I need to know."

"Ian?"

"You didn't believe him, did you? Even you should know better than that."

"God, you're..."

"Yes?" he prompted her. "Don't stand on ceremony now, we've no secrets left. Your whole life has been vindicated, please don't hold out on me now."

"You're despicable."

He laughed, pulling on his jacket. "You don't know the half of it."

And he went out the door, slamming it shut like a tomb.


John sat in the shed and waited. He did not have to wait long. Outside he heard the Fiat's engine start up. He got up and looked out. Margaret driving off in a fury. He went back inside and sat down. Eventually Ian came in, closing the door silently behind him, as silently as he did everything. "No, don't put on the light," John said as he saw him reach for it.

Ian walked over to him carefully. John stood up. "I know where he is," Ian said.

John heard the suppressed excitement, the jubilation. He was surprised for a moment to feel a nudge of pity for him under everything else. It evaporated like water on a hot stone. "I know you do."

Ian didn't seem surprised. "I want a promise."

"My promises are worthless."

"I'll risk it."

John didn't look at him. He could see Ian's feet as two vague shapes on the floor, standing before him. He could hear his breathing, rapid, unnatural. "Alright, Ian, a promise."

There was a pause then Ian brought his mouth to his ear. The words came out low and fast, getting it out in a rush. When he was finished John withdrew his head and said, "What makes you so sure I want him that much?"

"You don't want to hear me telling you that, do you?"

"No, I don't think I do." He stopped again, moved his feet.

"Well?" Ian demanded. His voice was urgent, charged with suspense.

"His mother is itching to spill the beans. She does and you'll be somewhere lower than I am, and I'm dog-shit numero uno. Your guarantees wouldn't buy my spit then. Everything would be right through your hands like sand."

"Life's full of risks. What's one more? Now, do you want to know or don't you?"

"You know, sometimes I almost like you."

Ian smiled in the dark. His heart lit up with exhilaration. "It won't last, John-boy. It never does."

"That's what I thought, I was just too polite to say so." He paused again. Ian's hands came out of the dark and lay against his chest. Like a woman's hands, loving him the same way.

"I don't suppose," he asked, feeling Ian's body move imperceptibly closer, "there's any point in asking you for the information now?"

"Oh no, John-boy, payment in advance. I insist. Better safe than sorry."

"I promised."

"Your promises are shit."

"You know, Ian, this could seriously be your last time. I don't like you so very much after all."

"Could be. They're so rare anyway, who cares?"

Ian made no further moves. John lifted his hands off him. "We don't touch. That's not on offer, savvy?"

Ian smiled, backing off. "Absolutely."

John nodded. "Shall we go then? I take it we are going somewhere?"

"Of course, always discreet with my big brother."

John patted his cheek. It was almost warning. "That's what I love about you, Ian, you make the shit taste so good. Lead on."


Margaret drove the car through a blur of water. She wasn't sure if it was tears or rain.

There were no lights on in the house. The living-room curtains were closed.

She let herself in, heart sinking. *He's gone. He's grown tired of waiting and gone.* "Danny?" she called. Her voice was soft, as if she feared he might be asleep. "Danny?" she called again, louder this time.

"Up here."

She peered up the stairs, following his voice.

"Up here," he called again.

She could see him now, silhouetted against the tiny stair window. "Why are you in the dark?"

"I felt like it. Come on up." His voice was low. He sounded...

She couldn't place the word.

Then it sprang suddenly into her head, unbidden.

*Dangerous.*

She shook herself like a dog, full of dread.

She climbed the steep stairs. He didn't move back. He seemed larger, darker, ominous in his featurelessness, his stillness. She stopped a few steps from the top, unable to walk on into him. Why wouldn't he move? "What's wrong?" she asked.

"Why haven't you found my money?"

"I've told you, I looked. What else can I do? I can't make it appear." She wondered how much of her face he could see in the dark.

"Come up."

"I can't, you're in the way."

He moved back a step then turned and disappeared. She followed him down the passage and into the room. There was only one panel burning on the gas fire. He turned and looked at her as she came in. "Close the door."

She pushed it shut and faced him again. His hair seemed purple in the blue light from the fire. His face looked cold, sinister, in the almost undersea colours.

"You looked in John's room?"

"I told you I did. I told you that last time I saw you. Against my better judgement, I might add. It was you that insisted." He wasn't quite meeting her eyes. She could feel his gaze like two points of pain in her right cheek.

"What did you find?"

"Nothing, I told you. Is there any point in going over this again, Danny? Am I under some kind of suspicion?"

There was a silence, a long silence, heavy with the hiss of the fire. Fresh bursts of rain threw themselves at the windowpane.

"On the bed."

Danny's voice made her jump. "What?" Her heart stopped, hung motionless for seconds.

"Look on the bed."

She looked at him, same unwavering stare. She crossed to it. There in the middle lay the photograph. Oh God. "Where did you get that?" she said, desperately thinking, trying to remember. It had been in her bag, the one place no-one ever went, sacrosanct. Mother's bag was always sacrosanct.

"Never mind where I got it. Where did *you* get it?"

She turned. He was standing, hands in his pockets, his eyes still watching her, always watching.

"It's John's," she said. "John took it."

He said nothing.

"Why don't you say something?"

"What should I say?"

"Your own brother has been taking obscene photographs of you and you're not shocked, not even surprised?" She could hear the disgust coming out in her voice and she couldn't stop it, couldn't stem the tide.

"My own mother carries an obscene photograph of me about with her, but that doesn't surprise me either."

She crossed the room in two strides, slapping him furiously, the whole body of her fear and anger coming out in one huge rush. "You've seduced them all. Him, Robbie, even..." she stopped.

"You?"

"You're filthy. You disgust me. You're no son of mine."

He shook his head. "Sorry, no amount of wishing will make that one come true."

"How dare you." She slapped him again.

She stood glaring at him, panting. He swallowed carefully, moistening his lips. He was looking somewhere over her shoulder, not meeting her eyes, like some insolent schoolboy reprimanded, punished and unrepentant. "I want my money." His voice was distant, uninvolved.

"I haven't *got* it."

"Then I'll go without it."

"You can't." Her voice was flatly emphatic.

He didn't answer her.

"If you would just learn some patience. Though God knows why I should help you, after the way you've behaved."

"Why don't you want me to leave?"

"It's not a question of you leaving."

"You've lied to me."

"I've lied to you? How dare you..." But she ran out of words. His eyes took all the words away.

"Why?" he repeated.

She shook her head. "The same reason as all the rest, is that what you're thinking?" Her voice was unsteady. "Something's happened to you, Danny. Somewhere along the line you've become someone else. I used to think this was all John's fault, but I'm not so sure any more. I don't seem to be able to remember who you were, all I can see is what you are now, this filthy hunger you bring out all around you. They're sniffing around you like a pack of dogs, all biding their time."

She took a deep breath, let it out again. Her voice was steadier. "I have never wanted anything from you, no matter what you believe." She looked at him, knowing what he knew, giving him a chance to condemn her, but he said nothing. His face remained immobile, unrevealing. She pressed on, more confident now. "I took that photograph to show your father, that's all. I wanted to give him his proof, but the more I thought about it the more I realised how futile the whole thing was. He wasn't going to believe me. I knew what he'd say, I knew who he'd blame, and John would get off scot-free all over again."

Danny turned his back to her.

"Danny..." She gripped his upper arms.

Danny looked into the darkness. How long was it since she'd been here last? It was getting shorter. Like a drug it was getting shorter all the time. Why didn't he care?

He turned slowly, meeting her eyes, holding them. She let her hands slide off bonelessly. He caught hold of them, took them to his chest with both hands, like a Victorian beseeching his beloved, then he pressed the palms flat and slowly guided them down over his chest, down over his belly, then down.

He took his hands away, leaving her holding him. She stood there. She did not know what to do. Her face burned. She felt frozen by his gaze. Was it always like this? Did he get an erection as soon as anyone touched him?

She let go carefully, trying not to draw attention to it, trying not to do anything that might make him react, but she was unprepared for what he did do.

He turned away, his face set in hard lines. "Get out."

"What...?" Her confusion was absolute.

"Go on, get out." He began unbuttoning his shirt, back firmly turned against her.

"I know where your money is," she said before she could stop herself. She was bargaining, only she didn't know anymore what she was bargaining for.

He turned slowly. All she could see was his chest, flat and hard. "Then why didn't you bring it?"

"I couldn't, Ian's got it."

He studied her face.

He thinks I'm lying, she thought.

Slowly he peeled off his shirt then began unbuttoning his trousers. He stopped. "What are you going to do, watch?"

She quickly turned her back, her face colouring up. She could hear him pulling off his trousers.

"When will you bring it?"

"As soon as I can get it."

"Tomorrow?" His voice was soft again, almost inviting, as if he was making a date.

"Tomorrow," she agreed limply. She felt used, like a dirty old rag. She had gained nothing at all.

"You can turn around." His voice came out of the dark, heavy with intent. Suddenly she was afraid again. She did not want to turn around.

"Come on, Mum, turn around."

She turned slowly.

He was standing there, stark naked, obscenely erect. He wasn't quite smiling, but it hovered there, like a suggestion around his mouth. "The real thing."

"*Danny*..." Her voice was numb, flat with shock. She felt her face flame.

"This was what you wanted, wasn't it? To see if I looked just the same? Don't you think it's better? In the flesh?"

She looked away, tearing her eyes off him, turning her body away. "Get dressed."

He laughed, low. "Come on, have another look. No charge."

She turned quickly, some dim notion of facing him down, but her mouth dried up at the sight of him.

"Why don't you touch it?"

She looked at his face, trying to read his expression. She didn't know who he was anymore. "No," she said in a whisper.

"Why not? Not moral scruples surely? Where were they two days ago?"

Her hand flew to her mouth like a comic book heroine.

"Another feel won't hurt, will it?"

She shook her head.

"She says no, but she means yes. Come on, be brave."

He jerked it. There, in front of her eyes, he made it jerk, flexing it like a muscle. It caused it to peel back on itself, revealing the head fully. "Look, he likes you. It would only be kind to give the boy a pat."

She saw his feet walking towards her. "No," she said to them, but they weren't listening. Then she smelt him, that same smell that had made her mouth water.

"That's it." His hand reached out to take hers. "There now, that was easy, wasn't it?"

She held it unmoving, huge in her hand, feeling the red heat come scalding off it. The veins were swollen so hard it felt inflamed.

166

"It actually physically aches." Although he was looking down at where he held her round himself it was obvious he wasn't talking to her. His voice was curiously flat, detached. It sounded as if he was talking about the affected limb of some fictitious patient on an operating table. "You don't know what that feels like, do you? You've never ached for anything in your life. What kind of a freak has a dick that comes up but won't go down? That can be tossed off six times in a row and still aches for more? Squeeze it," he grunted. "Really squeeze it." He pressed her fingers tight then said, "Sometimes I would even run cold water over it, rub it on the windows, trying to cool it on the glass. I used to sneak downstairs and rub ice cubes over it. Standing down there in the kitchen, this great red lump of meat sticking out in front of me, rubbing it all over with ice cubes. Bone weary, tossing off into a fistful of ice-cubes in the dark and crying afterwards because it was nothing, just a great, big, empty void of nothing. You talk about hunger. You don't know what that word means. You don't even *begin* to know what that word means."

She looked at his face in horror. *He doesn't even know what he's doing or who I am. There's no part of him functioning beyond his hand and that thing.* And suddenly she wanted to get it over with, see his face go slack as a stunned animal's, see him again as he had been two nights ago, spread out on the floor, helpless under her hands. She wanted that power over him, to see him destroyed by his own need.

She pulled his hand off hers and took hold of him. He said, "Oh Jesus," flatly, as if he had dropped a cup or made some unforeseen error. She took a firmer grip on him and her mind flickered instantly to John, feeding this need in him, cultivating it for his own ends.

"Oh Jesus," he said again as she inexpertly attempted to masturbate him. Already she was panicking, wanting it finished.

"Oh, Danny." The voice was deep, filled with angry pain. She whirled round in fright. She stood there holding Danny by the penis as if she was leading him by it.

"This has *got* to be your all time low." John lay back against the door, shaking his head slowly from side to side.

"John," she said meaninglessly, like she could explain something. But he didn't even seem to see her. His face was white. He'd lost so much weight so quickly he looked almost gaunt. *He looks like him,* she thought hysterically. *He can't look like him.*

"Why do you do it, Danny?"

Danny said nothing.

"John..." she said again, beginning to panic.

He looked at her suddenly, as if seeing her for the first time. "Let go of him."

She looked at her hand, half in surprise, and snatched it away, rubbing it furiously on her sweater, trying to wipe away the sticky feel of him.

"Why do you do it, Danny?"

She turned quickly to Danny and saw his face. It was grotesque, his expression full of an intense itchy-white excitement. It was like some curling filthy smile consuming his whole face. "Danny...?" she said, but it didn't reach him. She felt suddenly irrelevant, as if neither of these men even knew she was in the room. She had simply ceased to be.

John began to walk towards him, slowly, his face eaten alive by some ancient emotion.

Margaret turned back to Danny frantically. He seemed blind to his own danger, like some automaton locked into a totally inappropriate response, utterly unable to function correctly.

She stepped in front of him, barring John's way. He looked at her as if he didn't know who she was. "Move it."

"Leave him alone."

"I said, move it." And his whole hand clutched her face, pushing her aside as if he were crumpling paper.

"*No!*" she screamed, catching at his arm.

He didn't even bother to shake her off, instead he elbowed her savagely in the chest, sending her flying back to hit the floor, flat on her back, and bang her head sickeningly on the tiled hearth.

She felt nothing but a single jolt that broke her neck.


He slapped Danny twice, lightly, only leaving the vaguest of marks. "Now you can't do it again."

"Cunt," Danny said, enunciating it as if he'd lived for the moment. John looked down between his legs and smiled. It looked wolfish on his thinned face.

"Unfinished business, that's all this is for you. Even on the Day of Judgement you'll be standing up there looking for some poor lost angel just aching for a way to fall." He slapped him again, harder this time. "Anybody at all." He smiled again. "Well, I can oblige, baby."

He looked up at his face, eyes searching his intently, then he licked his lips. "Ask me then." John's hand slid round him, wrapping itself around his penis like a boa constrictor. He gripped it fiercely.

Danny shook his head slowly, his breathing rapid. Sweat stood out on his forehead, a slick oily film.

John looked at him steadily. He still held Danny's cock, now inconceivably larger, as if it had somehow inflated itself still further to combat the crushing pressure of John's hand. "It calls you a liar, Danny."

"No."

"It calls you a fucking desperate liar."

"No."

"You remembered, didn't you?"

Danny said nothing.

"That's why you came back here."

"You wish. You were fucking replaying it. You've been replaying it for months."

"Not all of it."

"I never did anything."

"No? That's memory and its tricks again for you. You were a little slut. Only six years old and already you were a little slut. Think he didn't know? Think he wasn't right? Look at you now."

"You told him it was the first time."

"Are you saying it wasn't?"

"It's you in the dreams. You chewed those fucking liquorice sticks all summer. That's why you took up smoking his filthy cigarettes, sticking your tongue in my mouth. To make me remember."

"Right to at least two. But that doesn't mean everything your diseased imagination dreams up is true."

"You liar."

"It's the truth. Rab was twelve, I was fifteen, you were six. He tried it out on me, I tried it out on you. The only major difference is we got caught. So it was no more baths, no more putting you to bed, and not because Dad didn't trust me either. After all what six year-old kid do you know would tempt his big brother into a blow job?"

"You took those lousy photographs."

"You really think so?"

"You bastard."

"Why? I could have done worse. Christ knows you'd have let me. Come on, Danny, be a little Christian."

Danny began to cry. The tears began to slide down his face effortlessly. "You greedy, vicious cunt."

"Not me. They're the greedy ones. I only want what's mine."

"Fuck off."

John nodded his head as if he was encouraging a mental sub-normal. "We had a pact, you and I. Time the deal was well and truly sealed." He pushed Danny back against the bed. It caught him in the back of the knees, making him sit down. John climbed on, pushing him back. "Here..." he reached down between their bodies, lifting himself slightly, undoing his clothes "...want to see?"

Danny jerked his head away.

John pulled himself out with a grunt of satisfaction. "Used to fascinate you, the sheer fucking size of it, all that hair. Come on, Danny, take a look."

Danny looked. And suddenly it was all back. In perfect detail. The smell of liquorice, the taste of salt, John making him take it in his mouth, the panic, but still, through it all, that pulsing excitement, knowing he'd get his reward in the end.

John showed it off, pulling it down, making it bigger. "Like it?"

Danny tore his head away.

John laughed, squeezing his penis. "Always did give you away." His voice changed. "Always was too bloody easy to make you stiff." His hand gripped Danny's jaw. "You know that it's me you've wanted all along, don't you?"

Danny shook his head again, fiercely.

John's hand gripped his face, hurting. "Say yes, Danny." And he pulled Danny's head up and down. "That's better." He eased himself over Danny's leg. "Much better." He made a low grunting noise like a man easing himself into a chair. "There." And he began to move against him, their genitals sandwiched together under his weight. He looked down into Danny's face. Danny tried to close his eyes, but he couldn't, because suddenly it was all there in John's eyes, naked for him to see. He felt his own response, huge, monstrous, worse than ever.

John whispered, "Your mother's lying dead on the floor, and what are we doing?" He was watching Danny's face avidly. Danny knew what he was watching for.

Fuck him... *no.*

"Come on, Danny, don't fight it." He whispered again, mouth close to his ear, "She's lying there dead. We haven't even checked. What does that say about us, Danny?"

"No, " Danny said fiercely, trying to struggle free.

John smiled, a smile of triumph.

"No," Danny pleaded, desperation making him beg.

John smiled, nodded, as if Danny was being very good. Danny was being splendid.

"John..." Danny moaned. He heard it, appalled, felt it come straight from his cock to his mouth – the need in his gut, his very soul, out there for everyone to hear.

"Come on, Danny," John whispered. "You know what we're doing."

Danny shook his head again violently, pressed his eyes tight shut, opened them again, the words trapped in his throat.

"Say it, Danny."

He moved against him slowly, tormenting him with that dreadful grinding friction and Danny knew it was no good. He felt it build up in him, better than it ever was before, better than it ever had been, his whole body alive with it. And John saw his face, read it there, and brought his mouth against his lips whispering, "You say it, Danny. Who do you love? I can make you say it. *Say* it."

Danny pressed his head back. "You cunt." But John followed his mouth, letting his lips just barely touch his, as if he wanted to feel the very vibration of the words when they came. Hearing them wasn't enough, not for John. And Danny knew he had to say it, there was no way round it, because he wasn't signing a pact and John knew it. He was acknowledging that his signature was already on it and had been for years. He was lying. He was telling the truth. It didn't matter, and John knew that too. All that mattered was he was going to do it. John had won, that was what mattered.

He closed his eyes and said it, a tense, gasped confession, so desperate it sounded real, trembling with false emotion – an orgasm masquerading as an oath – and John received it with his eyes sliding closed, mouth sinking onto his, becoming suddenly languorous in his thrusts. "Had to be, Danny. Had to be..."

And he came.

The Story Continues In
**DANNY 1 - Hope House**
ISBN 978-0-9567154-3-2

# THE DANNY QUADRILOGY

**DANNY 1**
Hope House

**DANNY 2.1**
Die Schwarze Engel

**DANNY 2.2**
Eilean Mhor

**DANNY 2.3**
Road Movie

**DANNY 3**
The Changeling

**DANNY 4**
Two Dead Boys

"There are not enough stars in this galaxy or any other to rate this series. It is simply... the most beautiful, haunting, frightening and complex story I have ever read."

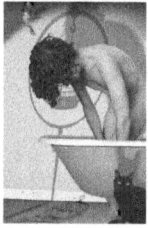  

**DANNY 1**
Hope House

**DANNY 2.1**
Die Schwarze Engel

**DANNY 2.2**
Eilean Mhor

**FOUR MASSIVE VOLUMES - SIX GIGANTIC PARTS**

# THE DANNY QUADRILOGY

## Chancery Stone
available in e-book & paperback

### "A sexually-explicit modern-day *Wuthering Heights*..."

**THE DANNY QUADRILOGY** is a huge stylistic achievement, a Jacobean drama on an epic scale, reaching into realms far darker than anything ever dreamt of in Shakespeare's philosophy. It belongs more firmly in the shadowy corridors of John Ford, the secret rooms of Christopher Marlowe, the feral imagination of John Webster - in short, in a place where gouging out eyes with steel spikes and unwittingly fucking your sister are commonplace tragedies.

For modern audiences, however, it may be imagined more easily as film noir, a long running soap opera from the dark side, something that HBO might commission as a creative pièce de résistance designed to out-swear *Deadwood*, out-abuse *OZ* and out-rape *Rome*.

It is the home of supernaturally compelling characters, blessed with the phallocentric charisma of sexed-up animals, goats in human form, satyrs. And they act out every sick fantasy in graphic detail, strutting their sex, violence, perversion and addiction as if they were proud of it.

It is beyond good and evil, it is simply necessary.

### "...a wonderful, unnerving, compelling and haunting collection of books of blood..."

  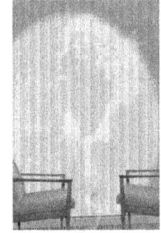

| **DANNY 2.3** | **DANNY 3** | **DANNY 4** |
| Road Movie | The Changeling | Two Dead Boys |

**Available on line from Amazon, Watersons, Barnes & Noble, Tesco and www.poisonpixie.com**

# POISON PIXIE PULP FICTION

*A new series of short, racy paperbacks in a handy pocket-sized format*

## SATYRICON

Chancery Stone

ISBN 978-0-9567154-2-5

Is Elmer Grant a satyr, a mythic beast unable to contain his own insatiable hungers, or merely a mortal man who brings infatuation, corruption and blood into the gossiping, fussy world of a well-known London department store.

Whatever his origins, Grant's entry into the staid halls of Smith & Wainright, manufacturers of fine fabrics to the Queen, is a match that ignites a powder-keg of sexual frenzy in this dark and animalistic fairy tale from the creator of **The DANNY Quadrilogy**.

Lean, mean and supremely erotic, it offers a sensual nightmare in a modern world, peopled with other-worldly creatures and a primeval hunger for *more*.

# POISON PIXIE PULP FICTION

*A new series of short, racy paperbacks in a handy pocket-sized format*

## BAD GIRLS

Max Scratchmann

ISBN 978-0-9567154-1-8

Bad girls, wicked women; lecherous, treacherous villainesses; hedonistic harlots, and plain old-fashioned bunny-boiling temptresses.

Immerse yourself in a feast of delectable depravity with these eight blackly humorous tales, spanning the familiar gothic grimoire of murder, lust and revenge with rapacious relish.

Lascivious lesbians, manipulative mad-women and gruesome gold-diggers are just a few of the bad girls that you'll meet in this fast-paced anthology, which proves beyond all reasonable doubt that the female of the species is definitely more deadly than the male.

# POISON PIXIE FICTION

## DELANEY 1.0
Chancery Stone
ISBN 978-0-9567154-8-7

Set in the avant-garde world of modern ballet, Delaney is a story of desire, greed and ambition amidst the sweaty bodies, nudity and backstabbing of a contemporary dance company.

Frank Delaney is a street lad training to be a boxer when he is seduced into dancing Nijinsky's most famous role: L'après-midi d'un Faune.

But company director, Jonathan Delmore, has plans for Delaney that don't include just dancing, and intrigue, jealousy and pure unashamed lust quickly weave themselves into an ever-tightening web around our intrepid hero.

**Available from any good bookstore, www.poisonpixie.com or via digital reader on Kindle, Nook & iPad**

# POISON PIXIE FICTION

Chancery Stone

**Twilight Tales** is a magical collection of dark fairy tales set in the shadowy woods of urban highways and faceless corridors. Skillfully painted in a Halloween palette of bonfire orange and steely grey, these mystical tales are a journey into an unrelenting darkness where the monsters are the beasts within ourselves...

Sister Esau: Beware the wolf, for he walks amongst us, even in the light. So just who is watching the comely Sister Esau as she walks the sterile corridors of the dental hospital with her stainless-steel bowls of teeth? The Cameo: In an old store in Paris, a tourist is fascinated by the cameo of a beautiful girl who seems to be looking right back at him. The True Story of Doctor Foster: An old man seeks for the way back to the tenth dimension in a rain-soaked Gloucester Road. Candy: A journalist goes in search of Violet Rose the rock-maker?s daughter under the salt-corroded colonnades of twilight Brighton. But all is not as it seems in this coastal underworld, and the lines between reality and fantasy become distinctly blurred in the hot nightclubs of this very erotic tale. The Waiting Room: Somewhere, deep in the festering rain, a little girl sits waiting in the waiting room, curtailing her hunger until someone finally comes. Citronella: A dwarf stalks a tall woman in spiked glass heels around the concrete forests of suburban London.

**"Chilling, atmospheric and erotic. An unholy alliance between Ray Bradbury's The October Country and Angela Carter's The Bloody Chamber"**

**Available from any good bookstore, www.poisonpixie.com or via digital reader on Kindle, Nook & iPad**

# POISON PIXIE FICTION

## The House at Ghost Elm Sands

Vanessa de Sade

Thirteen-year-old Victoria's world is turned inside-out when her mother dies and she is sent to live at her grandmother's house at the desolate Ghost Elm Sands.

But under the pale blue Kentish sky a mysterious teenage girl in a blood-red bathing suit haunts the deserted beach, and Victoria becomes gripped with a new infatuation in the midst of her grief.

A touching and emotional tale of loss, first love and infatuation, beautifully rendered by master story-teller, Vanessa de Sade, in this, her first young adult novelette.

## Tales from a Tangled Bush

Vanessa de Sade

**Tales from a Tangled Bush** is a dark collection of five previously-suppressed best-selling interfamilial taboo tales about the forbidden sides of human sexuality, all darkly romantic and highly erotic.

Curvaceous Babe is groomed to be the circus fat lady when she reaches her sexual maturity in this erotically explicit tale set during the lean years of the Great Depression; Cody gets busted for a joint in his locker and is sent off to the woods and his uncle, Ranger Dan; Penny and Cherry meet on the net in the wee small hours to share their deepest and most intimate secrets on a sexy webcam site; full-figure Cougar – Tabitha – has had to move to a new and much smaller home. But the walls of her new place are paper-thin and her hot and sexually active son, Marcus, is just next door; and, lastly, it's a real turn-on for curvy blonde Cindy to discover her fit brother, Aaron, is shaved below the belt.

**"Vanessa De Sade's stories are a godsend in a genre noted for its mediocrity and glut of unoriginality..."**

# Crimson Velvet
Vanessa de Sade

Two deliciously different erotic period novellas from master story-teller, Vanessa de Sade.

## The Hush
Leo travels to the stately home of Jack, his old school friend, in the blistering July of 1914, as the world stands hushed on the precipice of the Great War. But here, in the woodlands where the ravens cry, the two boys delight simply in each other's sun-kissed bodies, blissfully unaware of what is to come, and the only fly in this otherwise idyllic ointment is Jack's sister, Constance, who Leo can't seem to get out of his mind…

## First Blood
World War II England. A voluptuous girl is led from her towering iceberg-like mansion while the midnight sky is aflame with the sound of bombs and gunfire. Taken across a gleaming black lake she is left bound, naked, to a tombstone, waiting for whatever is roaming the derelict island cemetery to slake its lust…

# Melanchlia Falls
Vanessa de Sade

The derelict cemetery at Melancholia Falls stands perilously close to a dark and sinister reservoir, its black water lapping menacingly at the crumbling mausoleums and headless angels.

It is to this desolate place that Ellie comes to live with her dad, caretaker to the deserted necropolis that no-one visits, but the father and daughter's relationship soon begins to warp and mutate under the cloudless Georgia summer sky. And who is the pale-skinned young man in black who flits soundlessly between the tombstones, and why do the seasons never change and the birds never sing at Melancholia Falls?

# In the Forests of the Night
Vanessa de Sade

*Published by Sweetmeats Press*

**In The Forests Of The Night** is a darkly sensual collection of erotic fairy tales. Each story blends the magic and fantasy of the traditional fable with the carnality and lust we've come to expect from Vanessa de Sade!

Beautiful, visceral and devoutly debauched, **In The Forests Of The Night** explores a much more grown-up side of fantasy. The seven sexy stories within these pages offer up a mind-bending, pulse-quickening twist on a classic genre.

If you think you know how a fairy tale is supposed to end, this book will make you think again! Sexual and cerebral, magical and modern, **In The Forests Of The Night** is the ultimate collection of sexy, adult fables!

# POISON PIXIE HUMOUR

## My Rubber Hebrew Nose

Max Scratchmann
e-book & paperback
ISBN 978-1477635308

Meet the Pobble who has all his toes, share the Fish Supper of J Alfred Prufrock and discover the lost manuscript of a poem penned by Edgar Allen Poe on his visit to the Raven Hotel, Blackpool.

**My Rubber Hebrew Nose** is a hilariously insane collection of literary parody and nonsense verse in the great tradition of Edward Lear and Lewis Carroll, written and superbly illustrated by British humorist, Max Scratchmann,

Come and join some literary greats and their sexually deviant maiden aunts, as well as a stellar supporting cast of horrible children and errant vicars, proving, if proof were ever needed, that British comic verse is truly for life and not just for Christmas.

## Bodice Rippers & Carnie Strippers

Max Scratchmann
e-book only
ASIN B00513D8DC

**Bodice Rippers & Carnie Strippers** is an eccentric collection of miscellaneous and very funny poems about love and sex, an unruly and anarchic anthology of deviant doggerel, which frequently mutates into breathy love poems, lascivious limericks and terrible tales of out-and-out shameful shenanigans.

Meet a hilarious selection of vapid vampires and hardened harlots, voluptuous Lolitas and their grasping grannies; as well as a suitably epic supporting cast of adulterous vicars, lascivious lesbians and nubile nuns.

Read it as a guilty pleasure or gift it to a friend with a wicked sense of humour.

"a fun and witty compilation of poetry which is packed with light-hearted festive cheer"

THE PECULIAR POETRY BOOK OF

# FUNNY XMAS VERSE

EDITED BY PATRICK WINSTANLEY

Packed full of funny Christmas poems, parodies and pastiches, **The Peculiar Poetry Book of Funny Christmas Verse** distils the true spirit of Christmas - comic, misanthropic, dyspeptic, or sometime just sick.

The collection is presented chronologically, taking the reader in seven easy leaps from the eager anticipation of Christmas, through the fun and festivities, to the bitter aftertaste.

Meet Pip, the ineffably jolly penguin who gets on everyone's tits, revel in the feminist retelling of the story of The Three Wise Men and discover the feminine hygiene product set to be a Christmas sensation. On your travels, take a detour into the strange world that is nonsense verse or pause to enjoy The Interlewd, a selection of risque or rude poems.

Written by contemporary UK poets Paul Curtis, Patrick Winstanley and Poison Pixie's own Max Scratchmann, the **Peculiar Poetry Christmas Collection** is as warm, frothy and intoxicating as a pint of beer, and just as unsuitable for children.

Edited by Patrick Winstanley
Illustrated by Max Scratchmann

# the last burrah sahibs

Max Scratchmann
ISBN 978-1-904246-38-1

A warm and witty look at the unofficial last years of British Colonial Life as seen through the eyes of a small boy growing up out East in the dissolving remnants of the British Raj.

After being compulsorily retired from an Indian jute mill and returning to Dundee in the mid 1960s, Max Scratchmann's family cannot settle down to life in Scotland. So, when the chance of a three-year contract in East Pakistan (now Bangladesh) is offered, they promptly fly off to live the colonial life one last time.

Aided and abetted by the mischievous Mafzal, his paan-addicted driver, eleven-year-old Max rediscovers the forgotten lifestyle of his early childhood, and meets a cast of colourfully eccentric characters amongst both the émigré British and the indigenous population along the way.

On the surface, life for jute wallahs' children may seem to be an endless parade of swimming pool parties and badly-dubbed Italian art movies, but growing political unrest and brushes with street rioting show that these are indeed stolen years, and **The Last Burrah Sahibs** is an engaging and heartfelt chronicle of growing up in a culture that is now well and truly lost.

Published by **Steve Savage Publishing**

# SCOTLAND FOR BEGINNERS –
## LEARNING TO LIVE IN THE LAND OF MY FATHERS

Max Scratchmann
ISBN 978-0957192058

Max Scratchmann was born the son of a Dundee jute wallah and spent the first six years of his life in India before being taken "home" to Scotland in the bitter winter of 1963.

In **Scotland for Beginners** he tells the often painful, but very funny, story of growing up in the bleak grey-harled bungalows of Dundee's newly-built suburbs and learning to adapt to his native land in an era when the very fabric of the nation was changing.

Told as a series of humorous vignettes, **Scotland for Beginners** takes us on a sentimental journey through "auld Dundee" as Max struggles to decipher Scots dialect; buys school clothes from the formidable Miss Hannah at the Peter Street Co-op, and heroically endures the tortures of organised games at the Junior Boys Brigade.

Then, as the Sixties become the Seventies and the country is plunged into darkness by power strikes and the Three Day Week, the teenage Max goes girl chasing at the Ice Rink; falls in love with Sally the prompter at the church drama group, and finally blunders into a dodgy drug deal in a garishly-painted tenement in the Hawkhill.

# CHUCKING IT ALL

Max Scratchmann
ISBN 978-09571920-2-7

Named one of the twelve best travel books of 2009 by Worldhum, **Chucking It All** exposes the gritty reality behind all those twee bestsellers which extol the joys of sunny rural idylls.

With its remorseless true-life account of downshifting to a remote Scottish island, **Chucking It All** uncovers the frightening realities of relocating to "a magical island lost in the mists of time" as you follow the warts-and-all adventures of urban misanthrope, Max Scratchmann, as he valiantly tries to forge a new life in the windswept Orkney islands, and grumbles his way through unending winters with eighteen-hour nights, nocturnal visits from drunken farmers and booty calls from desperate divorcees.

From struggling to fit in as a temporary postman in a wilderness where houses don't display numbers or names, to attending drunken country ceilidhs with the island singles' club, or finding himself up to the neck in local politics while performing in the village pantomime, **Chucking It All** is an urbanite's nightmare and one of the most hilarious books that you will read this year.

Irreverent, sarcastic and bitingly caustic, **Chucking It All** still manages to be a grudgingly affectionate portrait of rural life through the eyes of a cynical outsider, and is one of the truest accounts of "living the dream" ever published.

"Does for downshifting what Lewinsky did for Clinton – only much funnier..."

**Available from any good bookstore, www.poisonpixie.com or via digital reader on Kindle, Nook & iPad**

# POISON PIXIE HOW–TO

## ILLUSTRATION
# 101

### Max Scratchmann
ISBN: 978-0956715463

Do you yearn to illustrate? Do you dream of being the star of the commercial art world? Then this is the book for you! In this fun-to-read manual you will quickly learn how to land Dream Commissions and wow Art Directors; get past the Scariest Secretaries; get loads of FREE Publicity; speed up Slow Payers; create killer newsletters and do a hundred other cool things to put your freelance illustration career straight into the fast-lane.

Yes, the classic is back! After over a decade in print the illustrator's bible is fully revised and enlarged with new chapters on marketing and self-publishing and crammed with oodles of new tips and trade secrets.

## HOW TO GRAB THE ATTENTION OF ART DIRECTORS

### Max Scratchmann
ISBN: 978-0953730742

Do you want to promote your art or photography to the world's top art directors and photo editors? Do you want to be in constant communication with decision-makers everywhere? But does your promitional budget read like a bad comedy script?

Worry not. Help is at hand! The picture postcard is one of the cheapest, easiest and most effective marketing tools invented for visual creatives, and this fun-to-read and easy-to-follow guide shows you scores of ways to generate lucrative commissions on budgets that very rarely exceed double figures.

Illustrated in full-colour throughout and featuring examples and breakdowns of real promotional postcards from some of the world's top photographers, illustrators and film makers, and written by award-winning illustrator, Max Scratchmann, author of the critically-acclaimed **Illustration 101**, this book could be one of the best investments that you ever make for your creative career.

# How to Write the Perfect Novel

Chancery Stone
ISBN 978-0954611576

There are hundreds of conventional writers' guides on the market, but none so scathing, cynical and downright cantankerous as this one. Forget toadying to publishers or obsessing over return postage - in this insider exposé veteran author, Chancery Stone, spares no-one's blushes as she strips the book world bare and reveals the true natures of publishers and authors alike.

Interspersed with laugh-out-loud parodies of best-selling thrillers, romances, crime, science fiction, erotica and even the Booker Prize, and naming names and showing no mercy to the perpetrators, **How to Write the Perfect Novel** will submerge you in such brain-numbing brilliance that you may never browse through a book shop in quite the same way again....

""The perfect antidote to the thousands of well-meaning, hefty writers' guides that currently flood the market"
**Essential Writers**

"A bitter look at how to succeed"
**Writers' Forum**

"This is the kind of book that you read for the humour, the scathing remarks and the blatant flaunting of all the rules. Yet it is so cleverly written that you find yourself learning things that, quite frankly, none of the other how-to books teach you"
**W H Smith**

**Available from any good bookstore, www.poisonpixie.com
or via digital reader on Kindle, Nook & iPad**

www.ingramcontent.com/pod-product-compliance
Lightning Source LLC
Chambersburg PA
CBHW061136200626
46817CB00016B/1656